A Medical Thriller by

VICTOR METHOS

When a man dies, a world is lost.

— Heraclitus

PROLOGUE

Undisclosed Location, Soviet Union, 1988

Michael Tippets had been with the World Health Organization for over eleven years, and never, not once, had he been as anxious as he was now.

Standing outside a bio-warfare facility in the heart of the Soviet Union, he wasn't certain what would happen. The only thing he could say with any degree of certainty was that the world wasn't prepared for what he was going to find when he got inside. The facility, known as Caucus 3, was a nightmare factory, one the world might not have known about if not for one particular man.

The Special Intelligence Section of the British government, better known as MI6, had recently encountered what they called a "walk-in"—a defector from a hostile government who wished to debrief and seek asylum. The man's name hadn't been released, but he claimed to be a microbiologist. Since no one at MI6 could verify anything the man told them about microbiology, Michael was called in.

The subject was debriefed in a room with a table, chairs, and a window looking down onto the grubby streets of London's south side, inside a building with a boarded-up pub on the ground floor, an office that no one would look at twice upon passing.

Michael took his seat at the end of the table as two MI6 operatives he'd been told were experts in debriefing and negotiation began to question the subject.

The subject appeared terrified, his hands trembling and his voice cracking. He chain-smoked during the entire debriefing and asked for vodka several times. The operatives informed him they didn't have any alcohol now but would be happy to take him to a pub afterward. A mistake, Michael thought, not to have alcohol. It might have weakened his inhibitions.

The man spoke in a thick Russian accent, though with perfectly grammatical English. He was a professor, he said, and enjoyed teaching. But the *Komitet Gosudarstvennoy Bezopasnosti*, the KGB, had other plans for him. He had been recruited in 1982 for a secret program known as the *Serviat*. The purpose of the program was to develop biological weapons for use in war.

Michael didn't have much to say. He knew most countries developed biological weapons and wasn't surprised. But then the subject said something that sent an icy chill up Michael's back.

"What specifically were you working on?" one of the operatives had asked.

"Smallpox and plague."

"What were you—"

"Excuse me," Michael interrupted, unable to hold his questions in. "Did you say smallpox?"

"Yes," the subject replied, looking at him for the first time.

"Are you telling me you have been working with live *Variola major*?"

He nodded. "Yes. The plague is just as deadly. We have heated it up."

Michael couldn't speak. His throat suddenly felt dry, though he couldn't bring himself to reach across the table and pour a cup of water.

The operative looked from the subject to Michael. "What's that mean?" he asked. "To heat it up?"

"It means that you evolve an antigen to be resistant to antibiotics. You take natural bacteria and expose it over and over to antibiotics. In a short time, you've evolved a new strain of the bacteria, immune to our only weapon against it." He looked back at the subject. "The Soviets have a strain of *Yersinia pestis* that is immune to the effects of antibiotics?"

"Yes."

The implications were horrifying. Plague, once known as the Black Death that had wiped out a third of Europe's population in the fourteenth century, and smallpox were not precision instruments like nuclear weapons. They were chaos incarnate in the form of organisms not meant to attack only military targets but civilian populations as well.

What Michael knew, that the Soviets didn't seem to care about, was that these agents couldn't be controlled. They would spread among whoever was attacked, of course, but diseases could not be contained. They would escape the confines of whatever nation was struck and eventually return home. Chaos did not sit still. Chaos did not have loyalty to its creators.

The actions the world had taken at that point were not entirely clear, but Michael had heard bits and pieces. President George H. W. Bush and the American intelligence community were taken aback. Within the CIA—and most intelligence services—to be informed of something so important by another nation's intelligence service was not seen as a success but a failure. The Americans weren't sure what to do exactly. But Margaret Thatcher was sure. Michael had heard she personally called Mikhail Gorbachev, yelled at him, and demanded that he open his biological warfare plants to the US and UK inspectors immediately. The leader of the most feared nation on the planet was awestruck, or intimidated, by the prime minister's boldness and agreed.

That was why Michael was here, standing outside the most secure facility in all of the Soviet Union. He'd been in the nation for five days now, and most of his time was spent in long, alcohol-laden meals waiting for the botched transportation to arrive and take him and his colleagues to their next destination. At first Michael had thought it was simply the inefficiency of communism, but now he knew they were stalling on purpose. The last three facilities he'd inspected were empty, but the equipment remained. He had no doubt that the Soviet Union was manufacturing the largest supply of biological weapons the world had ever seen and hiding the evidence.

And this, Caucus 3, was the surprise facility he had insisted on seeing out of order. It was too large for them to clear out right away. He had no doubt the evidence he needed to determine the extent of their program would be found here.

The massive steel double doors opened. A man in a smock and hardhat met them. He held out his hand and smiled.

"Dr. Tippets, welcome to Caucus Three. I'm sure you'll find everything in order. I am Dr. Volkovich. Don't hesitate to ask any questions if you feel so inclined."

"Thank you, Doctor. I'll keep that in mind."

Michael had a team of six with him, and they followed him into the facility. Volkovich spoke to them about friendship and cooperation, about a new horizon for the future in which the Soviet Union could count the US and UN as allies in the fight against tyranny and oppression. Michael wasn't really listening. He was more interested in the factory before him. He had been wrong.

They had cleared everything out. No workers were inside, and nothing was functioning. Only the equipment, too difficult or time consuming to dismantle and move, remained. But the equipment was enough.

Near the heart of the factory were two large vats. The vats were made of semitransparent plastic, perhaps a few inches thick, and topped with blue cones that had tubes thrust out from the apex of the cone. The vats were empty. Michael stopped in front of them.

"This is it," he said. "I would like to test the interior of these vats."

Volkovich swallowed. "For what purpose?"

"Because I believe these vats were holding a biological agent expressly prohibited by the United Nations resolutions, which the Soviet Union took part in crafting. I want them tested, now."

Volkovich shook his head. "There is nothing there of interest. Let me show you—"

"Doctor, I believe we were to be given a free hand in the examination of this facility. If you do not allow me to test these vats, I will have no recourse but to inform my government and the WHO that you refuse to cooperate and that I am of the opinion that the Soviet Union is engaged in large-scale production of biological agents for attack on civilian populations."

Volkovich looked down at the floor. He had a sadness in his eyes, like a man held hostage. Michael suddenly sympathized with him. He had likely been forced into this position against his will, probably with threats of violence and imprisonment. But these weren't rifles they were talking about, or some sort of new grenade. Smallpox and plague were the two deadliest diseases in history. To play with them was foolish beyond measure—a child playing with a gun.

"I'm afraid, Doctor," Volkovich said sadly, "that I cannot allow you to open and test these containers. It's for your own safety."

"What do you mean? We've been fully vaccinated against *Variola*, and plague does not survive long exposed to air."

"I'm afraid… your vaccinations wouldn't protect you."

Michael was silent a long time, processing what the man had just said. Why wouldn't his vaccinations…?

"No," he gasped. "No, you couldn't be so reckless. Not even you."

Volkovich shied away and sat down on a bench, leaving Michael staring up at the massive vats in front of him. They had done it. They had developed a strain of smallpox resistant to vaccination. They were no longer talking about wiping out thousands of people in a civilian center with plague. Michael now knew they were talking about the extinction of the human species.

"We're all madmen now," he muttered.

BOOK ONE:
The United States

Present Day

The young man noticed his fingers were turning white and loosened his grip on the briefcase. He sat in the passenger seat as the jeep bounced down the uneven road. Abandoned cars lined the shoulder like skeletons from a long-forgotten war. And out there, from somewhere, they were being watched.

The young man swallowed. "How much longer?" he shouted over the din of the engine.

The driver, a heavyset soldier in a gray camo uniform, didn't look at him while speaking. "Another five minutes, give or take."

The young man glanced up at the husks of skyscrapers, broken testaments to humans' ingenuity and their capacity to destroy themselves. "What exactly do we do if... you know, we're attacked?"

"I'm armed. They usually stay away from vehicles, though, something about the noise." The soldier finally looked at him and then turned his eyes back to the road. "What's your name?"

"Mitchell. Um. Dr. Mitchell Southworth."

"Well, Doc, I hope you know what the hell you're doin', 'cause you're about to be dropped into a war zone."

Mitchell watched the soldier for a long time. The man's face seemed carved from stone, a scar running down from the top of his head to his neck. Mitchell had scars as well, but his weren't visible.

The hospital looked like it had just barely survived a bomb blast. The exterior paint was chipped and cracked in spiderweb patterns, windows gaped, the shards of glass long since removed. Several military personnel, armed with large rifles, stood by the entrance. They were wearing full biohazard gear. A few more sat in chairs.

"This wasn't originally a hospital," the soldier said as he pulled up to the entrance. "It was just a clinic. But it's easier to guard—only two ways in or out. You learn both those ways, you hear me?"

Mitchell nodded slowly and then stepped out.

The jeep rumbled off, leaving him staring at the taillights in the early morning. A sign painted on a white sheet hung over the entrance: HOSPITAL, ALL WELCOME.

"Can I help you?" one of the guards asked.

"Yes, I'm here to see Dr. Samantha Bower. Oh." He pulled out his identification. "Dr. Mitchell Southworth with WHO."

"Yes, sir. Go right on in."

At the entrance stood two infrared scanners that had to be passed like metal detectors. *Heat*, Mitchell thought. *They were looking for heat. How clever.*

The first sign of infection with *Variola major*, specifically the strain of smallpox now known as Agent X, was fever. Detecting elevated heat given off by a person acted as a sort of virus scanner. Imperfect, of course, but it would probably do the trick most of the time.

Before Mitchell could pass by, a scream tore the air. He whipped his head around. A woman dashed for the entrance to the hospital. From head to toe, all he could see was blood. It seeped out of her eyes, ears, nose, and mouth—black thick blood. Her eyes were black as well, and the scream escaping her lips gurgled as she vomited.

The woman tried to jump on the first guard, still screaming. The second one lifted his rifle and, as casually as shooting a target at a firing range, blew the woman's head off.

The corpse collapsed with a wet thud. The blood spread in a widening circle. The whole thing had happened so fast that Mitchell's heart had only now caught up and begun to pound.

The guards pulled the corpse away, leaving a trail of blood and brain matter. Several large dumpsters sat on what used to be a driveway next door. One guard held the corpse's ankles and the other the arms as they lifted it and threw it in. One of them sprayed something into the dumpster and then lit it on fire. The guards stood around watching the flames as if they were in front of a campfire.

"Sir."

Mitchell turned. His throat felt dry, and his heart wouldn't slow. "Yes?"

"Are you coming or going?"

"Um… coming. Coming. I'm here to see Dr. Bower."

"Step through the scanners, please."

Mitchell walked slowly through them, afraid that setting them off might force him to share the same fate as the corpse in the dumpster. Compassion and mercy were no longer traits someone could expect from others.

Once past the scanners, he was told to head to the end of the corridor. Offices lined the hallways of the hospital, most of them turned into patients' rooms. Cramming several patients into each room seemed a bad idea to him because of the risk of cross-contamination. The limited space probably left the administration no choice.

In one room, several men and women in scrubs of varying colors sat around a circular table. The scrubs were stained, worn, and old.

Mitchell said, "I'm looking for Dr. Samantha Bower."

"Ain't seen her in a while. But she goes up on the roof a lot," one of the men said.

"Thanks."

The elevators appeared to be fifty years past their prime. The metal groaned, and an odd clicking sound emanated from the doors as they opened. Mitchell stepped in and hit the button for the top floor.

The doors opened to a corridor that led to the roof. He opened the steel door and saw a woman sitting at a table, an umbrella shading her.

"Dr. Bower?"

The woman looked at him. "Yes?"

Mitchell thrust out his hand, and Dr. Bower stared at it. Remembering that handshaking was not a custom adhered to anymore, he withdrew it. Mitchell looked over the city. It looked like something out of a third-world country, not Miami, not one of the largest cities in the richest nation in the world, but something dilapidated and abused.

"Amazing, isn't it?" he said. "How quickly things fell apart?"

"Depends on your perspective, I guess. Some people think nature's just taking back what's hers."

"We're part of nature."

"Are we? It didn't seem like we acted that way."

Mitchell sat down across from her, placing the briefcase next to him. He opened it, took out a digital recorder, and placed it between them before pressing the record button. "I'm Dr. Southworth. I guess you know why I'm here."

"I do."

"You were there at the beginning, Dr. Bower. That's why I asked for this interview. I need to know everything. I need to know how we got to this, how the world ended."

She shook her head, staring off at the horizon. "It hasn't ended yet, but it might."

He adjusted the recorder and leaned back in his chair. "Let's start from the beginning, please."

1

"The detonations were the beginning," Sam said. "The virus had appeared in South America and Hawaii before then, but we thought it was a fluke, the kind of aberration of nature that pokes its head out sometimes. A Spanish flu virus once appeared in the early twentieth century, killed three percent of the world's population, and then disappeared without a trace. There are things in nature we just don't understand, and sometimes they show us glimpses into that unknown, as if we can touch it.

"So after Hawaii, procedures were put in place, FEMA better trained on containment, and the Centers for Disease Control set up better communication with the World Health Organization and the United Nations. We saw that there really weren't individual nations any longer. Humans could travel as far as they wanted, faster than ever. A virus could appear in Bangalore and be in Manhattan by the end of the day. The speed of our travel has made us susceptible to contagion in a way we weren't meant to be. Hunter-gatherers didn't infect other bands of hunter-gatherers with their antigens. They were spread too widely. So when the poxvirus hit, the strain we now call Agent X, we weren't prepared for the speed it could travel.

"There are two measures to the spread of an antigen: R-naught and T scores. They both describe the same phenomenon, how fast a virus can spread. Ebola has an R-naught of one, meaning each person infected generally infects one other person during the contagious stage of the disease. Traditional smallpox is five. Agent X, the mutated strain of *Variola major*, has an R-naught of twenty, making it the most contagious disease in history. Only measles, with an R-naught of eighteen, compares. So after Hawaii, at the CDC where I worked as a virologist, I began running infection grids to predict the spread of Agent X if it ever appeared again. Another virologist there, Dr. Ngo Chon, worked with me to come up with the simulations. We discovered that human beings would have to live farther than fourteen days apart if we were going to slow the spread of the virus. That meant that one infected group had to be farther than two weeks' travel away from other hosts. Two weeks was long enough that the infected host would become immobile before coming in range to infect others. Living two weeks apart was practically impossible. We couldn't come up with a scenario where Agent X wouldn't spread to every population center in the world within three months.

"That's when the detonations occurred—four of them. It wasn't clear at the time who was responsible. I only saw bits and pieces of the larger picture. Two men tried to kill me, for reasons I still don't fully understand. Something to do with the fact that I was one of the virologists deemed most likely to develop a vaccine, which they couldn't allow. Six other virologists were on their list, as well as administrators and physicians, and they're all dead. I'm the last surviving virologist that this... organization... deemed a threat. And on top of the detonations, liquefied *Variola* was dumped from planes on other cities, onto large groups that had congregated for whatever reasons.

"After the detonations, martial law was declared in the United States, not just the four cities affected, but the nation as a whole. The problem with that is that the military is meant to fight off national threats, not act as a police force. When the military become the police, the citizens, by definition, become the national threat. Curfews were imposed. Thousands of people who wouldn't comply were arrested and held in military brigs. It wasn't chaos yet, but chaos was coming. I just wasn't paying attention. Chon and I were busy experimenting with liquid nitrogen. Agent X mutates quickly, so we thought that if we could slow the virus down, slow its mutations down, we might be able to develop a vaccine from the husks of the weakened virus.

"That autopsy after the liquid nitrogen experiments was at the CDC in the BS4 lab, the most secure laboratory in the world. I sat out in the hallway in a blue spacesuit, just staring at the linoleum and preparing myself for what I was about to find inside the autopsy room. We had been experimenting nonstop for so long, I'd lost hope. That autopsy was it. If it didn't work, I wasn't going to try again.

"I entered the autopsy room and found Chon and a pathologist named Tomomi Yashima standing by in their own spacesuits. The suits are connected by a hose to the walls, providing fresh, sterile air to the suits, in contrast to the negative air pressure inside the lab, which would supposedly keep any antigens out of the suits. It'd never been tested on a live antigen, but the theory calmed us down. Most of the scares that happen inside a Biosafety Level Four laboratory happen because of nervousness or carelessness, not because of the danger inherent in working with hot agents. So any placebo that would calm and comfort the scientists and aides in the lab got implemented. I think that's all the negative air pressure was, a pacifier so we wouldn't think too much about exactly what we were doing.

" 'You ready for this?' Chon asked me.

"His voice sounded otherworldly in his spacesuit, like he was talking through one of those old cell phones that resembled bricks. Even with the negative air pressure, the scent of the autopsy room permeated the suits, and I had a suspicion Chon breathed through his mouth. Every autopsy smells like human feces. 'Yeah,' I said. 'But if it doesn't work...'

" 'It'll work,' he replied, nodding to Dr. Yashima.

"The pathologist, a Japanese transplant who'd only been out of medical school a few years, had been promoted rapidly with the deaths of two senior pathologists on the CDC staff, men who had died after infection with pox, before we understood how contagious it really was. I could tell she was uncomfortable, but I knew she would do her job.

"In front of us on a metal gurney lay the body of a recent victim of the virus. Smallpox has devastating effects on the body, and it's something you can never grow accustomed to seeing. It was a white male, and his skin elevated away from the dermis with thick, oozing pustules, creating a texture that looked like a cobblestone road. Over half his face, the skin had filled with fluid, resembling a sack. The sack, had he lived longer, would have grown to cover his entire head, but he died from exsanguination before that could happen. Even now, we're not entirely certain what a patient infected with smallpox dies of. Usually it's something secondary like exsanguination, asphyxiation, kidney failure... but how the virus actually kills, no one really knows.

" 'Cross your fingers,' Chon said.

Dr. Yashima had a puzzled look on her face, and I realized she didn't understand the expression. 'It means hope for the best,' I said. She grinned underneath the thick, transparent faceplate before turning to the metal tray next to the gurney. Several stainless steel tools lay before her on a blue towel. She took a large scalpel and turned to the cadaver. Her eyes shifted from Chon to me. I nodded and said, 'Go ahead, Tomomi.' She inserted the scalpel just underneath the cadaver's nipple, and then cut along the chest. The cut looped up to the shoulder and then straight down the center. Her hands moved like a sculptor's, carving away at her mound of clay, no wasted movements, just pure concentration.

"When she stopped cutting, a Y had been carved into the cadaver's chest. Tomomi peeled up some skin and reached her fingers underneath. I pushed my fingers into the cut as well, and we pulled. The dermis came off like skin from fried chicken. We peeled it down to his stomach and flopped the excess to the sides. Dr. Yashima then took out a tool that resembled garden shears and snapped off the cadaver's first rib, then his second, then his third. She went all the way up one side and down the other until all the ribs formed a pile on the linoleum floor. Using the scalpel, Dr. Yashima then flipped up the breastplate like a Tupperware lid.

"Instantly, a river of thick, black blood flowed out of the cadaver, over the gurney, and onto the floor. Dr. Yashima took a ladle off the tray and began scooping the blood into a bucket underneath the gurney. I reached in and pulled the man's lungs up, then his kidneys. Pustules made them look like carved-up sponges. The liquid nitrogen hadn't worked, hadn't even come close to working. We had failed again.

" 'Back to the drawing board?' Chon said.

"I stared into the body cavity and the infected blood that had drowned the man. 'No, not for me, Ngo. This isn't working. There's something we're missing. Or maybe it's too smart for us.'

"Chon rolled his eyes and said, 'You're anthropomorphizing again.'

"He was right, but I couldn't help it. The virus adapted. It anticipated our movements, learned from our experiments. How could I not give it human traits, malice and human motivations?

" 'What else is there?' he said. 'We gotta keep hammering the LN. It's the only thing that's slowed it down.'

" 'Does this look *slowed down* to you, Ngo? We're not an inch closer to developing a vaccine.' He exhaled, a small puff of fog covering his faceplate for a fraction of a second before the pumped-in air cleared it. 'I'm done,' I said, taking a step away from the table. 'I'm going to help the people I can actually help. I need to get outta the lab and into the field.'

"Of course, I didn't realize at the time what was happening in the field. The four detonations and the planes that had released the liquefied virus were a distraction. The intent of the explosions was much crueler. Smallpox, in liquefied form, could potentially get trapped in clouds. The clouds would move, releasing rain and pouring down virus over entire cities. The poxvirus can live for nearly a day outside of a host. It wouldn't take long for it to infect massive swaths of people. And that's exactly what happened. Except that it had a modification that led to something I never could've dreamed..."

"I was busy at the time. A man I barely knew had me promise to watch his daughter. He was dying of the pox and he killed himself to prevent others from getting infected through him. So I promised him. His daughter was twelve, Jessica Burke, and she lived with me and my mother until my mother passed four months ago. I took care of my mother, fed her, bathed her, spent time with her. In a lot of ways, it was like taking care of a child. I didn't mind. I loved my mother and no one else would take her, though I have two siblings. When she passed, it felt like a little bit of me died, too, that part that held on to childhood memories. Every day I wake up, even now, and I expect that world, the world of my childhood, to appear before me. But instead, I get this one." She paused.

"During that autopsy, Dr. Yashima opened the cranium and studied the brain. That's the first time anyone had seen the lesions. She took photos, and later that day when I sat in my office, staring out the windows at the sky as I did all the time, she brought the photos in."

Mitchell pushed the digital recorder closer to her. "Tell me about the lesions."

2

Samantha grew uncomfortable and shifted in her seat. Out on the horizon, a bird drifted by, or maybe just a piece of debris. Garbage filled the streets now, and heaping piles of trash in parking lots or even the middle of the freeway weren't uncommon.

"The lesions first appeared as black dots, almost like leopard spots," she said. "The metencephalon and frontal lobes were most affected. In the cerebral cortex, there's a layer of what's called 'white matter,' but it didn't look white in this patient. It was nearly black. The white matter is what controls connections between different regions of the cerebrum. If something wanted to take control of a human being, those are the regions that would have to be affected, shut down our higher reasoning, turn us into mindless animals. As the three of us stared at the lesions, we didn't know what they were. I thought maybe it was hemorrhaging in the brain unique to that patient, but then something happened that changed that.

"That night, I went home. I live in a suburb of Atlanta, and when I was gone, my neighbor watched Jessica. She was a kind, elderly woman whose kids didn't call or visit her anymore, so she was happy to spend time with Jessica. When I got home, the two of them were sitting on the patio, drinking juice and laughing, watching the sun set like nothing in the world was wrong. I sat down next to them in a chair, my body exhausted to the point that I nearly fell asleep as they asked me questions about my day. I tried to answer as many as I could, but I had to tell them I was just too tired and had to go to bed.

"I went upstairs and got ready for bed. Water was only on for two hours each morning in an attempt to conserve it, so I couldn't take a shower, but I used some from buckets to get a towel wet and run it over my body. Then I lay down on the bed, and I was gone. I don't know how long I slept, but I remember what woke me: a scream; a brutal, primal scream.

"Jessica, her eyes wide with terror, ran into my room as I jumped out of bed. I thought perhaps something had happened to her or our neighbor, maybe burglars, which had become prevalent without a decent police force, but then I heard the scream again. The sound emanated from the house across the street. 'Wait here,' I said.

"I grabbed the revolver out of my closet before throwing on some shoes and running outside. No one else was outside. No one cared that a woman was screaming. I knew the home. It belonged to a family: parents, Eric and Beth, and their two children. I dashed up the porch steps and pounded on the door. 'Beth? You okay?' Another scream, and then the sound of crashing wood and breaking glass. But this scream cut off, as though the person's mouth had suddenly been covered. I looked around the neighborhood. Even now, no one was coming out. Calling the police was useless. They would take two hours to get out there if they came at all. I tried the doorknob and the door was locked, but a window on the porch leading to the front room opened when I pulled up on it.

"I stuck my head in and said, 'Beth? You okay?' Still no response, so I shouted, 'I'm coming in, and I have a gun.' I don't know why I said I had a gun, maybe to scare away any potential attackers, maybe only to make myself feel better. I don't know, but when I entered the home, a tingling sensation went up my back. I stood in their front room and scanned the surroundings. There were toys on the floor, family photos on the walls, food still out on the dining room table, two grilled cheese sandwiches only half eaten. I wrapped both hands around the gun and held it low, my finger over the trigger guard like I'd been taught in my concealed-carry class. I crossed the front room, the dining room, and the kitchen. I opened the back door and peeked out. The moonlight reflected off a glass coffee table on the back porch, and several hardcover novels lay on the glass. Other than that, the backyard was empty. Going back into the house, I saw the stairs leading up to the second floor. I was about to leave and call the police when I heard a thud, and then banging, pounding against a wall or a door. I swallowed, thinking a burglar had definitely broken in and was holding the family hostage. The police wouldn't be here in time. I was the only hope.

"Upstairs appeared much like the downstairs with the exception of family photos. The walls were bare. I went to the right first, past a bathroom, and looked into the first room. A child's room, decorated in posters of sports teams and cartoon characters. Another bedroom was the same but decorated with posters of adolescent boy bands, so I quietly walked the other way to the master bedroom. Inside… I saw something I would never forget."

Mitchell waited quietly a few moments before asking, "What did you see?"

Samantha pulled the sunglasses she had on her head down over her eyes. "I saw Beth's body. It'd been torn apart, like an animal attack or something. Her organs lay in tatters over the carpet, and blood was spattered everywhere, even on the ceiling. Her face had been ripped away from her skull, and her left arm was missing just below the shoulder. My first thought was that a bear or a cougar had gotten in. We'd never had an animal attack in the neighborhood, but that was my first thought. And then I saw her husband.

"Eric was bent over near the nightstand, hunched down like a gargoyle on a medieval cathedral. He was holding something to his lips and there was a wet, tearing sound. He didn't seem to notice me, but the hairs on my neck stood up. Rather than speaking to him, I began backing out of the room, the gun held firmly, when I ran into a floor lamp. It banged against the wall and Eric's head shot up, though he hadn't turned around. Slowly, he rose, his face still away from me… and I could see the blood. I didn't wait for him to look at me after that. I ran down the stairs and out of the house. I heard Eric screaming behind me, just a loud, guttural scream, and I could hear his footsteps as he chased me through the house. I made it out and slammed the door behind me. He pounded against it. The door wasn't locked. It was more as if he forgot how to open it. As I stood on their porch, the gun aimed at the door, he banged against it for a long time, snarling like a pit bull. As quietly and carefully as I could without falling over, I backed away, down the front steps to the sidewalk, before heading into the street and back to my house.

" 'What was it?' Jessica said as I ran in and locked the door behind me. Concern twisted her beautiful face. She'd been through so much already that the thought of more tragedy filled her with pain and despair. I could see it on her face clear as day.

" 'Nothing,' I said. 'Just something across the street.' I grabbed my phone, hurried into another room, dialed emergency services and reported that I thought my neighbor had killed his wife. They said they'd send someone out as soon as a unit was available. I knew that wouldn't be for hours. Most police officers had quit their jobs. The prospect of dealing with an infected person and taking the virus home to their own families wasn't worth the paycheck. For whatever reason, some officers chose to stay, but they were few, and the ones who did stay didn't stay long. As they saw their friends infected, droves of police officers left. A few months after the detonations, an entire city would be lucky if it had ten police officers.

"I ran back out to the living room and attempted to put on a brave face for Jessica as I stared out the window at Eric and Beth's house. My thoughts raced. Maybe the pressure of living such an existence had finally caused Eric to snap. Maybe someone else had killed Beth, and Eric just happened to be there when I came in. But that didn't explain his behavior. He was instantly hyper-aggressive, almost as though he wasn't human.

" 'Sam, what's going on?' Jessica said next to me, and I put my arm around her. I remembered what it was like to be that age, the things that concerned me. *Were my friends talking about me behind my back? Would I have a date for the school dance? Could I get good grades in all my classes?* But that wasn't what she had to worry about. For her, life had become nothing but survival. No other concern seemed important enough to consider. 'It'll be okay,' I said. 'The police will be here soon.' She didn't respond right away. Instead, we both stared at the home across the street before she said, 'I don't like the city. I want to move.'

" 'Move where?' I said, looking down at her. She pressed herself against me as though I could shield her from whatever was scaring her.

" 'I don't care. Anywhere. Just away from the city. Away from all these people.'

"I bent down and looked her in the eyes, eyes that should've been full of life and laughter but instead had settled into hardness and efficiency, a soldier's eyes in a twelve-year-old girl's face. 'You'll be safe, Jessica. I'm not going to let anything happen to you. Do you understand? Nothing's going to happen to you.'

" 'You don't know that,' she said, pulling away from me. 'You don't know what's going to happen. Everybody dies. That's what will happen. I'm going to die.'

"My hands were still on her shoulders and I felt her body convulse, a tremor of emotion running through her before the tears came. I wrapped my arms around her and brought her in, pressing her body against mine, making certain she felt my warmth. I kissed her on the head and said, 'You are not going to die. Do you hear me? You are going to live.'

"I don't remember what we did for the next couple of hours, maybe just sat in the living room and read, but the time came when the police arrived. A single patrol car manned by one officer, a grossly overweight man who parked in the driveway of the home across the street. He ambled up to the front door and knocked. Waiting a few moments, he knocked again and then tried the door. It opened, and he pulled out his gun and stepped inside.

" 'Stay here,' I said.

Jessica immediately grabbed my arm. 'No! Don't go. Stay with me. Stay here, please!' I bent down and looked into her eyes again, attempting to calm her. But the panic in her eyes had settled in, and she wouldn't hear anything I said. 'Jessica, I will be right back. I just need to make sure Beth and Eric are okay. You can watch me from the window.'

"She flung her arms around me. 'Please don't go.' But I had to get over there and verify what I had seen. I knew a logical explanation existed, something that would explain it in a way that would remove the ball of anxiety in my gut, so I left and locked the door behind me. I saw Jessica's face glued to the window before I crossed the street.

"The neighborhood was quiet and still. I wondered if anyone even cared that a police cruiser sat in one of our driveways, the lights spinning and illuminating the street red then blue, red then blue. I wondered why the officer didn't just turn the lights off. Probably to alert any burglars of his presence so they could run off and the officer could avoid interacting with a member of the public. I glanced into the cruiser as I passed. A shotgun lay across the backseat, and crumpled on the floor, a yellow biohazard suit that looked like someone tried to shove it under one of the seats. When I got to the porch, I stood there and listened. I couldn't hear anything from inside. In fact, I intended to wait on the porch when two loud pops went off. *Bang, bang!* With each bang, a flash of light through the windows. I still held my own gun but suddenly realized the officer might think I was a prowler and shoot me. So I put it away and stepped off the porch. I stood by the cruiser and waited.

"Nothing happened. Glancing back to my home, I saw Jessica's terrified face in the window. My first thought went to her. What would she do if something happened to me? She had no family left, none that she knew of, anyway, and no friends. Government programs like foster care and welfare had all but shut down for fear of spreading the virus. The military saw them as 'negative externalities', programs that diverted resources from the real objective of maintaining order and containing the epidemic. Jessica would have nothing and no one. I couldn't risk that. As much as I wanted to know what had happened, I couldn't risk harm for her sake. I backed away from the house, never taking my eyes off it. Halfway into the street, I nearly jumped when the door flew open and the officer tumbled out.

"He gripped his upper arm, panic written on his face as he ran to his cruiser. I could see blood pouring from a wound on his neck and out over the fingers he had around his arm. He placed a call on the two-way radio and then jumped out and ran to the trunk. Flipping it open, he then rummaged through everything back there until he found a first aid kit. His eyes fixed on me—large, wild eyes. 'I need help,' he shouted as he rushed toward me. My first instinct was to reach for my gun, but I forced myself to remain calm.

" 'I'm a physician. Sit down on the curb. Let me have a look at your injuries.'

"He didn't comply at first, instead he shouted, 'I need help,' again. Shock was setting in, and his face was as pale as the moonlight. I grabbed the first aid kit from him and sat him down on the back of the cruiser. I lifted his collar for a better look at the wound and saw the indentations, teeth marks. He'd been bitten, and a chunk of his neck the size of a silver dollar was torn away. 'What happened?' I said.

" 'Fucker ran at me. Just jumped out. I popped him twice, but I don't know if he's dead. Fucker just ran at me!' The officer's eyes told me he was going to lose it. The injuries, though pouring blood, weren't life threatening: one wound in the neck and another smaller one on the upper bicep. I glanced at the home. I pushed Eric out of my mind to tend to the officer. The first aid kit had plenty of gauze, and I pulled some out to stop the bleeding until emergency services could get there. Ambulances were even scarcer than police. When they were called, most of the time it was because someone was dying from the poxvirus. They would drive past, not even bothering to tell the victims why they wouldn't stop and help. I had once seen an ambulance allow a man to die in front of his hysterical wife because the driver confused vomiting from flu with vomiting from the pox. The man's blood was later tested as part of a lawsuit and found clear of infection. That's almost funny now, someone suing the government for letting a loved one die, considering everything that's happened.

"I slowed the blood as much as I could with what I had. Glaring at the house, I knew I had to go inside. I had to check on the children, who I hadn't seen when I'd gone in. 'I'll be right back,' I said, but the officer didn't hear me. His eyes had glazed over, and he stared at the ground. I hurried up the porch and inside the home. In the middle of the living room floor, Eric lay flat on his back, two bleeding holes in his chest. I approached him slowly. The stench of decay filled the home. A dead body has a unique smell. Nothing else in nature smells like a dead human body, and I smelled one just then. But it wasn't coming from Eric.

"Stepping over Eric's corpse, I saw something poking out of his collar. The only light on in the home was the one light I'd turned on in the kitchen, so it was difficult to make out. Track lighting on the ceiling provided a flood of bright light once I turned it on, and I bent over Eric's body. His eyes... His eyes were black with red circles in the middle, smallpox eyes. And what I saw sticking out of his neck were pustules. Eric had the poxvirus.

"I quickly jumped away and covered my mouth. *Variola* is transmittable through the air and the entire event played through my mind. Did Eric ever get a chance to breathe on me? Did he sneeze or cough? Did he spit? I looked out the front door to the officer who still sat on the back of the cruiser, his eyes not leaving the ground. The officer, without a doubt, was infected. A possibility existed that he didn't inhale droplets of saliva or mucus or blood, but the fact that he was bitten means the proximity between them was close enough that he in all likelihood did.

"My only thought was to run out as quickly as I could. The virus lived on surfaces, too. A house that had been inhabited by an infected person would have to be torn apart to get rid of the virus. The linens and furniture, carpet, rugs, hair products, toothbrushes, food, dishes and cups, anything that came into direct contact with someone infected would have to be burned.

"I headed for the front door when I heard another thump upstairs. It stopped me cold. Beth couldn't have survived her injuries. Someone else was up there. I turned around and headed up the stairs, pulling out my gun again. I hadn't grown up around guns. My father was a pacifist and wouldn't keep them in the house. It wasn't until I was attacked that I purchased one and made shooting at the range a regular habit, so I wasn't uncomfortable holding it, and I knew if I had to, I could shoot someone with relatively decent accuracy.

"At the top of the stairs, I stopped and listened. The thump came from the right, from the children's rooms, which I'd already checked. Cautiously, and with as little noise as I could, I went over to the first room, the boy's room. I flipped on the light and scanned from wall to wall, but I didn't see anyone. Another thud sounded from the wall. I looked over, instinctively bringing the gun up in front of me, and noticed the closet with the sliding doors. Breathing hard, my heart beating furiously, I went over to the closet and slowly slid open the door. Inside, Eric and Beth's oldest child, whose name I couldn't remember, lay on his back convulsing. Foam dripped from his mouth and blood soaked the closet floor, spilling from every orifice as though an invisible vise squeezed it out of him like water from a sponge. His arms were shaking violently, and his eyes rolled back into his head. I saw then for the first time that the whites of his eyes had hemorrhaged and turned black, the pupils red.

"In a flash, the boy was on his feet, still seizing, his muscles slamming him into the closet doors and walls. His eyes fixed on me, and I could see there wasn't any reason there anymore, no recognition that I was another human being. I backed away and closed the door, leaving the boy growling in the room. Soon, I heard the pounding against the door as he smashed his body against it. I thought if I could get him to a hospital, we could stop the convulsing and figure out the behavior later. Maybe it was some sort of psychosis brought about by dehydration. Most of the blood had left his body, as well as Eric's, and severe dehydration could alter a person's mind to such an extent that they could kill. Several case studies existed on survivors of shipwrecks or mountain disasters where they would turn on their fellow survivors after only days without adequate water."

Mitchell didn't move, and when Sam stopped speaking, he didn't ask her to continue. Instead, he put his hand under his chin, as though to support his head, and waited patiently a while. When Sam didn't continue, he said, "When did you find out about the lesions?"

Sam sipped the contents of her drink, lemonade that she had made herself from lemons that grew in a garden near the hospital. Grocery stores didn't exist anymore, and if someone wanted to eat, they had to grow it themselves or be given food in a handout by the government. "The next day. I went to the CDC and brought Jessica with me. It was the most secure place in the state, and I didn't want to leave her home until I figured out what was going on. She sat in my office and listened to music. Without radio and only a few places receiving Internet service, music was a rare treat. I had a collection of old CDs and a player with batteries, and she seemed perfectly content sitting in my office. I asked my boss, an assistant chief at the CDC, Dr. Fredrick Jared, to keep an eye on her while I went up to the BS4 labs and examined the bodies of Eric and his son, whose name I learned was Ryan." She paused. "I wasn't prepared for what I saw."

3

Mitchell waited until Sam appeared ready to speak. She was beautiful, and his mind kept going to her looks. It embarrassed him that after all his experiences and all the honors he'd received, he was still governed by man's baser instincts, though he liked to feel he could control them.

As Samantha sipped her lemonade, her eyes hidden behind her sunglasses, he thought of his own wife and the last few moments he'd had with her. He'd spent that time with her in a hospital while she vomited the last of her body's precious blood over her bed sheets. The treating physician had sedated her so she could die in peace. Both thoughts—that in this environment, in this time, he still thought about sex more than anything else, and that he had watched his wife die and still couldn't help but think of other women—filled him with guilt and shame.

He cleared his throat. "Tell me what you found, Dr. Bower."

Samantha leaned back in the chair, crossing one leg over the other. "Dr. Yashima, Ngo, and I performed the autopsies. Their body cavities had filled with blood, but not to the degree we'd seen before. Their organs weren't drowning in it. They could function. But the brains were much different than those of any other patients we'd seen. The lesions were eating away at the brain matter, primarily the frontal cortex, almost like a severe brain injury.

" 'What would this do to someone?' Ngo asked. He was what we called a *Mud-Fud*, which meant he had both a medical doctorate and a PhD. His specialty was research. I think, ultimately, he didn't enjoy working with patients, and despite his brilliance, he seemed to know little about how the human body actually worked.

" 'The prefrontal cortex is the seat of reason,' I said. 'When it comes to behavior, most of our higher functioning takes place there. So with damage like this, a person would…'

"Dr. Yashima interjected, 'They would become an animal.' "

Mitchell didn't speak for a moment before he said. "Did you have any inkling what was coming?"

Sam shook her head. "I thought it was a new mutation that just killed us off faster. I didn't know what the virus was doing. Most people think viruses attempt to kill us as quickly as possible, but that couldn't be farther from the truth. Ebola Zaire, the most deadly of the four genera of Ebola, kills us within days. In total, it has taken the lives of roughly seven thousand people throughout modern history. You compare that with a virus like HIV and AIDS. The AIDS virus has learned. It's adapted. People think that because of modern drugs, those living with HIV and AIDS are able to extend their lives now, sometimes by as much as thirty years after a diagnosis. But the drugs have nothing to do with it. It's the virus itself. It's learned, if that's the right word, to slow down the process of death so that the host can spread the virus as far and wide as possible before dying. That's why Ebola has killed seven thousand people, and AIDS has killed fifty million.

"That day, I decided to call a neurologist by the name of Luther Daniels. Luther was the head of neurology at Johns Hopkins, and I knew if anyone could give us an explanation for the lesions, it was him. I let Jessica hang out in the cafeteria. Some of the other employees had brought their children as well and I let her be with them. Interaction for kids was so rare... you should've seen her face. It lit up just at the sight of other kids her age.

"But anyway, I sat in my office and called Luther.

" 'Hello?' I could still hear the grogginess in his voice though it was well past noon.

" 'Luther, it's Samantha Bower at the CDC.'

"He chuckled. We'd always had a good relationship since medical school, and just at the sound of my voice, his mood seemed to lighten. I got the distinct impression that Luther was as lonely as Jessica.

" 'What'dya know, what'dya say?' he said in his New Jersey accent, something he'd gone as far as taking lessons to get rid of. 'I haven't spoken to you since Hawaii.'

"Luther had been one of the physicians I called for advice during the initial outbreak. Though he's not a virologist, I felt he had a deep understanding of how the human brain and mind interacted and the consequences of certain infections on the psyche. That's also part of any infection by a virus, the psychological effect. The research points to the fact that the attitude of a patient, particularly one suffering from a serious illness, plays a major role in their recovery… or their death. 'It's been hard to think about old friends lately,' I said.

"I heard him exhale as though saddened. 'I know,' he said, 'Lord, don't I know. Have you read the Book of Revelation at all, Dr. Bower?' He knew I wasn't religious. What he was really saying was that I *should* read the Book of Revelation.

" 'No,' I said. 'Not recently, anyway. My mother was deeply religious, and I'm sure she made me read it at one point. Why?'

" 'Because it contains everything you need to know about what's going on. Every generation since John the Divine has believed their generation is the one, the one generation John was referring to when he spoke of the seas of blood and the rain of fire. Every generation thinks itself special, set apart from previous generations. The difference for us is, we're it. This is Armageddon."

Samantha paused a moment. "You have to remember, this is before the world epidemic, before we labeled the four detonations the T-zero event, the moment when civilization was wiped out and started over. At that point when I was speaking with him, we had an epidemic on our hands, a bad one, but just an epidemic. I felt that we'd beaten smallpox before and could do it again, so all his mystical references didn't resonate with me. I thought he was just being a Christian, which he was. 'I need more than the scribbles of wandering tribes from thousands of years ago, Luther. Do you have access to a BS4 anymore?'

" 'No,' he said. 'USAMRIID revoked my top-secret clearance when I retired.' I hesitated before asking him. Luther had been a brilliant physician and, though he didn't receive credit, was on a team that had secured the Nobel Prize in medicine for their work using snake venom to combat brain tumors. But he had a wild side that, like his accent, he could never kick. I once heard he hired a stripper for one of his histology professors and had her perform a lap dance for him during the final exam. Medicine isn't the kind of place where creativity and spontaneity are valued. It's more like the military. He'd actually started work in the last place I could see him, the United States Army Medical Research Division, and as I could've predicted, he was forced to 'retire' within a year. It didn't seem to faze him, and he just moved to Johns Hopkins. 'I need you to come to Atlanta, then,' I said. 'You'll have full access to the BS4. I'll get you clearance. I need something analyzed.'

" 'What?' he said, the curiosity in his voice practically jumping out of the phone.

" 'Lesions,' I told him. 'Lesions on the prefrontal cortex of patients affected by *Variola*, by Agent X, kinda dark, almost black lesions. They look like burn marks and appear to have damaged the brain tissue. I was attacked last night by two of my neighbors who had become infected. The father was shot and killed by police, and the son jumped out of his bedroom window, breaking his skull open and bleeding to death. We have them here for the autopsies, and their prefrontal lobes and a few other areas are covered in these lesions.'

" 'Hm. Sounds mildly interesting. I don't deal much with the infected. Do they all have the lesions?' I shook my head even though I was on the phone and then felt silly. Putting my feet up on the desk, I tried to strike a posture of relaxation. Our posture affects our mood, so I always forced myself into more relaxing poses in the hopes that it would calm me. 'No, not that I've seen. This is a new phenomenon.'

"He made a few noises, as though he were lost in thought and mulling it over intensely in his mind, before he said, 'Okay, gimme a day and I'll get out.' I knew he couldn't decline, but I played along anyway.

" 'I really appreciate this, Luther. I know it's a sacrifice to cut into your research time. I promise I'll get you out and back as soon as I can.'

"He chuckled. 'No need, you know you were always one of my favorites. See ya soon.' I hung up and put the phone down. Downtown Atlanta wasn't too far and I could see the skyscrapers. Not that long ago, they looked like glimmering gems in the bright sun, clean and well taken care of. Now, they appeared like abandoned warehouses, dirty and empty."

"That night, I opted to stay home. Jessica and I would sleep in the upstairs bedroom and lock the bedroom door. When we were getting ready for bed, she stood in front of the mirror and brushed her hair. I sat on the bed and watched her. I had always wanted children, specifically a daughter. That prospect seemed a million years away now. Even the thought of bringing a child into this existence filled me with dread. I couldn't do it, so having Jessica there wasn't just for her benefit. It helped me, too. I don't think it's enough to just live, I think we have to have something to look forward to, something to live for. Coming home and spending time with Jessica was that something for me.

" 'I miss my dad sometimes,' she said out of the blue.

"The death of her father was not something we had discussed. She understood what happened and why he did what he did, but as far as both of us were concerned, it was one of those topics that was more painful to talk about than if we left it alone. She'd never once brought it up, but I suppose it was natural she'd want to talk about it with someone. 'I didn't really know him,' I said, 'but I know he was a good man. Sacrificing himself probably saved a lot of people. All he cared about was that you were taken care of.'

" 'I was mean to him,' she said, pulling the brush through her hair. 'I was mad because I thought he left me and my mom. So I was mean to him. I don't know if he knew that I loved him.'

"I was quiet a moment. The relationship I had with my own father was close, and imagining it otherwise was hard to do. Your father, at least I think for women, shapes who you date, who you want to marry, the men you're attracted to, and what to expect from them. Maybe that's why I haven't been married yet; my standards were set high because of my father. But I could see Jessica felt pain, and I wasn't sure what to do about it.

"She set the brush down and came over to the bed. She put her arms around me and lay her head on my shoulder. Outside, we heard tires screech and a crash, the sound of bending metal filling the street. I felt her arms tighten around me. The sound had startled her. I didn't move for a long time, just held her, made sure she felt at ease before I tucked her in and left the bedroom. I didn't even look out the window, because I didn't want her to think it was important, further frightening her. So I left under some excuse, running down to get some food or something, and then I went out on the front porch and looked up the street.

"Two cars had crashed. The door was wide open on both, and something was happening inside the one, fast, jerky movements." Samantha paused. "I never made the connection. It wasn't until much later that I realized what it was. So I just went back inside my home and locked the doors."

Mitchell had the urge to move a strand of hair that had fallen over Samantha's face, but he held himself in check and chastised himself for even thinking it. "What happened when Dr. Daniels came down?"

"Civilian flights were hard to come by, so it took two days for him to get down to Atlanta. Looking back on it now, I should have known something was happening, but I focused completely on the lesions and didn't pay attention to what was going on around me. Reports started trickling in from other cities, rumors started spreading among the staff of the CDC, news reports seemed to grow more violent. Something was happening, and no one was quite sure what.

"I distinctly remember seeing a report of a mob attacking and killing a family with their bare hands. Ripping away limbs and tearing them open with their teeth... the report went into detail about it. Someone had taken a video on a cell phone. A family sat in a minivan at a checkpoint. It wasn't as common as now, but checkpoints had been set up on all interstates, and if you were going to travel from one state to another, you had to verify the identity of everyone in that vehicle and submit to a search. A line had formed at this checkpoint in... I think it was Kansas City, and this crowd of people stormed the minivan. They came from the fields, their clothes in tatters, some of them nude. The driver's side window was open, and one of the mob reached in and pulled out the driver, the father. Several of the mob ripped open his belly and eviscerated him while the others tried to get into the van. I remember thinking that the doors were probably unlocked, and why weren't they just trying to open the doors? But that didn't even seem to occur to the mob. They just smashed the windows, and several got into the van. You couldn't see what happened to the family because... because blood coated the windows from the inside."

Mitchell knew the scene well. He'd seen a thousand just like it. "And you didn't investigate an attack like that further? The CDC didn't look into it at all?"

"How could we? Smallpox is the deadliest virus in human history, and this particular strain is the most adaptive and unusual we've ever seen. We felt—*I* felt—that our only mission was to develop a vaccine. The world could go to hell around us, we could always rebuild, but someone had to be around to do the rebuilding. And I felt developing a vaccine was the way to do that."

Samantha folded her arms and looked down at the table. "When Luther arrived, he excised portions of Eric and Ryan's brains and ran tests for almost a week. That week was… unusual. I'd go home every night and come to work the next day just like every other day, but something was different, almost like the air had changed. The days got darker… something.

"The reports kept coming in, mobs of people killing anyone they could find. It wasn't entirely unexpected. Whenever law enforcement breaks down, you can expect most men to satisfy their more wicked urges. Say what you will about Freud, he predicted that, at least. When a society loses the protections of law, like in Iraq after the American invasion when we dismantled the police and military, there's still an order behind the chaos. In Iraq, people were trying to get as much material gain as they could. If that meant killing people, they did it, but it was never purposeless. Even when it seemed like it was, we found out that the killing occurred because of feuds between tribes that went back centuries. The killing had an explanation, but the killings taking place here, they had no explanations, no reason behind them."

She paused, unfolding her arms and putting her hands in her lap. Mitchell glanced down at the digital recorder to ensure it was still on.

"I was driving to work one morning, and there was a jogger by my house," she said. "I don't know what possessed this woman to go out jogging during martial law, but she did. Maybe she thought that little bit of normality would help get her through the rest of the insanity during the day. I don't know, but she was attacked by two men. I saw it. They chased her down like lions after a gazelle. And this woman was in shape, skinny and fit, and the men were not. One was so overweight his stomach bounced over his belt, but they ran her down. It was like they were possessed and didn't care if they gave themselves heart attacks.

"I swung the car over to the curb and opened the passenger door for her to jump in. She was screaming, and I could see the look on her face, her eyes like marbles, completely devoid of the capacity to think. She got to the door before the first man reached her. He hit her like an NFL linebacker and took her down. I think even the impact might have killed her, but they didn't stop. They… they…"

Mitchell said, "If you need a second, you don't have to…"

"No, I want to." Sam swallowed. "They pulled her legs off. The strength they must've had to do that… now we know that it's because of the near-toxic levels of adrenaline pumping through them, but at the time, all I could think was that it looked like pulling the legs off a fly. Just snap, a few tears, and they came off. The woman lived only a few moments after that, in shock as she bled to death. The men began… tearing her apart."

Mitchell's throat felt dry. He swallowed. "Do you mean... eating her?"

"I don't know if I'd call it eating. Anything they swallowed was instantly vomited back up, along with a torrent of blood. I got to see it from up close. They weren't even paying attention to me. They were just focused on the legs. There was nothing I could do. I wasn't armed, and no one was around to help, so I drove away. I thought that I would call the military patrols and have them go by when they could. At least she would get a proper burial, and maybe they could even catch the two men that killed her."

Mitchell nodded. "That must've been traumatic to see. Surely by now you knew something new was going on? Not just a poxvirus, something much more violent?"

"Yes, I did. That's why I wanted to speak to Luther as quickly as I could. Those men were infected, but unlike most infected, they were faster and stronger. When infected with *Variola*, after the incubation period has passed, people are bedridden. They can't even go to the bathroom by themselves, much less chase down a runner and tear her limbs off. I suspected we either had a new strain of virus, or the old strain was doing something new. The lesions were of course my top concern, and I hoped Luther had something.

"When I got in to work, I found Luther in the general labs, the unsecured labs we took tour groups through, on the main floor. He was sitting at a terminal looking at DNA matrices. I came up behind him, standing quietly a few moments before saying, 'That bad, huh?' I knew that when he got a result, he liked to email me, or whoever he was doing the analysis for, right away. He wanted us to know what he found so that he could get the inevitable questions out of the way. The only time he didn't email with updates and reports was when the news was going to be something we didn't want to hear.

" 'It's not good,' he said. 'The lesions. They're not lesions at all.' He took off his glasses and placed them on the table. His eyes were rimmed red, and I saw the black circles underneath them that hadn't been there when I picked him up from the airport.

" 'What are they?' I said, sitting on the desk.

"He rubbed the bridge of his nose with his thumb and forefinger and said, 'They're rotting brain tissue. The brains of that young man and his father were rotting from the inside out.' "

Sam hesitated. "And just like that, everything was different."

4

"It seemed like one of those things," Samantha continued, "that once you know about it, it starts popping up everywhere. The CDC that day started getting more and more requests for autopsies, blood work-ups, biopsies, everything that could be tested, primarily from the military. They were the de facto police force, and the number of arrests and shootings to maintain order had skyrocketed. They thought something new had been introduced, but they knew even less than we did. Military intelligence thought that a radical terrorist group had infiltrated all facets of society and was attacking in large numbers. That's silly to even think about now. Why would a terrorist group use their bare hands, when weapons that could kill a hundred times more people were available? That was just one example of the flaw in their logic, but they had even deeper problems. Soldiers were not immune, and the biohazard suits barely seemed to help. They were exposing themselves to the infected and, in turn, becoming infected themselves.

"In one episode, a soldier had turned on his comrades in the middle of a patrol. Patrols went out in parties of six, and a single soldier had killed all five other men. When they found him, he was riddled with at least ten bullets. They shot him everywhere—the head, heart, kidneys, legs—but he hadn't given up. All he cared about was killing those soldiers, and he did it before he bled to death. So the military was thinking they would make great weapons. We're in the middle of the worst epidemic in history, it's not even close to over, and they're thinking, 'Gee, we can turn these monsters into weapons to fight the North Koreans.' So now the military has an interest in figuring out what's going on, and that's when the numbers hit, the numbers of all the people who had attacked others and were required to be killed. The FBI's Hazardous Material Response Unit had at least four thousand samples taken from around the country. They had known about this effect for five weeks and kept it to themselves. They said they didn't want panic. But I don't think that's the truth.

"The truth was that only a handful of giant corporations own the media and dominate the markets. When there's a crash, they're the hardest hit. They were just trying to prevent another crash, hoping this new behavior induced by the virus just went away on its own." She shook her head. "They were willing to let people die if they could just prevent losing any more money, as though money meant anything anymore.

"Anyway, once we determined what it was, a degenerative disorder of some kind brought about by the infection of *Variola*, where only certain regions of the brain were affected, we could see what was happening, the sheer destruction of it. Even in Atlanta, you'd see people dashing from place to place on the sides of the roads, screaming, blood raining out of them. But they wouldn't really attack each other. I noticed that almost immediately. Luther decided to stay and help at the CDC. One night we were running samples through the spectrometer and he said, 'This isn't found in nature. This is engineered.' The statement took me by surprise. I'd considered it, of course, but Luther had never intimated that his thinking was going down that path. 'That's the problem with man's arrogance,' he said. 'It destroys itself, too.'

"I didn't know what he meant at the time, but I do now. Whoever engineered the virus didn't prepare for its devastation. Maybe they had an antidote they thought would save them, or they just didn't realize how quickly it would spread, I don't know, but a biological attack is not like a nuclear attack. A nuclear attack is a precision instrument by comparison. A virus, once released, spreads everywhere. The country of origin isn't immune. I think the engineers just didn't realize it would come back to haunt them so soon.

"One thing we couldn't figure out, though: Why was the violence showing up now? Was it a new strain or a different virus entirely? Once we had completed a full analysis of Ryan and Eric's blood, we sent the results to Dr. Goldberg in Tel Aviv, Dr. Gam in Paris, and Dr. Arcand at the WHO. None of them could tell me anything. It was Luther who said something that broke it open, casually, as we ate pasta at my house with Jessica gulping chocolate milk, a treat Luther had arranged for her. 'What if it's the initial infection, but this trait is dormant for a certain time?' My mind reeled. How perfect that would be. Distract us with smallpox while infecting us with a virus we wouldn't be screening for, one that wouldn't cause symptoms for months or years.

"I had Jessica get a sleeping bag, and the three of us drove down to the CDC immediately. Darkness had fallen and few city lights were on. The government attempted to conserve resources wherever possible, and streetlights were not considered a necessity. But you could see *them*. Not swarms of them, not yet, but you could see a few of them just out in the piles of refuse or wandering aimlessly in the darkened streets. One man stepped in front of our car and screamed at us, bloody spittle spattering over the hood of my car, before he jumped onto the hood with both feet.

" 'Go!' Luther shouted. I hit the gas. The man flipped forward, his face against the windshield, leaving a smear of blood and bits of ragged flesh. Jessica had her eyes closed and was chanting something to herself. I looked at Luther, who appeared as if he wanted to pass out and was gripping the dashboard so tightly his fingernails were cutting into it. Luckily, the CDC wasn't far. I parked and, feeling as though I had a lead weight in my stomach, got out and hurried inside with the two of them. It was just like that, overnight. One night we didn't feel entirely unsafe, and the next night we couldn't drive down the street, but we didn't realize how much worse it was going to get, not then. My only concern then was to test Luther's theory that the infection had occurred months or years ago in Eric and Ryan and had lain dormant.

"Few staff were there at that hour, but I did find an assistant willing to help me. I set Jessica up in my office on the couch and was about to leave when she said, 'Sam?' I turned and saw the look of… *resignation* on her face. Not fear, not confusion, more like the acceptance of a belief she didn't want to believe. 'We're going to die, aren't we?'

"I sat down near her feet. 'No, we're not going to die. Epidemics have lifespans—that means they only last for so long. Then they stop spreading and begin shrinking.'

" 'They stop spreading because they've killed so many people, don't they?' I could've lied to her, but if I'd learned anything about her, it was that her ability to look at her circumstances without flinching exceeded that of any adult I knew. She would know I was lying.

" 'Yes,' I said. 'The virus kills until there aren't enough people to spread it farther. I think this virus is near the end.' I leaned down and kissed her forehead. 'Now get some rest.'

"Luther, the assistant, and I all went up to the BS4 labs. The analysis would take hours. I got some Diet Cokes for us, which was saying a lot because anything like that was a luxury at this point. When the data had been collected, we all sat out in the waiting room and drank our sodas and waited a good twenty minutes, just decompressing, I guess. We talked about mundane things. The weather, how much Luther missed professional baseball, where we got our shoes from. That was one of the first things that hit you when resources were scarce, but it was something you never thought about before: What if you needed new shoes? The stores were closed, and ordering online was impossible because so few mail carriers existed anymore, it being one of the jobs that interacted with the public so much that the government regulated who could deliver the mail to slow the spread of the virus, so what would you do? That hadn't been a problem for me, but the assistant said he had to trade a box of candy bars with neighbors for some new sneakers. That seemed to be how most people got the goods they needed, barter. Money was almost worthless now with hyperinflation, even though people were still fighting and killing for it.

"After resting for a bit, we ran the data. The results were… not anything I expected. The biopsies showed infection in every area of the body we tested, anywhere touched by blood. The virus spread throughout the whole body and assimilated into the cells. We ran antibody tests, viral antigen detection tests, and a viral RNA test. The antibody test tells us a ballpark range of how old an infection is." Samantha swallowed. "We estimated that Eric had been infected for nearly eight months, about the length of time that had elapsed since the T-zero event, and Ryan not too long after that. But we still couldn't identify the virus itself. It simply didn't resemble anything we'd seen before.

" 'Luther,' I said, as we stood over the terminal staring at the results on the monitor, 'could you do me a favor and test me for the virus, please?' He stared at me for a while in silence, and then nodded and went to retrieve the equipment. Once Luther had taken my blood, he hurried back to run the test and I was left with the assistant in the lobby. He was a younger guy, maybe twenties, and looked uncomfortable. 'You don't need to stay,' I said.

"He couldn't look me in the eyes and kept glancing between the floor and me. 'I just… I have to…' he said. 'I'm sorry.' The assistant rushed out of the lobby, and I was left alone, staring out the windows onto the street. I sat that way for a long time, but I don't know if it was minutes or hours. Time didn't seem to have the same meaning to me just then.

"Cars could sometimes be seen on the streets, but they were rare. So when I heard the engine, I was curious, and the stress of waiting for the test results, anything that could take my mind off it for a moment, was welcome. I went to the window and stared down into the street. A sedan sped by and then veered to the right as people swarmed into the street. The car attempted to get around them, and then it just decided it would push through them. The car had slowed down enough that it didn't generate enough force to plow through the crowd, though. One of the bodies got stuck in its passenger-side wheel well, forcing the car to skid to a stop.

"I don't know why I watched what happened next—morbid curiosity, I guess. Maybe just that the possibility that I was infected made me want to see, really see, what I had to look forward to. I don't know. But I watched.

"The crowd rocked the car for a while, tipping it nearly to the side. The strength they had amazed me. But they couldn't punch or kick, which is what they needed to break through the windows. Inside, I saw a couple. A man and a woman. They were screaming, helpless, like flies caught in a flytrap.

"Finally, one of the crowd broke through the back window. Just…forced himself through, pushing with his head against the glass. The screaming grew louder as the infected crawled over the backseat and bit into the neck of the woman, coming away with a chunk of flesh and sinew. The man opened the door and tried to run. He got maybe two steps before they took him down. I couldn't see what they did to him, but the screaming stopped. The woman in the passenger seat now had several infected on top of her. The only thing I could see was her leg, shifting around like it was bobbing in water.

"When they were through, the infected wandered around. It seemed random, purposeless. They would run into each other but never attack. Somehow they recognized one another.

" 'Sam?' I turned to see Luther standing behind me with his arms folded. He wasn't looking me in the eyes, and I just knew. Without him saying a single word, I knew… I was infected.

5

A breeze blew over the roof and Mitchell leaned back in his seat, farther away from Samantha. He didn't speak for a long time, but neither did she. They both sat while the breeze whipped their hair, pushing a few pieces of debris off the roof.

"So you're saying," Mitchell finally said, "that um... I mean, you're infected?"

Samantha nodded.

"Am I at... I mean, am I..."

"Chances are, Dr. Southworth, that you've been infected for months without knowing it. I wouldn't worry about catching it from me." Sam paused. "When I found out, with Luther standing there behind me, my first thought was of Jessica. Had I inadvertently infected her? Had I ended her young life without even knowing it? I've been in love, I've had friends, found purpose in my life... but she hasn't experienced anything. The thought of her dying so young filled me with anxiety and sadness, and all I could do was sit down in one of the chairs in the lobby. 'Luther, we need to test Jessica, too. And you should probably get tested as well.'

"He sat down next to me and said, 'I ran Jessica's blood while you were down here. She's infected, too. But I'm not.'

" 'Then you need to leave right now, Luther. As quickly as you can. The next plane.'

He grinned, his elbows on his knees as he leaned forward. 'And where would I go? Where could I go that those… *things* won't be? Iceland? Antarctica? You think I'm going to die freezing my ass off on an iceberg just to buy myself a few more years of misery? No, I'm staying. And we're gonna find a cure.' He said *cure*, not *vaccine*. Maybe someone else wouldn't have caught that, but I knew what it meant. It meant he thought I was going to die. A vaccine is preventive. A cure is postinfection. I was dying, and Luther had just told me that he was going to risk himself to help save my life and the life of the little girl that had come to mean so much to me.

" 'I can't let you do that,' I said. 'You have to save yourself.' He looked at me in a way that said, *What the hell are you talking about?* Then realization about something splashed across his face. 'You don't know, do you?'

" 'Know what?' He stood and held out his hand. I took it and he helped me up. It would of course have been customary to let go as he led me down the hall, but the warmth of human touch is… well, it's something that you need more than you think you do. We held hands as we walked to the front desk in the lobby and Luther pulled up some grainy video that he had downloaded onto his laptop. 'This is LAX, about two weeks ago.'

The video showed a plane that had just finished boarding and was getting ready for takeoff. The tarmac appeared clear, but the passenger walkway still attached the plane to the terminal. The plane yanked away, tearing the walkway from the building. Bodies spilled out of the walkway. The infected poured into the plane. The ones that couldn't make it because the plane pulled away jumped inside, hanging by their hands, clawing their way in. It was difficult to make out what was happening in the cockpit from the angle of the camera, but the pilots were frantically shouting into their radios. One of them rose and got a gun out of a box just as the door broke down. The infected rushed in, jumping on them both like ants over a bit of food. The man with the gun got off two shots, both into the chest of one of the infected, and it didn't do anything. He still rushed forward as though nothing had happened.

"Luther opened another file. 'This is Paris, about a week ago.' The video was a stadium of people. They huddled together, some of them with rifles or pistols, others clustered together in groups, vacant stares in their eyes. The scene seemed to be a calm one until the steel doors to the stadium burst open and the infected dashed in, the roar of the screams from both predator and prey forcing nothing but a high-pitched static sound to come through the speakers. The scene was… I can't even describe it. One man was sprinting, and one of the infected grabbed him from behind. It scalped him, ripping the entire top of his head away just like that. A young girl was torn apart in front of her parents. The father ran back to help and was decapitated when several of the infected bit down into his throat and worked their way through. Never in my life did I ever think I would see anything like that.

" 'And this is Tokyo,' Luther said. Another video, a crowded subway. People ran and screamed, someone recording on their phone as a mob of infected howled and chased them from car to car. When they reached the last car, the infected swarmed inside, and the video died. 'This is Mecca,' he said, opening another.

" 'I've seen enough,' I whispered. 'How was this kept hidden? Where were these reports when—'

Luther interrupted and said, 'Reports? There's no reports. The government and companies that own the media don't want this stuff out. They want you to think they're in control. If people felt they'd lost control, everyone would rely on themselves. The government would lose authority. They want to keep that authority for as long as possible but... I mean, you saw it.'

I stared at the still image of an infected. 'Why didn't you tell me?' I asked.

"He replied, 'I thought you knew.'

"I should've known. The world fell apart, and I'd had my head in a lab. Partly, it was done on purpose. I couldn't handle all the negative reports. I couldn't handle the death and the blood. So I told myself that the best way to focus was to cut myself off from it all and just concentrate on what I actually could influence, the development of a vaccine.

"Just then, screaming came from outside. We both looked back. They'd seen us. A group of infected were sprinting for the CDC building. The doors were locked, but they were just glass. Several of them screamed from the moment they began running until the moment they slammed into the doors.

"I jumped to my feet and ran down to the lower levels and my office. Luther ran right behind me, stopping only once to break the glass in an emergency case that contained an axe and a fire extinguisher. He ripped off the axe and caught up to me. Jessica was asleep. I grabbed her shoes and immediately pulled them onto her feet. 'What's going on?' she said, sleep still in her eyes.

"As I lifted her, I said, 'We're leaving.'

"Only two exits were built into the CDC building: the front parking lot where we had parked, but where our car was now overrun, and the back exit that connected to an underground lot for use by the top administrators. 'There's a parking garage on the lower level,' I blurted as we ran down the hall. Just below us a couple of floors, you could hear the screaming and the thuds from destruction of furniture, windows, and equipment. The screaming was the worst part, high pitched and nonstop, as if they didn't need to pause for breath.

"A loud crash echoed in the halls, and I knew they'd stormed the stairwell and gotten through the door onto our floor. I hit the button to call the elevator, and we couldn't do anything but wait. Jessica clung to me, and Luther gripped the axe so tightly I thought he might break the handle. We knew they were close from the screaming. A door flew open down a long hall, and I saw them flood the corridor. Many of them had died in a hospital and wore hospital gowns, but some had blood-soaked normal clothing: suits and jeans and workout clothes. Some were nude, and those were the worst. Their skin pale as morgue lights, missing breasts or genitals or hunks of flesh, covered with bullet holes or stab wounds or the charred flesh that said they'd made it through a fire.

"I hit the elevator button again and again. Luther searched the corridor for somewhere else to hide, another office. He found one, but I knew the door wouldn't hold. The elevator was the only way. I didn't even hear the ding over the screaming, but I saw the doors open, and we leapt on. I pressed the button for the bottom floor.

"Those five seconds as we waited for the elevator doors to close was the worst five seconds of my life. I saw their faces, the blood that poured from their mouths and eyes, and the wounds that wouldn't heal. I looked into those black eyes, sunken back into their heads, and I knew that humanity might not survive this, that maybe Luther had been right, this was Armageddon.

"One leapt, screaming. It landed a foot away and Luther swung with the axe, splitting its head in two. Blood spattered over the hallway, over Luther's clothing and face. He pulled back just as the doors began to close. He couldn't catch his breath, and his hands trembled so much the axe fell from his fingers. Lifting them in front of his face, he watched as the blood dripped down over his palms. 'We have to wash that off,' I said. Luther seemingly couldn't move or speak; his eyes were as wide as golf balls.

"The elevator stopped on the bottom floor and opened. I stepped out, Jessica still clinging to me. Quiet and dusty, the parking garage hadn't seen anyone in a long time. No one parked there anymore. I don't know why. I think it was something about being in confined spaces with other people. A hallway on the south end had another set of elevators, a drinking fountain, and bathrooms. We rushed over, Luther still unable to say anything. I pushed through the door and pulled him over to the sink. After turning the faucet on, I shoved his hands underneath and began wetting paper towels and scrubbing the blood off his face. I took off his jacket, which was spattered with blood, and tossed it on the floor.

" 'I killed him,' he muttered, his hands still trembling. 'I… I killed him, Sam. I killed someone.' I ignored him, focusing instead on cleaning off all the blood. Jessica stood away from us, and I motioned with my head for her to stand even farther back. I thought, *I don't want her to get infected*, and then a deep sadness filled me when I remembered. 'I killed him, Sam. I killed…'

"I lifted Luther's face with both hands, ensuring our eyes locked, and said, 'He was already dead.' This seemed to calm him, and I finished getting the blood off. When we were through, bloodied paper towels and pink, frothy water coated the sink. The three of us stood there, unable to move, listening to the sound of our breaths. Luther, powerless to hold the emotion back, leaned against the sink, his hand over his eyes, and wept. I placed my hand on his shoulder and allowed him to finish. Jessica folded her arms and stood against the wall, her eyes on the linoleum. Luther finally stopped and looked up. 'You must think I'm such a pussy.'

"The phrase, for whatever reason, maybe just to have a release, made me chuckle. 'Well, a twelve-year-old girl went through the same thing and isn't crying.'

"Luther laughed, nodding his head as he used a dry paper towel to wipe the last of the moisture off his face. He said, 'Whoever did this, whoever made this, they needed to start with live *Variola*.'

"I nodded. I'd run through this analysis a long time ago. 'There are only two places in the world to get it,' I said. 'Here, in the BS4, and a BS4 laboratory in Siberia where the Soviet Union held their stock.'

" 'Could someone have gotten into the stock here?'

"I shook my head. While anything was possible, the thought of someone stealing poxvirus from the CDC was insane, so unlikely as to be impossible. 'No way,' I said. 'It's locked in a steel crate, wrapped with heavy chains, and has two padlocks the size of my head. Only a few people even know about it, much less have the key. And the location changed every week. We had fifty-two different locations we'd cycle through, and only maybe five people knew where it was at any given time. Four of those people are dead. I'm the fifth.'

"Luther tossed the used paper towel into the garbage. 'Then it had to have come from Russia. Sam… whoever released this, unless they were suicidal, must've prepared for it. They had to have engineered a vaccine and a cure. They'd be insane not to. Otherwise they were signing their death warrants, too.'

" 'There's plenty of people who would kill themselves to bring about the end of the world.'

"Luther shook his head and said, 'Yeah, but not every one of those people would have the money, the knowledge, the facilities, or the patience to engineer a virus like this. This had to be a nation. And if it was a nation, they developed a vaccine and a cure. They wouldn't condemn their own people to this.'

"His reasoning was sound except for one thing: human beings weren't rational, not all the time. That's why economics could never be a real science. The fundamental basis of all economics is that people act in their rational self-interest. That's why economists can't predict anything. They don't realize how much we really are ruled by emotions. 'No,' I said. 'I disagree. I think they would risk it.'

"He stood up and walked to the door, peeking outside. 'We have to try,' he said.

"The possibilities of what to do next were limited. I had thought the best course would be to hide out in my house or maybe somewhere with sunshine. Spend my last days in a place near the ocean where I could watch the surf and lie under a blue sky. But then I looked at Jessica. I saw her youth and the terror in her eyes. She didn't want to die. She didn't think it was a way to bypass the horror the world was about to face. For her, the only thing left was to fight. So for her, I had to fight, too. 'Okay,' I said. 'We'll go to the lab.' "

6

Samantha waited a beat, lost in thought, before continuing. "Sneaking out of the parking garage wasn't difficult. All the infected were up in the parking lot outside or in the building itself. Under cover of darkness, we ran up the ramp into the open street and then down the sidewalk. Our car was gone, but we thought we might be able to convince a military patrol to give us a ride to the airport.

"The streets had an eerie calm to them, or maybe they appeared calm because of the chaos we'd just seen. You could hear every piece of trash flutter in the breeze, every cricket, every plane that drifted by overhead, and there were a lot of planes, both military and civilian.

"As I watched Jessica, I considered telling her about our infection—that the virus was dormant inside us but that when it was triggered, it would turn us into one of those… things. I knew she would want me to—she'd want the truth—but I just couldn't do it. So little of her childhood remained that I didn't want to take anything that was left by telling her that, so I didn't tell her. I didn't even discuss it with Luther. I didn't ask him how long the antibody test indicated I'd been infected. In South America, during the initial outbreak, I dealt with a canister that I believed at the time had released the smallpox virus. The canister later showed no *Variola*. But as we walked down the darkened streets, I knew then what had been in the canister: the real plague, the one meant to bring the world to its knees. That left the question of why I hadn't displayed symptoms yet but Eric and Ryan had. I wondered if I had received a more docile and slow-moving version of the virus, one that took years to incubate rather than months. And that made me wonder which form Jessica had.

" 'The detonations,' Luther said, 'the green clouds. You told me once that *Variola* could be turned into a mist. Is that what they did? Turned it into a mist to be carried on the breeze?'

"I shook my head, making sure I took a couple of steps away from Jessica so she couldn't hear what I said, and I spoke quietly. 'No, that's not what they did. They did turn it into a mist, but not for the breeze. They wanted it to be carried in the clouds. Once in liquid form, *Variola* can be carried by clouds. They shot gallons of it high in the air, and it was caught in the clouds and transported around the world.'

"He shook his head, staring at the sidewalk, which was cracked and dotted with litter. 'Amazing,' he said. 'Just amazing, the planning this all took.'

"Down the road a ways, we heard an engine. We ducked into a yard until it was obvious that the vehicle was a military patrol. I ran out into the road and held my arms up. The vehicle, a Humvee, slowed and then stopped. I ran over to the man in the driver's seat. 'I'm Dr. Samantha Bower with the Centers for Disease Control. Our facilities have been overrun with the infected. We need transportation to the airport for—'

"The soldier stopped me. 'Ma'am, that's a negative. We got a situation just outside the airport, and all units have been called in.' I looked at Jessica and Luther, who were out on the sidewalk now.

" 'Can you take us as far as you can?'

"He considered it for a moment, and I could tell he wanted to say no, but he caught a glimpse of Jessica and swore under his breath. 'Get in.'

"We piled into the Humvee and drove down the residential street before linking to the interstate. Once there, we took a bridge that gave us a view of the city. Fires raged across the cityscape, entire buildings engulfed. Black streams of smoke billowed into the sky, darker than the night. 'What happened?' I said to Luther. He stared at a skyscraper that was burning from the ground up and shook his head.

" 'I have no idea.'

"The airport, or just about a mile outside of the airport, was cordoned off. Up about two hundred yards, I could see the front line. We were witnessing a battle—one of the first major battles in a new type of war. The street had been narrowed with vehicles and sandbags, leaving a kill zone in the center. Soldiers were set up behind the sandbags, with others with large rifles posted in the empty buildings on either side of the street. Tanks flanked the soldiers, and green helicopters hovered in the skies like crows in the night. It was all for one purpose: to kill as many infected as they could. And there didn't seem to be any end to the supply.

"They rushed in through the kill zone by the hundreds. After being mowed down by the soldiers' weapons, most just got back up and kept running. It took complete devastation of the body to get them to stop. I could hear the soldiers shouting. They were asking the same kinds of questions we were asking: 'Why don't they attack each other? How are they so strong?'

"Luther sat in the Humvee like a blind man who'd just been given sight. His mouth was open and he didn't blink. 'Do you think they've retained memory?' he asked. The damaged prefrontal cortex has nothing to do with memory.

"I shook my head. 'I don't know.'

"We were quickly ushered out of the Humvee and ran over to the first terminal at Hartsfield-Jackson. The sound of rolling tanks echoed, and people were barking commands. The soldiers wore body armor and helmets. I didn't understand why. Their enemies didn't have guns. They stood right in the way of the rampaging hordes. The military just wasn't prepared. They thought this would be Iraq or Afghanistan. But the enemy they were fighting didn't care how many of them died, they couldn't be frightened, and they wouldn't stop, no matter what. I even saw a few of the infected that'd had their legs blown off or had been cut in half at the waist by rifle fire still crawling toward the soldiers before they bled to death.

"The planes leaving the airport filled the night air with the roar of their engines. I quickly recognized these weren't normal flights. These were escape rafts from a sinking ship. Only two planes remained by the time we ran into the terminal. The crowds of people took my breath away. They were smashed in like cattle, but even cattle seemed to have a sense of decency to the other cattle. There, I saw full-grown men kick little girls to get ahead of them in line. I saw the young injuring the old, the strong injuring the weak, the smart injuring the dumb... anyone with any type of advantage was using it now to harm everyone else around them.

"The poor clerks at the counter were shouting, trying to calm everyone down. Explaining to them that there was only so much room on the planes and that not everybody would be allowed to board. I don't know who fired the first shot, whether it was one of the airport police or one of the potential passengers, but I know that after that first one, a series of back and forth started. We ducked low and headed for the escalators as the sound of gunfire filled the airport and the crowds ran. But they weren't running away, they were running toward the gates and the last two planes.

"To take three spots on that plane would mean three other people wouldn't be able to leave. That didn't sit well with me, considering how many families were there. But Luther told me, 'You can't think that way anymore. You can't think about their survival or the survival of your friends. Look around you, Sam. This is the end of the world. You have to think about the survival of your species. And right now, you have the best chance of developing something that can stop this madness. You have to survive.' I don't know if I believed the part about me being the best chance to develop a vaccine or a cure, or even to find one that had already been developed, but I knew I had a better chance than anyone else at that airport. In terms of survival of the species, I had to get on one of those planes.

"The gates were guarded by several airport police, all with their guns drawn. You should have seen these men. Barely in their twenties, shaking, their faces pale with fright. They looked like kids in Halloween costumes. I don't think they ever expected for a second that they would have to draw their weapons. We ran to the first one, a young kid probably no more than nineteen. He swung his gun around at us and shouted, 'Don't come any closer!'

"I held up my hands. Slowly, I reached down to the lanyard around my neck that held my identification from the CDC. I held it up. 'My name is Dr. Samantha Bower with the Centers for Disease Control. I'm a virologist. I'm studying this outbreak and trying to find a vaccine. I need to get on one of those planes and get out of the city.'

"He glanced around but didn't budge. 'You're lying,' he shouted. 'You're all lying!'

" 'This is my identification. Look at it. It has a watermark. It can't be forged. This man next to me is a physician as well. He's helping me find a way to stop this.' I paused. 'I know you have family somewhere, family you're worried about. I'm trying to help them, too. The only way to stop this is if someone finds a vaccine. Otherwise, our entire species will become like *them*.'

"The boy swallowed and looked down at Jessica. 'Who's she?'

"I placed my hands on her shoulders. 'My daughter.' He stood there a long time, his gun aimed at us. The crowds grew more restless. Even with guns, the police wouldn't be able to hold them back for long.

" 'Okay,' he said. 'Back there, now. Now, go!'

"We ran. I clutched Jessica's arm, and we ran past the two officers in front of the gate then one of the airline employees. The crowds behind us became enraged. I could hear their roars. Shots were fired, and people screamed... but I didn't look back."

"On the plane, I could see that most of the seats were taken, but there were some empty ones. These quickly filled with employees of the airlines. No announcements came, nothing letting us know where we were going or how long the flight would be. The engines just started, and we pulled onto the landing strip and took off. The fires were more visible now, dotting the darkness below. I glanced around at the passengers. They weren't just some random cross-section of society. These were blue bloods; the wealthy. I could tell from the shoes, the purses, the watches, and the suits. I had no doubt that people had been bribed to allow them on. I could hardly complain, as I'd used influence to secure my place as well, but it didn't seem right that money could save your life. Maybe it always had, and maybe it was a naïve view to think money wouldn't be the determining factor. I don't know.

" 'Any idea where we're going?' Luther asked one of the passengers in front of us.

"The man, without turning around, said, 'JFK. And then the fuck outta the country.' I looked at Jessica, her face coated in sweat, her hair messy with bits of dirt and soot. She looked like the survivor of some natural disaster you see afterward on television, interviewed by the media and asked ridiculous questions like, 'How do you feel?' I placed my arm around her and leaned my cheek against her head. For some reason, the man's statement that he was getting out of the country seemed to make sense right then. I didn't even consider that the rest of the world was even worse off than we were."

7

A glass of water sounded divine right about now, but Mitchell didn't want to run downstairs to fetch it. The Miami heat in the summer was something else, particularly for someone who was born in Alaska. Mitchell glanced down at Sam's drink. It would take a gun to his head to make him take a sip of that, considering Sam's infection. Just this, sitting across from her, was something he could only do because he didn't have a choice.

"I'm really interested in what happened in Siberia. How did you find the people that developed the virus?" he said.

"It wasn't in Siberia. After landing in JFK, we had the option of taking a flight out of the United States. New York was disintegrating, but much slower than Atlanta. New York had already been through a major tragedy and had emergency response teams, logistics panels, and communication hubs set up. Emergency hospitals and quick-response crews were seemingly always on call. When the word came that the virus had spread to the East Coast, they were ready. But no amount of preparation could get them truly ready for what they were going to face. There was nowhere in North America with more people per square foot, crammed into a tighter space, than New York City. When the dormant virus finished its incubation period, millions were affected, millions that took to the streets.

"The military did the best it could. It choked off major streets and used snipers and helicopters for the majority of the fighting. In fact, the military was so successful at first that the civilian government thought cutting resources to the military and increasing resources for civilian protection centers wasn't entirely inappropriate. Of course, the powerful, those with influence, filled the protection centers, cutting everyone else off. The military couldn't even fully equip the teams it had. It seemed martial law didn't mean martial law. The military still had commanders beholden to people in the civilian government and did what they were told.

"They just didn't see what was coming. They didn't think. The dormant virus had infected the military, too. When its dormancy ended, an already-depleted military lost more than half of its force to the virus. Squadrons fighting in the streets would suddenly have to defend themselves from those in their own ranks. They would be fighting the infected and have to turn around and fire at their comrades. On top of that, no one knew who was in charge. The military said it was, the civilian government at the state level said it was, and the federal government claimed it was issuing orders directly to the states. Directions weren't followed, and regional military commanders began making their own decisions. In some regions, where they abandoned their body armor and traditional military fighting tactics, they did well. In other places, where they tried to stand toe to toe with the infected and just overpower them, they failed. Huge numbers of soldiers were lost to nothing more than their commanders refusing to recognize that they were facing a superior force, a force that didn't care if it lost. One of the generals told me that the winner of any fight is the one with the most to lose. But he didn't understand that the infected didn't think that way. They *couldn't* think that way. They just didn't care about the outcome or themselves. The winner of any fight isn't the one with the most to lose, it's the one with the least to lose.

"At JFK, we landed and got off the plane into a hub of raging death, not at all what I expected. The infected had attacked and the marines dug themselves in. Wave after wave of the infected, screaming, mostly nude, like some dark force from our nightmares, hit the marines' position over and over and over. The marines fought to the last bullet, and when no ammunition was left, they used knives and fists, trying to stab and beat the infected to death. That was another thing that wasn't planned well—ammunition. Everyone had a weapon, but not everyone had enough ammunition to actually use it against hordes of infected. We jumped into a transport, which was just a city bus used to move people away from the airport. People were rushing to get there, and as soon as they did, they'd have to wait in line to be rushed away. The marines couldn't hold the position for much longer, and as our bus left JFK, I saw them overrun.

"It looked like a tsunami flowing over the marines and taking them with it. A few stragglers tried to run and were quickly swallowed up. Some stood and fought and were taken down like ants. I saw one marine slam the butt of his rifle into the jaw of an infected, a woman, and her jaw snapped off, but she didn't stop. She leapt on top of him, attempting to bite into his face, but without her lower jaw, all she could do was pour blood down his throat from the wound—torrents of blood, right down his throat. I knew that not everyone would die from an attack by the infected. Many of them would become infected themselves.

" 'They don't die,' Jessica said, panic in her voice. I put my arm around her as the bus sped down the interstate and away from the airport.

" 'No, they'll die,' I said. "The human body can only survive about a week without water. They're not getting any water. Eventually, they'll all die of dehydration.'

"A man seated across from us said, 'That's where you're wrong.' The man had light black skin and green eyes. He wore jeans and a green army jacket, the handle of a pistol visible underneath the jacket. 'I've seen the way they kill,' he said. 'They don't just tear apart the flesh. They drink the blood, too, a lot of it. Most of it's thrown up, but they're learning. They're trying to retain as much as they can… they're trying to survive.'

"I held Jessica closer to me and Luther said, 'That's impossible.'

"The man shook his head. 'I wish it was.' The name on the breast of his jacket said JASON S. He turned his face toward the window and didn't speak for a long time. Neither did we. Everyone on the bus just watched the passing city out the windows. The fires had begun to burn across New York, too, just like in Atlanta. I didn't know how they started, but I later learned that the military had been given orders to burn the bodies of the infected. Sometimes, if there was an enormous number of dead in a building, they would just light the building on fire rather than drag the bodies out to a ditch or the middle of the street. Each fire I saw filled me with anxiety, and they kept increasing, more and more suddenly flaring up in the darkness. I imagined that's what oil fields that had caught fire looked like.

" 'You know a lot about this disease, considering how new it is,' Luther said to Jason. 'Like, you've seen them up close.'

"Jason frowned and looked at us. 'I have. The outbreak is only new here. It's been happening in parts of South America for almost two weeks, in regions of Western Africa for almost a month.'

"Luther shook his head and said, 'I haven't heard anything about that.'

" 'That's because you're not reading the right news. We hear and see what they want us to hear and see. You think some drunk slut in Hollywood is news? They want us distracted. Not paying attention. Bread and circuses distracted the Romans two millennia ago, and it hasn't changed that much since, just different bread and different circuses.'

"Luther watched him a moment. 'You've been there?'

"Jason nodded. 'Yeah, man. I been there. I was there in the beginning when we went into the Congo and found entire villages torn apart. Piles of limbs stacked up like firewood. The villagers didn't know what it was. They thought their relatives were possessed. They'd lock 'em up and then bring in the shamans to exorcise the devils. Second they opened the door, the ips would grab 'em, tear into 'em."

" 'Ips?' Luther asked.

"Jason nodded. 'Yeah. That's what we called 'em. I don't know where it came from. Maybe it meant Infected Persons, something like that.' Jason paused before saying, 'They didn't tell us what we were heading into. Our orders were to take out terrorist cells that were using violence to force the relocation of the native population. That's what they told us. I thought we'd be fighting Congolese guerillas. That first time we saw the ips, they were running out of the jungle. They sprinted right into our gunfire, even the kids. I had to fire at a boy maybe nine years old, maybe younger. I blew off part of his head and you could see his brains, just, like, exposed. He kept comin' at me. I had to put eight rounds into him before he went down, and even then he wasn't dead. I was firing at center mass and it just didn't do anything to stop them. And the screams... that's the part of it that wakes me up at night, the screamin'. They don't sound like human beings. And you'd be in the jungle, in the thick of trees and vines, and you'd just hear that screamin' from all directions and you wouldn't know where to fire. And they'd hit you like a tornado, and you'd hear your own men crying when they got pulled into the jungle... and then the screaming would stop.' Jason swallowed before continuing. 'Ten squads went in, Special Forces... Delta Force, SEALs, Force Recon...Ten went into the jungle and only one came out, my squad, with just me and one other man. That's when I knew it was over. There was no stoppin' it.'

"Jason's eyes ran down to my chest and made me uncomfortable until I realized he was staring at my lanyard. 'You with the CDC?' he asked. I nodded, and he said, 'What're you doing up here?' I looked at Luther, who had his gaze fixed on Jason. Something was happening between the two men, but I didn't know what. Almost like some sort of challenge.

'Same as you,' Luther said, 'running.'

"A moment passed between them where neither spoke. Jason finally said, 'I figured you guys ran for the hills. I saw some people with the CDC trying to collect samples from the ips at the airport. They were some of the first ones killed.' I glanced at Jessica, who stared at the fires in the city around us. 'So?' Jason said. 'Do you have a vaccine or not?'

"Luther said, 'Why would you think we have a vaccine?' Jason quickly looked around, making certain no one was paying attention to us. Everybody on the bus was so focused on themselves that I don't think they cared what anyone else spoke about.

'That's the rumor,' Jason said quietly. 'That y'all have a vaccine and just haven't gone public with it yet.'

"I shook my head. I'd heard these rumors my entire career at the CDC. That HIV had been cured, but the drug companies had bought us off so we wouldn't release it. That cancer was avoidable, but we didn't want to release the research on prevention because too many industries relied on the 'cures' they peddled. Any time people feared something, they needed to blame someone else for their fear.

" 'If we had a vaccine,' I said, 'I wouldn't be on this bus.'

"Something about him made me uncomfortable, the way he wouldn't blink, maybe, and I looked out the window rather than keep eye contact. But the city wasn't much better, not for a few hours, until we got upstate and away from major population centers. The buildings turned to barns, and soon we were surrounded by forests rather than skyscrapers. Traffic clogged the roads there. No one knew where to go. Every talking head on television told them something contradicting the last talking head. MSNBC said to run to the cities. Fox News told them to get to the country. CNN told everyone to stay where they were and that government rescue operations were underway."

Samantha grinned and shook her head, taking a sip of the drink before taking off her sunglasses and putting them on the table. "There were no government rescue operations. The government was as clueless as everyone else. We were fighting an enemy who didn't care about morals or standards, who didn't care about harm to themselves, who had no problem wiping out civilian populations. Our government didn't know what to do. They were still thinking in terms of the old world, the pre–T-Zero-Event world. Politicians fought just so opponents across the aisle couldn't get something done. But the rest of the world was changing. Generals disobeyed the president because he hadn't served in the military, and they didn't respect him. States tried to assert their authority over the federal government as much as they could. The governors of several states even declared their states would be seceding from the Union. All federal programs were shut down. The governor of Arizona said that illegal immigrants carried the virus over onto US soil, and he used people's fear as leverage to build a wall. That's how the Rio Grande Wall began construction, a nineteen-hundred-mile wall with armed guards every two hundred yards, at a price tag of only five billion dollars. The ips, a term I began using after meeting Jason Shafi, were killing us in our own homes, and the government cared about whether Mexicans sneaked across the border.

"Driving near Albany, New York, we saw a line of people, handcuffed, with blindfolds over their eyes. It was just like that, too, like you see in the cartoons, when Bugs Bunny is almost executed and then saves himself. The only things missing were the cigarettes dangling from their mouths. We stopped near them. The military checkpoint couldn't let us pass until they verified the identities of everyone onboard. I don't know why they cared who we were; maybe they thought terrorist groups were attempting to take advantage of the chaos and attempting further attacks. Maybe they'd bought the Arizona governor's line that illegal immigrants had spread the virus and were rounding up everyone without proper ID. I don't know. But they made us sit there for almost half an hour. So I had a good view of the line of people.

"They were crying and trembling, some of them young, really young, preteens. The soldiers lined up in front of them didn't seem that much older. I could see them, too, because of some floodlights illuminating the area. They appeared almost as frightened as those lined up in front of them. And then, without warning, someone barked an order, and the soldiers lifted their rifles. I pressed my hand to the glass and said, 'No.' But it was just an instinctive reaction. I knew I couldn't help them now.

"The soldiers fired, and all but one of the people in the line dropped. The one that didn't drop was one of the preteens, a girl. The soldier in front of her hadn't fired. He held the gun in position but refused to fire. His CO barked orders at him, got in his face, shoved him, but the man just lowered the rifle and then dropped it. I couldn't hear what they were saying, but I could see his lips. All he said was, 'No... no.' Finally the CO picked up the rifle and shot the girl himself. He tossed the rifle at the soldier, bouncing it off his chest. The soldier stood at attention, and, though it was difficult to make out, I think I saw tears on his cheeks.

"Somewhere the order had been given that what was termed the 'pre-infected'—those who had the virus and were beginning to show symptoms but hadn't reached the point of attacking others—would be executed. To house them in prison, feed them, and take able-bodied men away from the fight in order to guard them was determined to be a drain of resources." Samantha smirked. "A nineteen-hundred-mile wall was deemed necessary, but allowing sick citizens to live was deemed a drain of resources.

"We crossed the border that night into Pennsylvania and then Ohio, where we transferred to another bus. Wyoming was the least-populated state in the nation and someplace Luther and I decided we could hide until we figured out a way out of the country. All international flights had been cancelled with the exception of military flights, and no one was going to give us space on those flights.

"Jason Shafi came on the other bus, too. He sat across from us again. Late into the night, when Luther and Jessica were laid out on the seats asleep, I noticed him staring at a photograph. 'What is that?' I asked. He glanced up from the photo.

" 'Just someone I lost.' He paused. 'You're looking for a vaccine, aren't you?'

" 'What makes you say that?'

" 'What's the likelihood that two scientists are on the same bus at the same time? Poindexter has that look about him, that look of certainty. That's the hubris of science, you know. Science isn't a history of developments like people think. It's a series of revolutions, complete upheavals of knowledge. After a particular revolution, the previous theories are laughable. And without their certainty, people lose themselves. So they cling to the next thing and are so certain about it that they'd fight to the death to protect it... until the next revolution. That's the look he has, as though he knows everything, but, just underneath, he's uncertain about everything.

" 'You don't speak like any soldier I've ever met.'

"He leaned his head back on the seat and turned his eyes out the window again. Skyscrapers, then farms, and now cornfields and great open valleys. 'My degree is in engineering,' he said. 'I thought that I'd be the best asset to the army that way.' He smiled. 'Haven't used it since the day I graduated from college. Shows how much I know.'

"I shifted in my seat. We'd been on the bus so long that my legs were falling asleep. 'This is a civilian bus, but you're military. What's a soldier doing with civilians?'

"He grinned. 'Tit for tat. You're looking for a vaccine, aren't you?'

" 'Yes. Now you.'

He put the photograph in the breast pocket of his jacket. " 'Let's just say I didn't agree with my orders.'

" 'You're a deserter.'

" 'It's not desertion to want to live. They were sending my team to our deaths, and I'd seen enough death.' He paused. 'Few days ago, I found out the team was killed to the last man. There wouldn't have been any use me dyin' with 'em. The brass don't see it that way, though. I'll be shot if they ever find me. How do you plan on finding a vaccine?'

"I didn't know who this man was or why he wanted to know what we were doing. My initial discomfort with him had faded. We'd all developed it, everyone that had lived through T-Zero, a general distrust of strangers. I tried to fight that distrust. 'We have a few leads,' I said.

"He chuckled. 'We're about to live in the desert together and eat cactus three times a day, but you don't think you can trust me with your big plan to find a vaccine for something that's already infected half the world? Doesn't seem too smart to me, especially since I can help.'

" 'How can you help?'

"Jason leaned forward, holding my gaze, our eyes locked as he said softly, 'Because I know where a vaccine is.' With that, he leaned back into his seat and closed his eyes, settling into sleep and leaving me staring at him."

8

Samantha gazed out over the buildings, hardly remembering Mitchell sitting in front of her. She glanced down to the digital recorder and then back out to the horizon. "That's what he told me, that he knew where a vaccine was, and then he just went to sleep like it was ordinary news, as though he were telling me who won the soccer game last night. Of course, I couldn't sleep. I wanted to wake him up right then and make him tell me what he was talking about, what he knew, but I didn't. Somehow I understood that he wouldn't tell me then. He would at some point, but not right then. So I closed my eyes and tried to get some sleep, too.

"When I woke, we were in Iowa. The farther we got from the coast and the cities, the less damage we saw. No waves of infected barreling through the towns, no tanks, no constant thuds in the sky from the helicopters raining bullets down onto the ips. It seemed almost… normal. We even stopped at an open diner still serving food. They took barter or money, and hyperinflation hadn't touched them. Eight dollars for an omelet and an orange juice. Nothing I've ever had in my life had ever tasted so good.

"After we ate, we were back on the bus. Luther and Jason didn't really talk much, but Jessica was fascinated by him. She asked him questions about his background, the places he'd been, how many infected he'd killed. 'Too many to remember,' he said. Jessica then asked if he had a family. His went silent for a while then said, 'Not anymore.'

"Luther calculated that Niobrara County in Wyoming would be the ideal location for us to set up and plan our next move. It was the least-populated section of the state, which meant there likely wouldn't be any infected. Jason watched us with a detached curiosity and never said a word about our plans. Not until we were in South Dakota. Driving through barren fields, watching the empty canyons and the way the sunlight reflected off a flowing river next to the road, I wondered how many more buses like this one there were. How many other civilians were they shuffling from the cities to the more rural counties in the Midwest and Rocky Mountains? My guess was a lot, which meant they didn't yet understand that not everyone with a dormant virus activated at the same time. Jessica and I weren't showing any symptoms, and the hope grew within me that maybe the virus would simply stay dormant.

"After days on the bus, having to refuel three times at government gas stations and stopping for the bathroom at least five times a day, we finally reached the Wyoming/South Dakota border. The dirt was dark brown, with the odd cactus growing between rocks and on the sides of cliffs. Luther said, 'I bet we can rent a cabin. Maybe stay put while I try and arrange a transport out of the country.'

" 'Ain't gonna happen,' Jason said.

" 'Why not?' Luther replied, not even bothering to look up at the man. I had noticed that Luther had a particular disdain for anyone trying to tell him what to do, and Jason seemed to be that man. Jason felt like he'd already lived through this once in the jungle and gave off an air of being an expert on the infected, which seemed to drive Luther crazy. Luther was used to being the one everyone looked to for answers, and to have someone like Jason challenging him sent him into miniature tantrums.

" 'How long you planning on hiding out in Wyoming?' Jason asked.

" 'What business is it of yours?' Luther replied. He had been examining a map and put it down on his lap, his eyes rising to meet Jason's. The two men stayed silent for a second before Luther said, 'And by the way, what are you doing here? Sam and I caught the bus heading this way on purpose, and you just happen to follow us? And you were on the first bus and just happen to sit across from us again? That seems like too much of a coincidence, and I don't believe in coincidences.'

"To his credit, Jason didn't take the bait. He just smiled and said, 'I wanted to come. I think she's got a plan that might stop all this. If she does, I have an obligation to help.'

Luther laughed. " 'Obligation, huh? Men like you don't have obligations. You just have opportunities, and nine times out of ten, you take the opportunity that benefits you the most and screws everyone else.'

" 'That so? And how many men like me have you met in that lab of yours?'

" 'I know your *type* really well. You're the ones who fight just to fight and run away when it gets too hard. The ones who believe you have to have regular wars to keep a nation healthy. You try to justify your inherent violence with imaginary arguments, unable to face the fact that you're just barbarians that find living in civilization difficult.'

"Jason leaned forward, pointing his finger at Luther. 'And I know your type, too. You think everyone else is so far beneath you that they become numbers. And you can do whatever you want to numbers. I may be violent, but the greatest atrocities in history weren't committed by people like me. They were committed by people like you, people who thought they knew what the greatest good was. That's your battle cry: the greatest good for the greatest number, and you justify every slaughter with it.'

" 'And you still haven't answered my question. Why are you on this bus?' Luther set the map aside as though he were going to rise up and punch Jason in the face. I thought I might actually have to restrain him. But Jason just chuckled, and Luther soon followed. I still didn't understand what it was between them. Some sort of primal, alpha-male nonsense, I guess.

" 'I'm on this bus because I can help you end this,' Jason said.

" 'How?' Luther said. 'You gonna club the virus to death?'

" 'Better. I know a place that Samantha would be very interested in. Shangri-La.' Jason paused. 'And it is real. I know because I've seen it. I've been there.'"

Samantha folded her arms again, lost in thought a moment, the breeze blowing over the tops of the skyscrapers, before she said, "I had heard rumors of Shangri-La before. It was a place somewhere in the world where everyone was immune to the virus, the initial Agent X. Different reasons for it were given. Some people said the townspeople had a natural immunity, some said they had developed a vaccine, others that they had a cure. A cure... You don't really know how far you're willing to go to save your life until your life is threatened. Having a cure to a virus is a one-in-a-billion shot. We don't even have a cure for a cold or the flu, much less a destructive supervirus like Agent X and whatever this new strain was, but at that time, in that moment, when Jason said 'Shangri-La,' I knew I would go. I would have to. No matter how long it took or what the cost was, I would try to live.

" 'Bullshit,' Luther said. 'Might as well go visit Santa Claus and see if he has a cure.'

" 'Ain't no myth, man. I've been there. I've seen it. I've seen the town, and it's not a lie. It's in the middle of the jungle, and there's ips all around them, but no one in the town's infected. They know how to fight it, if you can find them.'

"Luther folded his arms. 'And where exactly are they?'

" 'Western Africa. The Congolese jungle. About as far from civilization as you can get.'

"Suddenly, I didn't believe in coincidences anymore, either. Jason Shafi didn't look like someone running from something, he looked like someone running to something. He wore his army jacket proudly. He wasn't hiding from anyone. 'You already knew who I was, didn't you?' I asked him. He grinned.

" 'I may have heard you'd be on this bus.'

" 'How?'

" 'When you checked in for the transport, they told me who you were. I'd been looking for someone that could help me. I've tried going up command, but the army's such a mess that no one knows what to do. I went to the medical research division and told them about Shangri-La. They didn't even care. It wasn't that they didn't believe me. They didn't care. The only thing they cared about was making sure they weren't the ones blamed for this outbreak.' He shook his head, staring out the window. 'They actually told me to leave the science to them and just go shoot some ips, which was the only thing I was good for.'

" 'And your plan is what?' I asked. 'Take us across the world to look for a town that you may or may not be able to find?'

" 'Oh I can find it,' he said. 'I remember it really well. They saved our lives coming out of the jungle. We were out of water, out of food, and out of rounds. They took us in for more than two weeks, until one day they showed us the way out of the jungle. They have a leader, a woman with this, like, blood-red hair. Complete red, not like you see here in the States. She spoke English, a white woman, and said her name was Tristan. I asked her how they weren't infected, and she just smiled and said that God had favored them above all other people. Wouldn't talk about it again.'

"Luther said, 'And you think they have a vaccine or a cure? They probably just weren't exposed to the virus properly. Or if they were, maybe they just killed off the infected before it could spread.'

"Jason shook his head. His eyes moved between the window and Jessica, and the way he looked at her, the sadness, I wondered if the picture he'd been staring at was of a child. He swallowed and said, 'They were exposed to it every day. The ips would run out of the jungle, come screaming through town. Sometimes they'd take a chunk of someone, cover them in blood, but that person never got infected. Tristan told me one night they don't get infected. They must've found a plant… something. I pressed her hard, and that's when they asked us to leave town. They don't want the world to know what they know.'

"Luther now appeared enthralled by what Jason said, that glimmer of hope that the damned get in their eyes when someone gives them something to hope for. He looked at me and then back to Jason before he snorted and said, 'I'll believe it when I see it.'

"A few hours later, the bus broke down. It was just a city bus from New York, after all, really old. We pulled over on the side of the road, and I could see the smoke billowing from the engine. The driver called it in, and they said they might be able to get someone out there by tomorrow, so we'd all be sleeping on the bus. My back and legs ached, so I stepped off and stared in every direction. It all looked the same: sand, dirt, brush, and hills. Other than the road, you wouldn't even know you were in America. We were in the middle of nowhere and stuck. You have to understand—now I know better. Now I know that the government, in an emergency situation, considers most of the population expendable. Each politician looks out for their powerbase, the people that keep voting them into office. But most of the people in this country don't vote, and they don't call their congressmen or legislators for favors. They're abandoned first, just like the major donors are taken care of first. I didn't realize it then, but no one was coming. The buses were expected to be a one-way trip for relocation in sparsely populated areas. If we made it, we'd have to fight for our survival there. If we didn't... just fewer people for the government to worry about.

"A desert wind blew and whipped my hair. After being crammed on that bus with only a few inches of open window providing new air, the wind smelled fresh and clean. The blue sky was painted with the contrails of the jets and commercial planes that had sped across the sky but weren't there anymore, the sky as empty as the desert before me.

" 'What do you think?' Luther asked as he came out behind me. 'We wait here or walk? The driver told me there's a town about four miles up. We could be there before it got dark. Or we could wait here for help. I think wait here.'

"I nodded. The thought of trudging through a desert without food or water seemed a death sentence as certain as going back to the cities. Jason came out, too, holding Jessica's hand. She had this demeanor that made me think of her as an adult occasionally. But right then, that demeanor dissipated, and she ran across the road to a patch of desert flowers, scarlet flowers with yellow centers. Instantly, she was a child again.

" 'It's not a good idea to wait here,' Jason said when Jessica was out of earshot. 'No rescue's coming.' Luther, at this point, ignored him. He turned away and leaned against the bus, which was fine because Jason was really only speaking to me.

"I disagreed with him. I still held on to that old-world view that, if possible, the government would help us. The military would help us. Being betrayed by both seemed about as likely as suddenly being able to fly. 'The driver said to wait and that he'd radioed it in,' I protested. 'We have food and water here, and other people. There's no reason to risk the desert.'

" 'There's at least thirty people on this bus. How many people do you think can fit onto a transport chopper or a jeep? Seven or eight at the most. The nearest base is two hundred miles from here. You think they're gonna send an Mi-17 four hundred miles three times to rescue civilians on a bus? I don't know when the decision's going to be made or if it already has, but some people are going to be abandoned. The brass knows they can't save everybody, and they're not coming out to Buttfuck, Wyoming, to rescue us.' He looked around. 'We're wide open. You might as well put a target on the bus. Ips ain't all we got to worry about. The law doesn't exist anymore, especially out here. No cops to enforce it, and you can sure as hell bet there's no military patrols. You wanna live, we gotta get to that town.'

"Luther pushed himself off the bus. He put his hands behind his back and turned to Jason, facing him square, and said in a flat, even voice, 'We're not going anywhere. We're waiting here until help arrives.'

"Jason didn't fight. He simply nodded his head. He must've expected us to react like that. What he basically told us was that the world didn't work the way we were accustomed to it working anymore. In a flash, almost overnight, that world had changed. It began with the T-Zero event, but it wasn't until the dormant unidentified virus became active that the world really changed. I think Jason knew we would have to see this new world for ourselves, that no one could explain it to us. So instead of arguing, he strolled over to Jessica and began describing the different types of flowers and bushes.

" 'I don't trust him,' Luther said. He had a knack for understatement. The tension between them had more to do with ego than trust, but I didn't tell him that. I think in a way, Luther was jealous. He'd had this grand plan that we would, the three of us, fly off to Russia on some great adventure seeking out a vaccine. Even if we did, Luther wasn't a fighter. He'd never held a gun, as far as I knew. Couldn't fistfight or scavenge if he had to. Luther was an academic, most comfortable in a classroom or a laboratory, and this new world we were just thrown into didn't have much use for academics. 'And why's he so damn interested in Jessica?' he asked.

"I watched the way he played with Jessica. He knew children, was accustomed to them in a way only those who had them could be, and Jessica couldn't have been happier. Maybe she had a small crush on him. I didn't think that at the time, though I can see it now, but the most likely explanation for her affection was that Jason reminded her of her father. It became apparent to me how much his absence had left a hole in her life that I couldn't fill no matter how hard I tried.

"I looked up to the sky and the sun, which would begin setting in a few hours. 'We better eat something,' I said. 'It'll be dark soon.' Luther glanced up to the sky as well, but his gaze returned to Jason and the laughing child who couldn't be separated from him."

9

"Night fell in the desert in a way I wasn't used to. I couldn't believe how quickly the sun set and how cold it got. That was the most surprising part, I think, the cold. You would think the desert would retain heat, but that wasn't the case at all. The wind howled, and it made your skin feel like ice. We had eaten outside, just some MREs stocked on the bus, but as soon as the sun went down, we couldn't stay out there anymore. We and the other passengers climbed back onto the bus and settled in for what we knew would be a long night. The seats weren't exactly comfortable, and sleeping in them upright sounded miserable. I let Jessica lie across my lap and ran my fingers through her hair until she fell asleep. Luther had his arms folded and drifted in and out. It seemed he wanted to stay awake, but exhaustion took him. Jason was the only one of us who didn't seem tired. He sat stiff as a board, his eyes glued to the windows.

" 'Who's that photo of?' I said quietly so as not to wake Luther or Jessica. He looked at me and didn't say anything right away. Even the mention of the photo brought pain to his eyes. I don't think he was the type of man to display emotion, so the emotion he did display must have been involuntary… unwelcome.

" 'My daughter,' he said softly.

"The way he said it, I knew what had happened. I could see the entire ordeal in my mind already. He'd been away, and he couldn't protect her. That caused even more pain, the feeling that he had failed her as a father. I regretted bringing it up, but he continued to talk about it.

" 'You know the worst part?' he said. 'I didn't get to say goodbye to her. The phones were out, so I rushed back when her mom told me she was sick. But by the time I got there…'

"I swallowed. 'This was during the initial outbreak?'

"He nodded, pulling out the photo and gazing at it. His eyes grew moist before he exhaled loudly and slid the photo back into his pocket. 'Nine months ago. She was eleven, right about her age,' he said, motioning to Jessica with his chin. 'What's her story?'

"I ran my fingers through her hair again. The way she slept was beautiful, her lips and face softening from the hardness she wore during the day, the protective wall she'd put up around herself to convince the world she was fine dropping away while she slept. Now she really did look like just a child. 'Her father died during T-Zero, and he asked me to look after her. I don't know why I said yes. Maybe I thought I could find a way to get her to people who actually knew how to raise a child or something, but that first night at my house, she threw her arms around me and cried, a long cry, as though all that pain had to come out and she couldn't control it anymore. She hasn't cried since then. It was like she had to get it out once and then put on a brave face for the rest of the world. She's been with me ever since.'

"Jason nodded, grinning before he said, 'You know what she told me today? When we were outside playing with those flowers? She said she hoped that you and me got married because she doesn't like seeing you lonely.'

"I don't know why that statement hit me hard, but it did. I think I blushed and looked away. I had been lonely, a deep loneliness that I didn't even know I had until Jessica came to stay with me, and I realized how much I liked the sound of someone else in the house with me. I was going to reply when Jason turned back to the window. His fingers reached down to the pistol he had tucked in his waistband and his eyes narrowed. 'What is it?' I asked.

" 'Somebody's out there.' He rose, and marched off the bus."

"I didn't wait long to follow him outside. I slowly laid Jessica down on the seats as I slipped out from under her and went outside. The air had grown even colder, and the winds were like jet engines in your ears. The clouds were black now, and I knew a storm had come in. I stood in front of the doors of the bus, looking out into the blackness of the desert, when I felt a shiver up my back. I thought it was the air at first, just the coolness of the wind getting down my collar, but it wouldn't go away. 'We should go back inside,' I said.

"Jason stood still, his hand on his pistol like some Wild West gunslinger. 'Be right back,' he said, and then he strolled into the desert and out of sight over a small hill. I was left searching the night for him, and I debated running out there to find him. I glanced back into the bus to check on Luther and Jessica, and as I did so, I noticed the arm reaching down to me from the roof.

"The fingers gripped my collar and pulled so hard the cloth wrapped around my throat and strangled me. I began fighting, pulling at the hand on the collar, trying to break away. I spun around to get a good look at my attacker, and I saw it.

"Its nose was gone, maybe bitten off, maybe rotted off. The skin on its face drooped, missing in some parts and thin in others. Its mouth opened, revealing blood-soaked teeth that had bits of ragged flesh hanging from them. It snapped at me from the roof, toppling over, nearly taking me down with it, before that scream escaped its lips. I ripped myself away from its fingers. As I turned to run, another one ran around the bus and tackled me.

"I hit the ground on my back, the weight of this… *thing* on top of me. It had once been a man. That's the hardest thing about ips, that you still see them as human. That you imagine their lives and families… that you think you can talk or reason with them. And then you see their eyes, completely vacant, washed-over eyes, pox eyes, like looking at two flashlights or something, just nothing there.

"It tried to bite me. I shoved my arm against its throat, pushing its head back, the teeth snapping a few inches from my face. Blood dripped down over my cheek and hair. Luther had rushed off the bus, but he was the only one. Everybody else just watched from the windows. Luther grabbed it and pulled it off but only for a second. It was back on its feet and rushed him. I rose, gagging from the blood that rolled down my face. It had Luther by the throat and pinned him against the bus. As it snapped forward, its teeth headed for Luther's shoulder, suddenly half its head blew off, bits of brain and bone spraying over me and into the desert sand. Jason came around the bus with his pistol drawn. The ip fell to its knees and then to its side.

" 'Get on the bus,' Jason said. 'Now!' We didn't have to be told again. I dashed for the doors and Luther followed… but the doors were locked. I pounded on the glass and the driver just shook his head. I screamed, 'Let us on, you asshole!' but I may as well have been speaking a different language. He didn't care at all. The other passengers were no help, either. They stared at the violence going on not five feet from them with a type of detached curiosity. I saw Jessica's head pop up, sleep written on her face. Behind me, I could hear Jason's pistol popping and the screams that encircled us in the darkness. I didn't look back. I kept pounding on the glass. Jessica's face contorted in anger and confusion, and she rose and dashed for the doors. The driver grabbed her around the waist and pulled her back. She kicked and clawed at him, but he didn't let go.

"Fear got the better of me, and I had to look back. At least thirty ips were sprinting for us, screaming in the darkness. Jason took his time, picking his shots carefully, firing each round deliberately. I didn't know how much ammunition he had, but I guessed it wasn't over thirty rounds. I pounded on the doors harder, hoping they'd break, or that someone would change their mind and help us… anything. No one moved, no one except Jessica. She bit down into the driver's hand so hard she drew blood. He yelped loud enough that I heard, and he let go. She quickly opened the doors and Luther pushed me through. Jason backed up into the bus, still firing, and closed the doors as the ips were on top of us. One of the ips got his head in, vomiting blood over the steps as we tried to pull the door closed. Jason shot him in the top of the skull, creating what looked like a canoe, before he kicked the ip in the head and sent him flying onto his back. We got the doors closed, but they were glass doors. They wouldn't hold forever.

"I jumped up and grabbed some luggage. Bags and suitcases, gym bags, whatever I could get my hands on. I tossed them to Luther and Jason, who began stacking them against the door, piling them high. The windows were too high off the ground for them to climb through, and other than that, there was no other way onto the bus with the exception of the windshield. The ips didn't seem to figure that one out, and they kept pounding against the door. We heard the glass break, and Luther and Jason put their backs against the luggage, pushing against the ones trying to get in. A few of the other passengers ran over and tried to help, but most of the people sat there, wide eyed and scared, unable to lift a finger to help. I grabbed Jessica and pulled her to the back of the bus. The infected pounded at the bottoms of the windows, shrieking, spattering blood against the panes of glass. I could see them clearly now, civilians, dressed much like us. A few of them wearing Yankees or Giants T-shirts and jerseys, clearly from another bus from New York, one that didn't make it.

"I searched the bus for weapons and couldn't find anything but a set of golf clubs. An entire bus escaping a war zone, and no one bothered to bring weapons on board. I locked Jessica in the bathroom and told her to wait there, giving her one of the golf clubs. I hugged her and she said, 'Don't leave me here.'

" 'I have to, but just for a bit. Don't come out, no matter what you hear.' I shut the door and turned around to see the driver hobbling to the back of the bus. He pushed past me and tried to get into the bathroom, probably because he knew it was the one place with a lock. I shoved him away from there and he swung at me with a fist, barely missing my jaw, and then grabbed me by my hair and tried to take me down in the aisle. I still held one of the golf clubs, and I swung at him, hitting him in the ear, which made him wince but not let go. I swung again and hit him in the eye. My swings couldn't generate enough power to really hurt him, not until he reached back to strike me, which gave me room. I hauled off and hit him hard in the temple. It must've caught him off guard, because he stumbled back, and I pulled away. I lifted the club like a baseball bat and swung with everything I had, catching him on the side of the head, bending the club. He fell onto one of the seats, disoriented and bleeding from the head. I lifted the golf club… and then stopped. I dropped it to the aisle and ran over to help keep the ips out.

"Several men, including Luther and Jason, had their backs to the luggage. There wasn't room for me. So instead I ran to the driver, pulled the keys out of his pockets, and ran back. I tried starting the bus, but the engine wouldn't turn. One of the infected out in the road saw me. Our eyes met… another woman. She sprinted for the bus and threw herself up against the front, clawing at the windshield as though it were a piece of fruit she could get through. Her nails scraped against the glass, a few of them ripping away, leaving a smear of blood and skin."

Samantha could tell that Mitchell was absorbed in her story, even if he had seemed apprehensive since she'd told him about her infection. His eyes were locked onto hers, and when she stopped speaking he said, "Um, how did you get out of that?"

Samantha said, "It's getting later in the afternoon. You wanna break for lunch?"

"No," Mitchell said. "I'd like to hear how you got out of there."

"As much as they threw themselves against the windshield, they couldn't break it. They would sprint, jump onto the windshield, and slide down. If one of them had even thought to pick up a decent-sized rock, they could've broken through, and there wouldn't have been anything we could've done about it. But that thought didn't cross what was left of their minds. The only thing ips think to do is to attack, attack, attack, attack, nothing else.

"I left Jessica in the bathroom a long time. Hours. I wanted to be sure none of them would get onto the bus. I would check on her and tell her just a little longer and then leave her another hour or two. I didn't want her to see what I was seeing, men pressed up against the luggage, the only things separating us from them, hellish figures throwing themselves against the windows, shrieking like beasts... We shut all the windows, of course, but you could still hear them. Most people didn't want to sit on the seats because the faces of the infected would be pressed against the glass, so they huddled in the aisle where there was room. I don't think anyone slept that night or the night after.

"We took turns leaning against the bags, but on that second day, it seemed like the ips weren't trying as hard. And after three days attacking the bus, they were hardly more than moving sacks of meat. Too much blood expelled from their bodies. That's why they were so frantic to attack; they were terminally dehydrated. Blood raced out of every orifice of their bodies, not to mention the torrents that would spew out with their vomit. Without someone to attack and replenish that blood in their bellies, without some source to hydrate them, and an inability or aversion to drinking water, all their strength left them with their blood.

"That was the first time, that morning on the third day, as I stared out at the ones that were still standing and jumping at the bus at a snail's pace, that I had any sense of hope. We had to starve them of their sustenance, or just outrun them long enough to let the virus kill them. They were in the process of dying, and if we could keep clear of them, we might be able to survive.

"When the sun hung above us in the sky, Jason took a step away from the bags. He lifted his pistol and said to the few men that were helping him, 'Move the bags.' The men hesitated a moment and then did as he had asked. Several of the ips were outside the doors, and Jason fired at each one, one at a time. They collapsed like bowling pins. He opened the doors and stepped outside. Only a handful of them were still functional, and they were so out of it they didn't even seem to notice him. He hopped back on the bus and gathered his one black bag and motioned that it was time to go. I grabbed Jessica and Luther and followed him out. We quickly left the bus and walked up the road. One of the ips tried to follow us, an overweight man in a velour suit, and Luther said, 'Shoot him.'

"Jason shook his head. 'Why waste the bullet?'

The town was four miles away and the sun so hot that my neck began to burn within minutes. I knew it would be a long, difficult walk.

10

Mitchell swallowed when Samantha finished speaking and then looked at his digital recorder. He had two gigs of memory, plenty to capture the entire tale, but not much battery power left. He turned off the recorder and pulled out some fresh batteries.

"If it's all right with you," Samantha said, "I'm going to grab something to eat."

"Sure, yeah. If you could get me a bottle of water, that'd be great."

When she was gone, Mitchell leaned back in the seat and watched the sun in the sky. As a kid, he remembered seeing on a show, maybe *Reading Rainbow* or something like that, that the sun had about ten million years of energy left. After that, it would die down and eventually go supernova. That bit of knowledge had haunted him his entire life. He knew he'd be long dead, but just the thought that humanity wouldn't live on, that in ten million years there'd be nothing in the solar system but cold rocks, filled him with dread. He remembered thinking about that a lot, so much that he stopped paying attention in school and began devising ways that humanity could potentially survive.

Samantha placed a bottle of water on the table, snapping him out of his thoughts, and he mumbled, "Thank you." He turned the digital recorder back on while she took a bite of her sandwich. "The town was Clover, Wyoming, right?"

"Yes," Sam said.

"Tell me what happened there."

She took another bite, chewed, and then wiped her lips with a napkin before finishing the drink in front of her. "The walk was terrible. Jason had managed to smuggle a few bottled waters off the bus, but I could've drunk those in one sitting. So we sipped. And the heat barreled down on us. I don't think it would've been as bad if we were someplace safe, but every sound I heard, every stone that happened to roll from the wind or brush that moved, was an infected ready to rush out at us. We walked in the center of the road, and the road heated up so much I thought the soles of my shoes would melt. It was the most anxious time in my life.

" 'Have you seen any of the reports from other countries?' I asked Jason, more to occupy my mind than anything else. He looked down, the sweat rolling off his face and splashing in small droplets on the black tar, where it would evaporate in a couple of seconds. He glanced at Jessica and I said, 'It's okay.'

" 'The democracies were the hardest hit. The dictatorships probably could've taken steps to prevent the spread, but dictators don't really care about the population. Most of the warlords in the African subcontinent used the virus's spread as a chance to strengthen their regimes. In Cameroon, the president for life, because they don't call themselves kings, declared that the virus was an invention by Europe, Israel, and the United States to wipe out the sovereign people in Africa and replace them with puppet regimes. Without education or access to outside materials, people believed him and rallied to his side. When the US dropped aid over the hardest-hit areas, the people burned it, thinking it was a ploy to spread the infection further. The next week, we still dropped aid. People burned the goods we sent them and we still sent more, because it's easier than going through the process of cancelling the aid. That's why the infected overran the military. For the majority of the military, thinking outside the box isn't a favored trait. The people who *do* think that way usually aren't given commands. It's the people who follow the orthodoxy who rise in the ranks and command our armies. That's why we'll never have a Hannibal or Alexander the Great.'

"He paused a moment, either lost in thought or catching his breath. That was something else that you would never have guessed about the desert: the heat made it unbearable to breathe. The air seemed much harder to suck down, as it was less oxygenated. Jason stopped and took a sip of his water before speaking again.

" 'My father was in Korea during the war,' he said. 'There was this hill the commanders wanted taken. He advised against it. They were in a good position to just wait. The hill was surrounded and the Reds couldn't get food or water up there. But the commanders wanted it now. So they ordered them to charge the hill. The soldiers were picked off like flies from higher ground. If they had just waited a few weeks, the Reds would've surrendered. My father was the one who told me people thinking outside the box aren't promoted.'

" 'But you still went into the military,' I said.

" 'Yeah,' he said, looking down the road. 'Had nowhere else to go. I think that's the town.'

"Just out maybe a mile, I saw what looked like a mirage, mall structures surrounded by glimmering water. As we neared, the water began to shrink and I could make out the individual buildings much better.

" 'China's doing the worst,' Jason said. 'They denied the existence of the virus for so long that everyone was caught by surprise. Beijing was devastated. We're talkin' 90 percent loss of human life in a city of almost twelve million. It was a… nightmare. Rivers of blood flowed in the streets, and the screams filled the air morning until night. I was only there for one day on a transport through the city, but I can still hear the screaming, like it came from the earth itself.' He paused. 'I saw a man trying to dangle off a bridge, hang there with a rope wrapped around his waist so they couldn't get to him. Running wasn't an option. During the first day or two after the infection takes over, especially if they stay hydrated, ips can run about as fast as the fastest humans could. So the only option in Beijing was to hide. This guy got underneath the bridge and thought he was safe, and the ips grabbed the rope and pulled him up. I saw his face when they started doing it as I rode by. It was just utter shock, complete disbelief. Before I could look away, he unfastened the rope and fell about four hundred feet onto the rocky shore of a river below.'

"I took a moment before speaking. Mostly because I was sucking breath so hard that speaking came with real effort. 'I think we can wait them out,' I said. 'They dehydrate so quickly, if we starve them of any fluid, I think we can wait them out. Even if they learn, or remember, to drink water, they'll just bleed to death.'

"Jason shook his head. 'I don't think they bleed to death. I don't know why or how, but I don't think that's the issue. It's the hydration, but I think they can survive without blood in their bodies, at least for a short time.'

"Luther said, 'That's impossible.'

"Jason looked at him and then away. 'You say that a lot for someone caught in the apocalypse.'

"When we arrived at the town, I was surprised how quaint it was. Like a town from a Western movie, with shops on both sides of the main street going through town and homes on the outskirts. About the most welcoming thing I saw was an ice cream shop, but the doors and windows had been boarded up. Didn't stop me from looking through the cracks, just to make sure, but it looked like the store had been abandoned for a while. In fact, the entire town was empty. We searched every store, every home, and every car in the street or in garages. No one was there.

"And it hadn't been four miles. Based on the time we left the bus to the time we arrived at the town, I estimated that we'd walked about six miles. Still not an impossible feat, but in that blistering heat, it felt like a hundred miles. I sat down on a porch and took off my shoes, just resting, when I realized something. We hadn't asked anyone on the bus to come with us, and no one had followed. I don't think it was intentional, at least not for me, but it just never crossed our minds to get everyone else to come with us. They had been prepared to watch us die last night, and I think a clear line had been drawn in the sand between us and them, so we went our separate ways. I never did learn what happened to them, whether they made it out or not, but it still haunts me.

" 'So?' Luther said, sarcasm dripping from his voice, 'What now, fearless leader?'

"Jason opened the door to the shop I sat in front of. It was a small grocery with no more than five aisles, all the shelves empty, but with a few boxes of crackers or cookies, and bags of chips that had fallen on the floor. It appeared someone had left in a hurry and tried to pack as much as they could as fast as they could. I forced myself up and into the store with him. I grabbed the first box of cookies I saw and took a bite; they weren't stale and had at least another year before expiring. I took the box out to Jessica and handed it to her. She dug into them like a man lost in a desert who'd just came across a Gatorade and mumbled, 'Hank blue,' with a mouthful of cookie.

"Near the cooler, bottles of beer, water, and soda littered the floor. I bent down and got a bottle of water. I knew I had to drink slowly, to sip the water, because when the body is in dehydration mode, taking in too much fluid too quickly causes vomiting. It was hard to resist, and I still chugged half the bottle before pulling it away and setting it down. A bag of chips lay on the floor near me and I reached over and ripped them open, knowing full well they would make me thirstier. 'They abandoned the town,' I said to Jason as he searched behind the counter for something. 'Looks like in a hurry.'

" 'Maybe. They could all be dead, too.' He found what he had been looking for: a shotgun. The black weapon looked heavy, but Jason twirled it in his fingers before he grabbed a box of shells from underneath the counter. He loaded the weapon and laid it on the counter. 'Why would they leave a shotgun?' he said more to himself than to me.

" 'They might not have had room,' I offered. The explanation was ludicrous, I know, but right then I didn't want to think about it. I just wanted to accept this gift of a place with food, water, and bathrooms without having to question it. Jason didn't seem to feel the same way. He picked up the shotgun and walked into the back, searching from room to room. When he was satisfied no one was hiding from us, he came back out and sat on a stool behind the counter, his attention outside, on Luther. 'What do you know about him?' he asked.

" 'Luther? He's one of the top researchers I know, focused his entire career on the limbic system, the part of our brains that deals with instincts and basic body functions, the part we share with other vertebrates. We met in medical school. Why?'

" 'Somethin's off about that guy. He dislikes me a little too much for not knowing me. What's he been doing the past few years?'

"I didn't understand where he was going with this, but it made me uncomfortable, as if he was gathering data on him or something. 'What's with all the questions?' I said. 'You can't stand the guy one second, and now you want to know everything about him?'

" 'I like to know my enemies.'

"I couldn't help but laugh. The idea of Luther as someone's, anyone's enemy was so absurd that I couldn't even picture it. He was a pacifist by nature, and I was certain he'd never even raised his voice at anybody, but having said that, I thought it made his behavior around Jason odd. Why did he so passionately dislike him without even knowing him? More than distrust had to be at play. Distrust wouldn't make you hate a person right off the bat. 'I think—'

"Before I had a chance to finish my thought, a scream came from outside. Jason and I looked at each other just a fraction of a second before Jason grabbed the shotgun and ran out. I followed him. I knew that scream. It was Jessica's.

"Jason came out with the shotgun ready to fire, and I had picked up a pair of scissors from the counter. Jessica and Luther stood under the awning and pointed to a man ambling toward the store. He wore mostly gray, with a ski mask or something similar wrapped around his face. As he got closer, I could see it was a scarf, and he used it to shield his face from the harsh winds that picked up sand and debris. The man looked up, and his eyes caught ours. He froze a moment, just a second, and then began walking again. When he was within a dozen or so feet, Jason lifted the muzzle of the shotgun and pointed it at the man 'Think that's far enough, partner.'

"The man stood in front of us, maybe ten feet away, the desert wind whipping sand against his clothing, which consisted of a long overcoat and gloves even though it must've been nearly a hundred degrees. The man raised his hands slowly and peeled away the scarf around his face. He was Asian, probably Chinese, with ruddy checks and cracking lips.

" 'Do you have any water?' he asked in accented English.

" 'Who are you?' Jason asked.

"The man sighed, as though the effort of speaking drained him, and he tossed his gloves and overcoat on the ground, sat down cross-legged, and his eyes dropped to the ground in pure exhaustion. I thought he might pass out right then, but he kept himself upright. 'My name is Shui. I am not infected. I need water. Please.'

"I went back inside and got a bottle of water. Jason clearly wanted to protest when I came back out. We didn't have an endless supply of water, and giving some to a stranger who we didn't *know* wasn't infected seemed like a waste. But I didn't care. I'd lost almost everything else. I didn't want to lose my humanity, too. I tossed him the bottle and he ripped it open and drank nearly half before he capped it again and stuffed it into a pocket of his overcoat. 'Thank you,' he said softly.

" 'You're welcome. What are you doing out here, Shui?'

"Sadness came over him then. He remained quiet a while and then said, 'Hiding.' He scanned the town and pointed to a building across the street. 'I will stay there. Away from you.' With an enormous grunt, as though his knees were buckling under him, he rose and gathered his coat and gloves before going across the street. Jason lowered the shotgun.

" 'He might be infected,' Jason said. He looked at me. I didn't know what he meant, so I nodded as if he were just making a statement that we were all thinking. But that wasn't what he had in mind. I could tell from his eyes that he wanted to kill the man for nothing more than the off chance that he was infected.

" 'No,' I said, shaking my head. 'No, I won't do it.' I folded my arms, prepared to battle Jason on this issue. We were still human beings, and as long as we were, we would treat other human beings like we always had.

"Luther, who'd remained quiet this whole time, finally said, 'As long as he stays over there, what's the problem? Besides, he looked like he might die from exhaustion before the virus kills him.' With that, he went inside, probably to find something to eat. Jessica sat, wide eyed, and I went and sat next to her on the wooden bench out in front of the store. I could see what this town must've been like then: quiet, a place where everyone knew everyone else. I pictured the storeowner sitting out on this bench saying hello to people as they passed by, sharing a few stories or quips, discussing the weather or other trivial things. Now the only things passing by the store were weeds ripped out of the ground by the wind and tossed haphazardly through the streets.

"Jason leaned the shotgun against the wall and said, 'Hope your mercy doesn't come back to haunt us.' He turned and walked inside without looking back. I put my arm around Jessica, and we watched the weeds tumble."

11

"That first night at the store, I couldn't sleep. The wind howled nonstop. On the second story of the building, an apartment had been carved out with two bedrooms, and we set up there. Occasionally, the wind would throw a piece of debris—garbage or more likely a twig or pebble—against the windowpanes. Jessica would wake up crying, and I'd wrap my arms around her until she went back to sleep. Eventually, we just slept in each other's arms.

"In the morning, I saw Jason go out with the shotgun, probably to explore the town for supplies. As I watched him out the window, Luther came in and said, 'You're not gonna believe this. They have running water.'

"Before I could reply, Shui came out of the building across the street, wearing a T-shirt and the same pants from yesterday, and stretched on the porch. He noticed me looking down at him from the window and waved. Despite how silly it seemed, I waved back.

" 'That guy again, huh?' Luther said, watching over my shoulder.

" 'He seems harmless enough.' I turned to Jessica and said, 'Why don't you take a shower while we still can.' She got up and left the room, and I heard the door to the bathroom close. When the water was running, I said, 'What are we doing, Luther? Traveling to Africa to find some tribe that allegedly isn't infected? Even if we found them, what facilities would I have in the Congo to analyze their antibodies? The only place I could do what I needed to do would be back at the CDC in Atlanta. So we have to go into the most dangerous jungle on the planet, find the tribe, and convince them to give us their blood, and then come back out again and go to a place infested with ips.'

" 'Ips?' he said with a look of surprise. 'You're really buying into Jason's tall tales, aren't you?'

" 'You think he's lying?'

" 'I don't know what to think, other than we shouldn't trust anyone, including him. Maybe especially him.'"

Mitchell pulled a package of gum out of his pocket and offered a piece to Samantha. She took it, gently unwrapped it, and placed it on her tongue. Gum wasn't something easily found anymore. "Shui…" he mumbled. "Is that Dr. Zhang Shui?"

Samantha nodded. "Yes, but I didn't know it at the time."

"He's one of China's greatest mathematicians. He just happened to end up in the same small town in Wyoming you were hiding out in?"

"Shui had come to the United States hoping to find answers. That day, that first day, we decided to stay in the town a bit longer. Jason thought that he could get one of the abandoned trucks running again, so we could get to the airport. He kept saying that if we could get to Francis Warren airbase near Cheyenne, he could secure transport out of the country. It seemed like a decent plan at the time, though more and more that day, I thought we should stay in town and forget the Congo. There was enough food to last us months. 'We can't,' Jason said when I talked to him about it. 'This isn't going to stop. We can hide out for a hundred years, and when we get out, we'll still be seeing ips. You wanna stop this thing, Shangri-La's the key.'

"He seemed so… *confident* in what he was saying. Like he just knew that this was the path we had to take. At the time, I was a ball of confusion and stress. I didn't know anything, much less how to save the world. But he was convinced we had to go to the Congo. The key was there. 'Why are you so confident?' I asked him out on the porch when we were alone.

" 'Because of the Soviet Union.'

" 'What about them?'

"He glanced at me, like he wasn't certain he could reveal such a great secret, and then hesitantly said, 'In the eighties, they ran experiments on the use of smallpox against civilian populations. Smallpox and plague, bubonic plague. They did experiments in the Congolese jungles, where the US couldn't find them.'

"I already knew about the Soviet experiments. They produced massive quantities of biological weapons, and after the fall of the USSR, the storehouses all but emptied, and no one knew where they went. We knew for a fact that the Soviet Union produced about forty tons of dry anthrax, but no one has been able to locate it. Some, no doubt, has been funneled to North Korea and Cuba, maybe Iran, but not forty tons. That's enough to wipe out a country, if you dropped it from small planes over the large cities. When I'd first been hired by the CDC, they briefed me on all this, and I volunteered for six months on the WHO's SWRP, Soviet Weapons Recovery Program. It was just an initiative to try to find all the lost biological weapons from the Soviet Union. Health Department officials from various Western countries would take turns interning at the WHO and assisting in the program. They told me it was going to be a needle in a haystack, but it was more like a needle on a sandy beach. Officials, even after the fall, were still loyal to the Soviet regime and refused to cooperate or would stall when we flew out for inspections. Some of them outright lied, and a few even ran. But I had never heard of experiments with smallpox in the Congolese jungle. 'I know a lot about the history of biological warfare, Jason, but I've never heard that,' I said as diplomatically as possible.

" 'Well, I know it happened. I knew someone who was there. A man named Hank Kraski. He was in charge of the Soviet biological warfare program, hardline KGB, no remorse, no pity… more like a machine than anything. He defected to the United States, and they adopted him into the intelligence community. Fucking KGB operative working with the Defense Intelligence Agency. Eventually, they gave him his own show. He was in charge of monitoring the Russian biological and chemical weapon programs and tracking down lost stores of hot agents, like smallpox. He grew really powerful in the intelligence community and became a power broker, selling state secrets to the highest bidder. When the DIA found out, they tried to arrest him, and he disappeared.'

" 'What does he have to do with the Congo?'

"Jason hesitated. 'He said they would vaccinate villagers and then experiment with different strains. They wanted a strain that was resistant to vaccines. I think he found it, and he also happened to find a way to protect an organism from the virus. That's what Shangri-La is. It's the one part of the world he left alone. I think he's there, and if he is, he knows how to stop this.'

"We sat quietly for a while, the sun up in the sky and Shui across the street from us, hanging his newly washed clothes on a clothesline. He didn't seem to mind that he was nude in front of strangers. That type of modesty didn't seem to exist in a world where anyone could die at any second. 'How do you know all this?' I asked.

" 'Because… I used to work for him. Robert Greyjoy worked for him too… and Ian. He sent them to kill you… and I was supposed to finish what they couldn't.' "

Mitchell froze. He blinked a few times and then put his hands on the table. "You telling me, Dr. Bower, that Jason Shafi was an assassin?"

Samantha nodded, stretching her legs out and then recrossing them. "Yes. When he told me that, that he had originally been sent to kill me, I didn't know what to do. I thought he was confessing before getting the job done. I rose and began to back away and he said, 'No, I'm not going to hurt you.'

" 'How do I know that?'

" 'Because I've had a million chances to do it if that's what I wanted.'

"He was right about that. He could've killed me at any time since we'd met, but he hadn't. So I didn't run just then because I didn't want Luther coming out. With the tension already between them, I didn't want to spark an altercation. Luther was no fighter, and Jason could clearly kill him if he was so inclined.

" 'Hank sent me to find and kill you,' Jason said, 'because he thinks you're the best shot at stopping this. But when I saw what the virus did... I couldn't believe it. When I told him about my girl... he said that sacrifices had to be made. *Sacrifices.* As if my daughter was a sheep whose throat we slit to the gods.'

"Realization came to me just then when he said that about his daughter. I had always wondered who would release something like this on humanity. What kind of person would kill off not only their enemies but themselves as well? 'It was a mistake, wasn't it?' I said. 'He didn't think it would get this bad.'

"Jason nodded, staring down at the ground. 'He told me he thought it would spread among the population of the Western countries and South America, decimate them, and then a new world would be built from the ashes. A world like glass, that's what he always said, but I don't know what he meant. Maybe a world that was free of conflict or something. He thought he had immunized the allied countries—North Korea, Russia, Cuba, China, and Iran—but that didn't happen. The virus mutated after it'd been released, and it kept mutating. It spread to every country on the planet, and he had to go into hiding, so when that happened, he just decided to run with it, to find someplace to hide out until it was over.'

" 'Why kill me, then?'

"He shook his head. 'For that, we'll have to ask him.'

"For the next few days, Jason spent the bulk of his time in the garage next door working on the old truck. Luther, for the most part, kept to himself, reading what books he could find, which were just some paperback novels in what used to be the town's only gas station. Jessica and I would spend our days walking around the town, exploring. There's something kind of mischievous in walking into other people's homes and being able to go through their things, seeing how they lived, what they did for fun. One overwhelming trait I saw in the town was the lack of televisions. A few people had them but just old color TVs with the bunny ears, nothing modern. I figured in a town like that, they'd spend as much as they could on TV, but apparently they had other things to do.

" 'One night, I saw Shui sitting on the porch of the building across the street. We'd been in the town already four or five days, and we hadn't exchanged any words since that first encounter. I felt sorry for him, for the fact that he was alone, so I went over and sat down a few spaces away from him. 'I noticed you reading earlier,' I said. 'What were you reading?'

" 'Reports from the Ministry of Health in Shanghai.'

" 'And what do the reports say?'

"He shook his head, turning his eyes away from me. 'Nothing good.'

" 'Your English is excellent. Did you study here?'

"He nodded. 'I receive medical degree from UCLA before returning to China.'

"The word *China* sent a spark of emotion through his face. We sat silently a few moments before I asked him, 'Shui, what happened in China? How did you get over here?'

" 'When outbreak first occur, the president said we were safe and that nothing would happen to us, the People's Army would take care of menace and round up infected. Of course, the outbreak was blamed on Western powers, Great Britain and United States. We were told you had released the virus, but people who were infected were easy to identify, easy to see who was infected and who not. Government say they would be rounded up, army would come to a village and take the sick, but they did not understand incubation period. They did not care. It was their arrogance. They had been told for so long that they were the greatest army that had ever existed, in the most powerful nation in the world, we had no rivals. They developed what you call a God complex and did not think harm could come to them. Do you know I saw some of the soldiers dealing with the infected without proper protection or containment? They just held them by their arms and carried them to trucks.

" 'I was a professor at Jiao Tong University, and they came one day for the students who were infected. We had heard horrible things about what they did with those who had the virus, so people began hiding from them. They would run away. Several of my students left the classroom and hid in the bathrooms. To gather and imprison them was a poor plan and one that anyone could see was going to fail, but the National People's Congress thought if you could eliminate the threat by force, nothing else was necessary. That was their failing in diplomacy as well. They wanted to get rid of their rivals by force and didn't understand that the use of force doesn't work, that it hurts the person using it in the long term just as much as the victim it is used against. They were hurting their own people worse. It would have been better had they not done anything. That way, the sick would have gathered at hospitals rather than hide, but that is what they did—they hid.

" 'In two weeks, the State Council went on all the television stations and said that the threat had been contained, that all those who were sick were now in resettlement camps away from the population, but it was too late. Those who remained hidden spread it to others, and those to others. We were in pandemic, and president was on television declaring victory. Again, it was arrogance, arrogance in his own superior abilities and a misunderstanding of how far people go to fight off an invader. Because that's what the army had become in every city, an invader ready to gather the sick and put them in cages. That's when I knew our nation was lost, when the government told me it was saved.

" 'The attacks began small at first. You heard things at the university of people killed by thieves for their possessions, women raped in the streets, a crime wave. That was the way they explained it to themselves, but I saw the crime wave very close. Several police officers went into a home where it was reported that a man had walked inside and killed an entire family. It was close to the university, and I stood across the street and watched. I had heard the screams earlier and called the police myself. I heard gunshots and more screams, and one of the policemen ran out of the house, covered with blood from his head to his feet. Another man, one I had not seen, jumped out of the house and chased him, like a fox chasing a rabbit. He leapt at him and bit his neck, through the neck so the policeman's head rolled down the street, and the man, if he was a man, lapped at the blood like a dog. His eyes raised when he saw me, and I ran. I have not stopped running since.'

" 'But why here?' I said. 'Why the United States?'

" 'It was rumored that because you started the plague, the United States was safe. I had to see for myself if there was such a place. It seemed to me the entire world was ending. When I cast off at the harbor, men were killing each other for space on the boats, but it didn't help. The jiangshi—that's what we called them—were more agile than most men. They filled the boats, and I saw people leaping into the water to get away from them, but they were in the water, too. I would see someone swimming for the shore and then they would disappear under the water and not come up again. I got onto a small boat that took me to Japan and then the Hawaiian Islands, but it was no better there. We are being pushed to extinction, and I don't even know why.'

" 'How did you end up in this town?'

" 'I was traveling with a group here. Everyone is coming here. They know it is the least populated state in America. Soon, it will no longer be so.'

"I didn't understand then the implications of what he was telling me. I thought we, the American people, were organized and by and large in the same general state as before the outbreak, as if it were some sort of bad year that we would recover from. People don't relocate entire cities because of a bad year. I still held that naïve belief that everything would be taken care of, but by that time, we were already scattered and planning a general retreat. The droves of infected that wandered the streets didn't really need to eat or resupply. They didn't care about water, food, or casualties. They just attacked. And a lot of the people they attacked, if they lived, would then turn to them within days. It was an army that grew in numbers the longer a war went on, unstoppable. That's the first time, right around when I had met Shui, that the military presented thermonuclear warheads as a viable option. They wanted to somehow drop a bomb that would wipe out entire populations and thereby save the rest. That was then, and is now, the stupidest idea I could've conceived. This strain of the virus had infected the entire planet. You could wipe out whole countries and it wouldn't matter. The infection would just continue to spread.

"The people had seen the writing on the wall, and they were fleeing the coasts in a mass exodus. Wyoming, New Mexico, the Dakotas, Utah, and Montana were the states they were traveling to. Tens of millions of people fled for them, everyone from Hollywood socialites and celebrities to retirees living on the beaches of Florida. The nation was terrified and sought refuge in the open plains.

"Shui was just the first. Within a week, three more people had shown up in town. I continued to share our water and food with them. Finally, when the fourth and fifth people came, a couple from Oregon, Jason put a stop to it.

" 'You can't give them anything else,' he told me one day when I went out to see him while he was still working on the truck. 'They're draining our resources, and we're going to need more still to get to the airbase.

" 'I can't turn them away.'

"He stopped his work and sat on the hood of the truck, wiping his hands on a dirty blue rag. 'Do you know who the best leaders are when there's an emergency? It's not the most compassionate. It's the one who's willing to kill ten people to save a hundred. That's why Rome, a republic that hated tyranny, granted dictatorial powers to a single individual in times of crisis. You have the potential to develop a vaccine. These people don't. You have to survive. They don't. It's as simple as that.'

" 'I'm sick of hearing about a vaccine,' I said. 'You're putting too much faith in me.'

"He looked out over the horizon. 'Storm's coming, much worse than it is now, and when it hits, we're gonna need to hang on to whatever we can. I'm hanging on to the belief that we can still fight this, and I think you're the best shot. If I let that go, I may as well just go out there and let them finish me now.'

"I didn't think those words would affect me, but they did. I saw Jason then not as some assassin, not as a soldier, but as a frightened man, a man uncertain of what would happen in the future, and I was the anchor he held on to for that future.

"The crowds continued to swell. Soon, the population of the city was somewhere around a hundred people, all vying for the resources Jason had hidden away somewhere. That nice couple from Oregon were meeting with people in secret, convincing them that it was unfair that we controlled the supplies. They wanted to take them from us by force if necessary. I only found out about it because one night I heard a tapping at the window on the second floor and looked out to see Shui throwing pebbles at it. I went down and opened the door for him. He sat at the table, waited for me to shut the door, and then said, 'They are coming for you.'

" 'Who?'

" 'Everyone else. Tonight. You must leave. They will kill you if you fight them, and if you do not fight them, they will use all the water and food and kill us all.'

"I looked over just then to see Jason standing in the doorway, his arms folded, his eyes on mine with a look of 'I told you so,' though he wouldn't say it. He disappeared and came out a moment later armed with the shotgun and his pistol. 'No,' I said. 'I don't want anyone to die.'

" 'Too late for that.'

"Jason went out on the porch and sat down, leaning the shotgun against the rocking chair. I stared at Shui, who kept his gaze low, unable to look me in the eyes. I checked on Jessica, who was sleeping upstairs. Just in case, I packed as much food and water as I could find in a duffle bag I'd found earlier in the week and went into Luther's room. He wasn't there. I ran down to the porch. Jason rocked slowly back and forth, his eyes narrowing on the crowd I could see up the street, a group of maybe fifty people. It looked like something out of *Frankenstein*. They didn't have flashlights, or if they did, they didn't want to waste them. So they had torches they'd handmade, and when they began marching toward us, the light bounced off the darkened buildings, casting shadows like phantoms against them.

" 'Let me talk to them,' I said. I still believed all humanity hadn't left our species yet, that they would be open to reason. I was willing to have a more democratic control over the food and water, but to just unleash a mob onto our only resources would be foolish. So I intended to let everybody cool down and have, I guess... like a town council meeting about it in the morning. But as they neared with their torches, I saw Luther. They had him tied up with his arms behind his back and a rag over his mouth. A man behind him poked him in the back with a rifle, forcing him to march as quickly as they were.

"Jason stood up. 'Go inside.'

" 'No, let me talk to them.'

" 'They're not here to talk. Sam, go inside.'

"Though ultimately I knew he was right, I couldn't force myself to go inside. I had to believe that they would be open to discussion. How could they not understand that our resources were limited and had to be rationed, that we couldn't just let people gorge themselves on our food and let everyone else starve… but I was wrong. As soon as I saw their faces, I knew nothing I could say would convince them otherwise.

"The nice couple from Oregon were at the head, the husband with a pistol in his hand. He took a step forward and said, 'I don't want to hurt ya. Just step aside and no harm will come to you.'

" 'I'm not hoarding resources. I'm open to putting everything in a communal spot and voting on how to distribute them. I always have been. I want everyone to get their share.'

"The man grinned. It was like this horrible mixture of sadistic joy and the pleasure someone has when they know a secret others don't. It was just… malicious. 'No, no more talk. You've been holding out on us, stuffing yourselves in there while the rest of us live on crumbs.'

" 'That's not true. We have rationed everything and shared as much as we could.'

" 'Shared?' the man said, 'Who the fuck made you queen so that you could share the food with us? The food belongs to whoever can take it. And I'm not gonna ask you again. Move the fuck aside, or we'll take it by force.'

"Jason stood up next to me. He held the shotgun with one hand, low, the barrel pointed at the ground. He bellowed loudly, 'Any man or woman who tries to take this food by force I will kill. I won't hurt, I won't threaten. I... will... kill *all* of you, if I have to. Count yourselves lucky that we share *anything,* that you have a roof over your heads, and that the ips haven't shown up yet, which they will. You can't move this many people without them following, so you need to save them bullets for the ips, not for us.'

"The man from Oregon considered this a moment and then smiled and said, 'Kill him first.' "

12

"The crowd didn't move. Everyone stood motionless. We even held our breaths—at least, I think I did. Jason held still, too. The only change in his demeanor was that his eyes narrowed.

"Finally, the crowd broke forward with a roar. People shouting, swearing… they kicked Luther over into the dirt. Jason lifted the shotgun and aimed directly at the man from Oregon's face, when suddenly a sound tore through the air, clear and loud as a jet engine. It came from the dark, just past where we could see with the torchlight, a scream.

"It was like the air had been sucked away and no one could breathe. The crowd wasn't loud anymore. They didn't actually move other than looking in the direction of the scream. Jason lowered the shotgun and turned. He marched back inside the building, but I stayed to watch the crowd. Just like that, they dispersed. They ran into buildings and slammed doors, drew blinds, put out torches. A few ran into a barn on the outskirts of town. In less than a minute, the entire street cleared, a ghost town. I stayed on the porch, peering out into the darkness. The scream had triggered something in me. I was forgetting about everything I'd seen, maybe not forgetting, but learning to deal with it. And that one sound brought it all crashing back, a cold, gray feeling in my stomach. I looked up to the sky and the blanket of stars. That was one thing about the lack of outdoor lighting that I could never grow accustomed to, how clearly you could see the stars. They looked like shimmering jewels encrusting the ceiling of a darkened room, much brighter and closer than I would've thought possible.

"I suddenly remembered Luther and quickly scanned the street. He was still lying on the ground, unable to get up. I ran out to him. His hands were tied with strips of cloth, and I ripped them away. The rag covering his mouth had probably once been white and now appeared brown from the dust and dirt. When I pulled it off, he coughed so violently that I could see the veins in his neck, even by moonlight. I helped him up and we staggered back to the store. Jason hovered over the dining table, the bright light of the kitchen making me squint as I sat Luther down in one of the chairs. Jason had laid out everything that could conceivably be used as a weapon: the shotgun, two shovels, a pickaxe, a hatchet, and several large kitchen knives. His pistol, as always, was tucked into his waistband near his right side.

" 'They'll be here soon. There's wood in the garage next door and hammers and nails. We need to board up all the windows,' Jason said.

"We worked frantically. I ran back every once in a while to check on Luther, who had a glass of water and some ibuprofen and said he felt fine. They had jumped him while he took a walk around the town, tied him up, and stuck him in the barn. 'They wouldn't have left us alone,' he said. 'Once they got the resources, they needed the room in the store. We would've been sent out into the desert.'

"When the ibuprofen kicked in, he joined us, and the three of us nailed thick boards over every window. And there were a lot of windows. By the end, drenched in sweat, my muscles ached, particularly my back. We got some water, just a cupful each, and sat on the porch. Jason scanned the surrounding area. 'Maybe it was something else,' I said hopefully, 'an animal or something? I had a cat that would scream like that when she was in heat.'

" 'Maybe,' Jason said. He looked back at Luther, who had dirt caked on his face, an outline of where the rag had been clean on the skin, making him look like he'd overslept in a tanning booth with a rag over his mouth. 'How you feelin'?' Jason asked.

" 'Fine.'

"Jason nodded and turned back to the darkness. 'Something's different about them,' he said softly. 'They're not just sick, it's something else. The way they attack, how it consumes them… something else is going on. It can't just be a disease in their brain… it can't.'

"Luther said, 'The brain is the soul. When the brain is damaged, so is the soul. They're just people that can no longer control themselves.'

"I looked from one to the other. 'Are you guys talking about the people in the town or the infected?' Neither of them responded.

"I don't remember how long we sat on the porch before going back inside, but when we did, we moved the furniture up against the doors. All three of us went through the store and then the upstairs apartment, checking and rechecking doors, windows, vents… anything that a person could conceivably crawl through into the building. When we were satisfied the place was as tightly locked down as it could be, Jason said, 'We'll sleep in shifts. You two sleep first. In two hours, I'll wake you, Sam, and then two hours after that you'll need to wake Luther.' None of us argued or made suggestions. In fact, whatever had been happening between Luther and Jason seemed calm. More pressing matters had taken our attention away.

"I went up to the apartment and into the bedroom. Jessica snored so loudly that I knew she'd have a sore throat in the morning. I thought about making her turn onto her side but didn't do it. She was in that state of sleep only a child can get to, one where the rest of world isn't just held at bay but actually ceases to exist: utter peace. Instead, I sat by the window and stared out at the dark town in front of me.

"Reading stories as a kid, I always tried to picture what a real Wild West town would look like, and I was never sure I got it right. Sitting there, staring at the blackness, I could see that I'd come close. This town could've been put in the West a hundred and fifty years ago and, other than the gas station and store, wouldn't have seemed that out of place. I pulled my knees up to my chest and leaned against the wall, my eyes glued outside, and slowly, I drifted to sleep."

"A soft hand on my shoulder woke me two hours later. I inhaled a deep breath and wiped away the strand of drool that I felt on my lip. He smiled at the little gesture and I smiled back. I stretched my arms, looked at Jessica, and then rose and followed him out of the room. He took out his pistol and handed it to me. 'Just in case. But if you hear anything, come get me. I'm gonna camp out on the couch.'

"I held the gun in my hand. It seemed heavy for how small it was, a silencer that I hadn't seen before clipped to the end. 'Did you really see that place, Jason? Shangri-La?'

"He nodded. 'Yeah, I saw it. It's in the middle of the most beautiful jungle you'll ever see. Thick green trees and vines, thousands of different animals and insects you've never seen before… it could be paradise.'

" 'But it's not, is it?'

" 'No, it's not. There are roving militias in the jungle. Some of them are cannibals, really vicious types. Tristan does what she has to in order to keep her village safe.' He paused. 'I once saw her kill four people, just line them up and shoot them in the head like they were livestock, because she felt they weren't contributing enough to the community. She made their families watch, and she didn't even blink. She has that focus, that ability to do what needs to be done.'

" 'To kill ten to save a hundred.'

"He nodded. 'Come get me if you hear anything.'

"He went into the front room of the apartment, and I headed down the stairs. The silence in the apartment was deafening. I guess that's the word for it, that kind of silence where it's uncomfortable because you just can't hear anything. With all the windows boarded up, I didn't really have much to look at. So I went to the small rack of magazines the store had. Everything was at least two months old and nothing I would normally read, a few celebrity gossip magazines and the rest about hunting, fishing, and guns. Behind the cooler, which had to be kept on to preserve the milk and other perishables that Jason hadn't stashed away, was the office. I hadn't ever gone back there, so I decided to explore.

"The office smelled like mildew, a small space where the owner shoved everything he didn't want the customers to see. Up on the wall, a calendar of nude women hung next to a work schedule. An old computer sat on the desk, and I got into the chair and flipped it on. It still worked. I tried connecting to the Internet, but the server was down, so I just flipped through a few files before noticing he had Minesweeper on there. I played for about twenty minutes before I heard something outside.

"I couldn't be sure what it was, but it made my heart race. I remained perfectly still, even holding my breath, and then I slowly rose and went out there. On one of the windows, a space of about three inches let in moonlight. The space between two boards that hadn't been nailed flush. I peeked out between the boards. Standing in the middle of the street, a man in a white button-down shirt and slacks stood staring at nothing. The shirt appeared almost black with blood, either the man's or someone else's. As he moved, his gait was slow and awkward, and I could hear him making noises before he screamed. His voice had gone hoarse, and the scream wasn't much louder than normal speech. Out of his mouth, a thick strand of black fluid leaked down over the shirt and into the warm dirt.

"In the garage next door, someone else must've seen him too, because a noise came from there. Like banging metal. I think someone saw him and tried to hide, accidently knocking something over. The ip immediately turned toward the sound, and though his movements had been slow, he sprinted over to the garage and slammed into the door. And he didn't stop slamming into it. Boom! Boom! Boom! He must've broken every bone in his shoulders and arms, but he didn't stop slamming into the wooden sliding door. Finally, the wood creaked and I could hear splinters, and then screaming from inside, the screams of women and children.

"I rushed over to our front door, which hadn't been boarded up, and started throwing furniture aside to get out there. Luther and Jason both stomped down the stairs. Luther said, 'What happened? What's going on?'

" 'They're trapped,' I said, not looking back. 'I have to help them.'

"Jason ran up next to me, making certain I looked into his eyes. 'You can't help them,' he said. 'They're gone.'

" 'No,' I said as I threw a chair away from the door. 'I'm not leaving them out there to die.'

"The screams grew louder. I could make out three distinct voices now, a mother and her two children. I pushed myself harder to move everything aside and then grabbed the couch, the heaviest item, to push aside, and Jason put his hand on it so it couldn't move. 'You're not going out there,' he said softly.

" 'Jason, get away from the door. I'm not kidding.'

" 'Neither am I. We don't know how many of them there are. If you open that door, I'm going to have to close it behind you, and I don't want to do that.'

" 'Do whatever you have to do, but I'm going out there.'

"He sat on the couch, making it nearly impossible for me to move. He weighed a ton, and with his feet planted on the ground, he resisted every one of my pushes and pulls. The couch wasn't getting moved. Outside, the mother screamed for someone to help her just as other screams joined her from the darkness. 'Luther, help me,' I said. But Luther didn't budge. He just averted his eyes and stared at the floor. I ran over to the window and peered through the opening between the boards. A group of infected surrounded the barn now. I had always thought their screaming was a product of their damaged minds, just the sound a brain injury might make. But I saw now that's not the only thing it was. It was communication. They screamed so the infected behind them would come running, and the ones behind them screamed so the ones behind them would come. I couldn't even imagine how many infected were about to descend on the town. Everyone in the area, I guessed.

"I made one last effort to move the couch, and Jason didn't move. He just said, 'I'm sorry,' quietly, so quiet I almost couldn't hear it. I could tell it wasn't an easy decision for him. But the decision had to be made. Even now, I don't agree with him. I understand that droves of infected attacked the barn and that we didn't have enough ammunition to take out every single one, but we could've done something…

"I sat on the couch next to him, listening to the screaming of the mother and children. A loud crash followed. The ips were in the barn. The screaming increased in pitch, and then... she prayed. She screamed out for God to help her as they tore her apart... Within seconds, her screaming and the screaming of her children stopped, and there were only the horrible sounds of the infected."

13

Mitchell noticed the sun for the first time in an hour. He had been enraptured in her story, and it was a compelling one. The world was filled with them, people from all walks of life that came from nothing and had to suddenly become warriors fighting for their lives. He never tired of the stories.

"How did you survive?" he asked.

Samantha rubbed her arms as though she were cold, but Mitchell thought it was quite pleasant. "It wasn't…" she said, not finishing her thought. "That night, none of us slept except Jessica. Even the screams hadn't wakened her. We sat still as glass. Every once in a while I would go and look out the crack between the boards. A lot of the infected were still in the barn, but there were so many now, and so many more pouring in, that the entire town would be filled with them soon.

"I went upstairs to get a better view of the town from the window in the bedroom. The infected were like ants, crawling over every space. They broke into homes, jumping through windows and bashing down doors. I saw one leap through a window in what must've been a kitchen. He made himself into an arrow, shattering the glass. Inside, I heard the screams from whoever had been hiding in there. Everywhere was the same. The infected hunted down the people in the town one by one. Some were able to hide, but many were not. And then I'd hear those horrible screams that filled the air. The window was thick, and the other homes far enough away, that Jessica didn't wake the entire night… but I could hear every single scream and every single prayer.

"I'd never seen death like that. Not ever. And I'd been in the middle of Ebola Zaire outbreaks in Western Africa, smallpox epidemics in South America… and I'd never seen anything like it. They systematically killed dozens of people. At one point, several tried to break into the store. They pounded against the boards, broke the windows, but they didn't hear anything, as we were utterly silent. Eventually they lost interest and moved on to easier prey. I could see it all from the window. One man… and I think about this at least once a day… one man almost got away. He ran out of a building and sprinted straight for the desert. I don't know why he thought he'd have a better shot in the desert in his boxer shorts, but he did. He seemed like an older man, but it was hard to tell in just the moonlight.

"He was fast and agile, darting between groups of infected, ducking and rolling when he had to. He got all the way to the edge of town when one of the infected flew out of the darkness of the desert like a ghost. He slammed into the man, taking him down, and then he grabbed the man by the hair and dragged him back into the town. I'd never seen that before, seen an ip act that way. It could've been random, again, just his damaged mind, but it certainly didn't look like it. It looked planned... methodical, almost as though he wanted the man to suffer with terror while being dragged back to the town.

"The old man was tossed into the center of the street. He rolled a few times and then lay on his stomach, just breathing. I could see his back move up and down with each breath. I think he knew right then it was done. Fate had issued its decree, and that's a hard thing for anybody to accept, but given the circumstances, he seemed to accept it with honor. He sat up and looked at the sky as the infected circled him. They didn't attack right away. They were savoring it. Then one ran at the old man and clawed at his back, leaving four streak marks across the soft skin. Another bit into his head, taking a chunk with him. They were like piranhas, each one taking a little piece. Soon the man dripped so much blood that he glistened in the moonlight, and that's when they jumped on him... like a pack of wild dogs. I had to turn away, but I can still hear those gory, wet sounds at night sometimes, and it wakes me up.

"Later on, near sunrise, I heard crying from outside. I peered through the window and saw a young woman, maybe eighteen or nineteen, stumbling through the street. She cried and howled with sobs and every few seconds would shout, 'Please help me!' Jason came up behind me and we watched her.

" 'I can't just let her die, not her,' I said. 'I have to do something.'

" 'Look over there,' Jason said, pointing to the darkened corners of the buildings. In the dim light of early morning it was difficult to make out, but if you looked closely enough, you could see it. The infected were still there, hiding in every darkened stairway and alley that could shield them. 'She's bait,' he said.

"If I hadn't seen it myself, I wouldn't have believed it. There's this overwhelming belief that the infected had lost their minds, all sense and reason, but here they were, laying a trap for anyone left in town. They let this young woman live so she would cry for help and draw anyone else out."

Mitchell stopped her and said, "Wait, wait, that can't be right. That's displaying intelligence, even problem-solving intelligence, forethought. It's been proven the infected, past a certain point in the incubation, lose all these traits."

Samantha shook her head. "Not proven, just believed. Like how nobody's actually proven that if you eat fewer calories you'll lose weight. What if you eat a thousand calories in donuts versus a thousand calories of vegetables? Will your body process them exactly the same? Will you lose the same amount of weight? Of course not, and we all know it. But we've bought into this belief that a calorie is a calorie no matter what. But a calorie's a measure of heat; it has almost nothing to do with the way our body processes food. But everyone *believes* it does. I saw the infected plan and think. They knew we would respond... they remembered what it was like to be human.

"When we didn't come out, they attacked her and killed her the same as everyone else. Jason had been right; they were drinking blood for hydration. Though they would still vomit, it wasn't as much as I had seen... they were learning. So that morning, nothing was left of the town. Maybe a few people hiding here and there, but I couldn't see them. And then I looked across the street at the roof and saw movement, a man lying flat on his belly. It was Shui. He saw me, too, because he did a sad little wave, letting me know it was him. I waved back, acknowledging that I saw him, and tried to mouth the words, 'We'll come get you. Don't move,' to him. He nodded, but I don't know if he actually understood.

"Jessica woke and I sat with her. 'I heard things last night,' she said. 'People dying.'

"I ran my fingers through her hair, placing my chin against her head. 'I know... I know.' Luther came in just then and went to the window. He stared out for a long time before I said, 'What?'

" 'I'm just wondering if they've moved on. I haven't heard them for a couple of hours.'

"Jessica said, 'Can I take another shower?'

" 'I don't think we should make any noise, sweetie. Just stay here and I'll get you some breakfast, okay?' She didn't respond, but she lay down on the bed, her eyes blankly staring out the window. Luther followed me out, and as we descended the stairs, I said, 'We can stay here. We have enough food to last us months, and the water and power are still on.'

" 'I agree. Maybe we can even search for a phone once those damn things leave.'

"Downstairs, Jason sat by the door, the shotgun between his legs. He had piled some more furniture against the front door, a fridge and a desk. He sat maybe five feet away, and though no noise came from outside, his eyes were narrowed with concentration. I knew it wasn't the type of concentration anyone just had. It could only come with hard, painful training. I'd always taken everything Jason told me with a grain of salt, unsure what exactly to believe and what not to, but right then I knew he wasn't lying about his training… He was a killer.

"I stood next to him and said, 'I need some food for Jessica. Where'd you hide it?'

"He exhaled, breaking his concentration and turning toward me. 'In the garage next door.'

"My stomach dropped. I had thought he'd hidden it somewhere in the store or upstairs, a place we could easily get to it, although we could've easily gotten to the garage yesterday. But today was a different day. 'How are we—'

" 'I don't know yet,' he said. 'I may just have to go out there.'

"Luther said, 'I haven't heard them in a while. Maybe they've left?'

"Jason shook his head. 'No, they're still there. We've got some pastries and stuff down here. Give her that for now. I'll go out at night.'

" 'Why at night?' I asked.

" 'I have no idea which of their senses are functioning well, but I bet their eyesight is the best one. We got the greatest shot of getting in and out in the dark.'"

"I can't tell you what it felt like that day, knowing we were going to open the door and head outside. We didn't hear a peep, of course, but I had a sick feeling in my gut. If they were smart enough to have a young woman act as a lure, they were smart enough to hide until nightfall. That first night, I convinced Jason not to go. That we should wait one more day before heading out. He agreed. The next day was spent doing not much of anything, looking through the same magazines, talking, and taking naps because we couldn't sleep at night. I checked on Shui a lot, and he didn't move, just stayed on the roof. I wanted to throw something to eat to him, but I knew I couldn't make it all the way over there from the window.

"Thoughts of a vaccine and Shangri-La at this point were almost completely forgotten. We were just trying to survive. It's amazing how much of your thought processes and brainpower are devoted to surviving when your life is at risk. It's as though you can't focus on anything else.

"That evening, the one when Jason was supposed to go out, I sat on the couch that was blockading the door and Luther came and sat next to me. He looked weaker, pale and thin. He wasn't a man used to strife, and his body wasn't taking it well. 'I don't know if we should be going to Africa,' he said. 'I think maybe I just want to go home.'

" 'To Boston? We haven't heard anything about what's going on out there. It could be overrun like Atlanta.'

" 'I have friends and family there. I don't even know if they're alive. I'm tired, Sam. I just want to be somewhere familiar. I don't know whether or not you or anybody can develop a vaccine, but maybe some things just aren't in our sphere of influence. I don't feel I'm adding anything to that or taking away. You won't miss me.' He looked at me and grinned. 'You should come with me, you know. Look out for yourself and that girl. Forget Africa.'

" 'If there's even a possibility… I'm already dead, Luther. I'm infected. So is Jessica, and maybe even you by now. If there's even a possibility I can save us, I have to try.'

"He nodded. 'Just make sure you're not putting her more at risk in the process.'

"Jason came down later. He gave Luther the shotgun. We stared at each other for a second and then he nodded. I rose from the couch and helped him move it away, along with everything else we'd put against the door. We worked as quietly as we could. Jessica came down and stood at the bottom of the stairs with her arms folded, her eyes wide with fear. I smiled at her, trying to comfort her, but I doubt it did much.

"Once the furniture was clear, Jason peered out into the darkness. He looked back at me and said, 'Five minutes. If I'm not back, barricade the door.'

"I nodded, and he opened the door and ran out into the darkness. We shut the door behind him, and Luther locked it and moved the couch against it. We stood there silently. We couldn't think of anything else to do. My stomach was in knots. I could see the garage from the crack between the boards on the window. I finally gathered the strength to move and went over there. I saw Jason sneaking around outside the garage. He stayed low and wasn't wearing his shoes. The garage door had been left open. He slipped through quietly, and I couldn't see him anymore.

"Those few minutes, I felt like vomiting from the anxiety. I couldn't believe I'd let him go out by himself. I should've gone with him. I could've stood at the entrance to the garage and made sure no one sneaked up behind him. As I was considering going out, I saw him slip out of the garage with two duffle bags and sneak back over to the store. Luther and I quickly pushed the couch aside and opened the door for him. He was maybe ten feet away when we heard the first scream."

14

"When it's as black at night as it was, your brain can't process sensory information well. It can't orient itself as quickly as normal, so it was difficult to tell which direction the scream came from. It seemed like it came from everywhere, as if the night itself screamed. Jason froze, his head whipping around in the dark. Finally, he sprinted for the store. And out of the alley between two buildings across the street, one of the infected dashed for him with almost superhuman speed. Jason got all the way to the door before he had no choice but to turn around. The infected leapt at him. He turned, pulling out his pistol as he fell back into the store's entrance.

"The rounds hit the ip but didn't do that much. He landed on Jason and clawed for his eyes. Jason had his arms up, blocking his face, which seemed to be the ip's target. I grabbed the first thing I could, a small chair the clerk had used to sit behind the register. I lifted it over my head and slammed it down into the ip's head. He jolted and looked up at me. His eyes were black from the hemorrhaging with little red, bleeding centers. He screamed and jumped at me. Luther fired, and a spray of blood went over the room and the entrance. The boom of the shotgun had deafened me, and all I could hear was a ringing sound. Then the screams from outside slowly came into my consciousness, hundreds of them, all rushing for us at the same time.

"Jason pulled himself up and slammed the door. 'Hurry!' he shouted, his back to the door.

"We scrambled to get everything against the door. We blockaded it in under ten seconds, but it almost didn't matter. The boards on the windows were creaking as the infected tore at them. I grabbed Jessica and sprinted up the stairs, Luther and Jason behind me. We got to the bedroom and shut the door, moved the large bed against it, and looked out the window. Swarms converged on the building, surrounding it on all sides, a sea of bloody faces and bodies. Shui watched everything from across the street. I hoped he'd make a run for it. With the infected distracted, it might've been his only chance.

" 'The window,' Jason said. The window was maybe two feet from the roof. Jason held out his arms for Jessica. I hesitated a moment. When you're in that spot, you don't think clearly. You cling to anywhere that offers even a second of safety. So I thought maybe we could stay in the bedroom. A ridiculous thought, now. They would've gotten to us in a few minutes. Luckily, Jessica didn't leave room for debate. She jumped into Jason's arms. He lifted her out the window and to the roof. He then held out his arms for me. I didn't move. Everything was in slow motion. Even the screams outside were dulled. It took Luther pushing me to get me out the window. The two of them pushed me up, and I climbed to the roof. I turned and helped Luther, then Jason handed up the guns before climbing up himself.

"When we were all on the roof, we backed away from the edge. Out from the desert, more infected sprinted for the store, shrieking like crows. I don't know if you've ever seen a swarm of infected attack a single target, but it's monstrous. They cared nothing about their bodies, about living or dying. Their bodies were just instruments to them, and they threw them into the building like they were invincible. Some even broke through the walls and then couldn't get back up because they'd shattered probably every bone in their bodies.

"We heard the door to the bedroom break, and then the ips flew out the window. They just piled out the window, one after another after another. They wouldn't stop. And when they hit the ground, they just got back up again and ran inside the house.

"I scanned the town. A few people ran out of the homes and sprinted into the desert opposite where the infected came from. But you could hear screaming from all around the town. They were coming from every direction, called by the screams. We had no escape route, no way to get anywhere. My first thought was that we would die from the elements and dehydration up there. But I saw that the ips were piling on each other. It wasn't inconceivable that they would pile high enough to get up here in the next few hours. We were alone in the dark, without food or water and with only a handful of shotgun shells and bullets left.

" 'Well, this is just great,' Luther said. 'Just fucking great. I'm so glad we decided to follow you, Jason. We couldn't have gotten to this point without you.'

"Luther seemed manic, twitching, rage building inside of him. 'It wasn't his fault,' I said. 'Everywhere's overrun. It would have been like this no matter where we went.'

" 'Really? How do you know, Sam? You've seen Atlanta, New York, and this shithole, and nowhere else. How the hell do you know?'

"Jason turned away from the infected and looked at Luther now. 'Take it easy, man. We're doin' the best we can.'

"Luther spit. I saw his hands trembling and his lip quivering. He looked wild then, feral. It was something I saw a lot of in the coming months. Society crumbled around us. All the institutions and formalities we knew were gone. People turned quickly to their baser instincts. I saw that in Luther that night.

"He stepped close to Jason, so close I worried he might push Jason off the roof. The two men squared off. I rose and stepped between them. 'Sit down, Luther,' I said.

" 'This man,' he spit, 'has led us to our deaths. We're going to die up here, Sam, all of us, in the worst way possible, and it's because of him.'

"I pushed against Luther, getting him to back up a few inches. 'No it's not. We're here because of a bug. That's all it ultimately is, Luther, just a microbe. It has no emotions, no sense of vengeance or evil. It just exists, and this is the result,' I said, motioning to the crowds of bleeding, screaming sick that surrounded the house. 'It isn't the fault of anyone here.'

"Jason didn't attack Luther. He just checked the number of shotgun shells he had left—seven. Not enough to do much of anything… except one thing. He looked at me and then Jessica and Luther. He didn't even have to speak. I knew right then what he was thinking, so I said, 'No, we can't.'

" 'Not yet,' he said, 'but they'll be up here soon. I can do you three and then myself if you need.'

" 'No, that's crazy. That little girl deserves to live. She's had nothing but a life of pain already. She deserves to get out of this.'

" 'I told you, *deserve*'s got nothing to do with this. If you'd feel more comfortable being the one to do it, I understand. I was trying to save you the pain.'

"I couldn't believe what I was hearing. My mouth literally fell open and I stood there like an idiot, staring at him. I think he asked me a few more questions after that, but I couldn't hear them. The image of him killing Jessica filled my mind. Somehow, the world had become such a mess that killing her would actually be the merciful act. I don't know how we got to that point. I don't know what happened that sent humanity on that path. Maybe all species go down that road and it was our time. I knew that 99.9 percent of all species went extinct. That was the natural order of things, and in the back of my mind, I always knew humanity's time would someday be up, but most species got roughly a four-million-year run before extinction wiped them out. We'd barely been on the earth two hundred thousand years as *homo sapiens*, and here we were on a cliff looking down.

"In the end, I wasn't sure we had a choice, but I didn't even want to consider it. Luckily, before I really could, I heard something, a roar. And then the truck burst out of the garage next door. It was a larger truck, an F-250 I think, meant for hauling massive loads. It looked almost like a monster truck. Behind the wheel, Shui tried to control it as he plowed through crowds of infected. They looked like dolls as they flew through the air or were crushed by the immense vehicle. A few jumped onto the hood, and he spun the wheel, causing them to fly off, before plowing through another crowd and coming near the store. He then sped away and spun back around. He would slow down whenever he neared the house.

" 'He's slowing down so we can jump,' I said.

"Shui flipped around and came near again. I took Jessica's hand and all I said was, 'Ready?' She nodded, and we leapt off the roof. We landed hard in the bed of the truck and it hurt my ankle. Pain shot through me, up my knee and into my hip. But I didn't have time to stop and consider it. I had to pull Jessica out of the way so Luther and Jason could jump down.

"Before they could, an ip jumped up onto the side of the truck and grabbed Jessica's hair. He pulled her toward the edge, attempting to lift her out. I kicked at his face with both feet, everything I had. It snapped his head back, but he didn't let go. The truck sped away again, twisting in the dirt road with enough torque to send the ip underneath the rear tires. The truck heaved up and thunked back down as we ran him over and sped back for Jason and Luther to jump down. I glanced back. The ip had been cut in half and was still screaming.

"By now the ips had caught on. Maybe not intellectually, but instinctively. They knew what was happening, and they left the house to swarm the truck. Shui couldn't slow down. He sped by the house, going enormously fast, and Luther jumped and hit the bed of the truck on his side. Jason leapt and nearly missed the truck entirely. He hit the gate and almost rolled off but held on with one hand, the shotgun in his other. I scrambled over there and grabbed his hand. He tossed the shotgun in, and I pulled him up as the swarm dashed after us. Their speed was the one thing I never could get used to. Several managed to catch up to the truck, and Jason had to slam the butt of the shotgun into their faces to get them off. One grabbed him by the collar, and he lifted the shotgun and blew off its head. Luckily we were going so fast that all the blood and gore fell downwind.

"Eventually, we beat them. We were too fast for them to catch up to. We sped between the buildings and up the main road. I saw some people, uninfected people, in the doorways of the homes, but there was no stopping now. The horde was right behind us. They had hidden from them this long, so they could hide a little longer. I was determined that I would send help to this little town as soon as we got near civilization.

"Luther started laughing. 'I can't believe that ac—'

"No one saw him. He must've been waiting on the outskirts of town in the darkness. And he moved like a panther. He reached into the truck's bed as we sped past and grabbed Luther. Maybe if Luther had been stronger… I don't know. Luther was dragged from the truck screaming, slamming into the bed before the infected had him on the ground. I didn't see exactly what happened, exactly how he died, but the horde was on him in a few seconds, their screams mixing with his.

" 'No!' I can't believe I did this, but I stood up and tried to jump out of the truck. I don't know what I would've done once I was out, how I would've fought them, but that didn't matter. My only thought was that I had to get to my friend, my friend that I had brought out to Atlanta when he should've been in Boston with his family.

"If Jason hadn't wrapped his arms around my waist and pulled me back down, I would've gotten out. Instead, I just shouted for Luther as ip after ip swarmed on him. As we fled the town, I collapsed. Either from exhaustion or the shock of Luther's death, I don't know, but I fell onto my back, and the sky swirled above me, and it just went black."

15

Mitchell checked the battery life on the digital recorder. The sun still hung in the sky, though it was evening now and the temperature had cooled. He felt both hungry and thirsty, but neither of those sensations mattered much to him. He would have preferred to finish this business today than eat and finish tomorrow.

"I had heard about Dr. Daniels' death," he said. "I just assumed he'd perished in the initial outbreak. That's when most of the population died, those first two days. I hadn't realized he lived for so long." Samantha didn't respond so he continued. "What happened when you fled the town?"

"We were in the desert, flat and hot, just like you'd imagine a desert to be. Every once in a while we'd see a caravan. There's no other word that really describes it: long lines of people trudging through the desert with all their belongings in tow, usually pulled by a horse cart or something similar. We stopped a couple of times and spoke with them, where they were headed, what the latest news was… I couldn't really pay attention. I kept seeing Luther's death. When I would sleep, which wasn't often, but when I could actually drift away, I saw torn, bloody faces coming at me, biting into Jessica, pulling Luther out of the truck. I saw my mother as one of them, a risen corpse with no soul, coming after me. I would wake up with a start, panicked, and Jessica would calm me. She never really said much, just put her hand over mine or lay next to me.

"One night, when Jason was asleep, I stared at this gun he had next to him. I thought it'd be so easy, just pick it up, put it in my mouth, and finish it. What did I have to look forward to, anyway? Another year, maybe two, of starvation and hiding before the ips finally won, or maybe the dormant virus in my veins would suddenly trigger and I'd actually become one of them, neither one of which was something I wanted to see.

"I think my hand actually came up to get the gun, and then I felt something. Jessica had wrapped her arms around me. She was asleep, but my motion had caused her to stir. I gazed at her face a long time. Even in all this muck and blood, it still had that childhood innocence… and I knew no one else would take care of her. Jason thought only of the greater good, and if that included leaving a little girl behind who couldn't contribute much, I wasn't entirely certain he wouldn't do it. I was all Jessica had. So I lowered my hand and placed my head against hers.

"Every fifty miles or so we'd come across a gas station. Not a government-owned one, but an actual gas station. They were all abandoned, of course, but we'd find scraps of food or some gas left in their storage tanks. It kept us going.

"Sometimes at night you could hear the ips out in the darkness. Howls and shrieks would echo through the valleys, but we could never see them. They were just shadows out in the blackness of night.

"Eventually, down to our last quarter tank of gas, we reached the Warren airbase. It didn't look like any airbase I'd ever seen, and since the initial outbreak, I'd seen a few. The airbase held maybe ten planes, and most of them didn't appear to be functional. A skeleton crew remained on the base, and almost all of them were armed. The only one who wasn't was a captain who came out to greet us.

" 'Who are you?' he said. He had a stern face and didn't want any chitchat. I thought he looked like a man who had been making hard decisions for a long time. He clearly thought this was going to be one of those decisions.

" 'Can we talk in private, Captain?' Jason said, jumping out of the truck. The two men walked off, leaving us in the bed of the truck. Shui came out. He smiled, a warm smile that spread across his plump face.

" 'I have something for you,' he said to Jessica. He pulled a package of cupcakes out of his pocket and handed it to her. She hadn't eaten much that day and tore into them.

"Jason came back a few minutes later. 'They'll take us as far as Florida,' he said. "They got a transport heading out that way to pick up some grunts. We can hitch a ride to the Congo from there.'"

Mitchell leaned back in his seat and crossed his legs. His lower back ached a bit, but he ignored it. "That seems rather odd, Dr. Bower. That you would just follow this man you barely knew into the most violent jungle on the planet."

"What other choice did I have? Atlanta was overrun. At the airbase, they had a real-time digital map of the war. That's what the military was calling it at this point, a war, not a pandemic. The map showed the green zones, which were the safe zones, and the red zones, those overrun with infected and considered lost. The coasts of the United States were almost entirely red, with splotches of red spattered over the country itself. A few wide spaces of green existed, like in the Mountain West, but even they were dotted with red. The rest of the world was even worse.

"I know there's been a lot of theories as to why the United States could hold off the swarms the longest. The NRA said it was because we were the most well-armed nation, and our citizens could fight the ips with guns. The liberals said it was because we had a lot of government programs that were already in place, like welfare, that could distribute goods quickly. Conservatives said it was because each state was an independent entity and so decisions on the local level were made quicker and more efficiently... but I don't think that's it at all. Have you ever walked into a room full of people from different countries? I can spot the American right away. They're usually the most outgoing, the most gregarious. It's a confidence we have, I think. We're not shy about making friends or making fools of ourselves if we have to. Someone told me once—I think they were from Russia—that we're the only people on the planet that expect to be happy. No one else expects that. I don't know if that's true or not, but whatever it was that allowed us to survive that initial two weeks, I think it was internal, not due to anything outside of ourselves.

"So when I watched the map at Warren and heard the conversations around me about the state of other nations, I wasn't surprised. The communist nations seemed to be doing the worst now. Their governments denied the pandemic for so long that the infected were at everyone's door by the time the government warned people. Once they warned people, they told them everything was under control, that the great leaders would take care of everything. This wasn't true, of course. What they wanted was for panic to be delayed long enough for the leaders to get themselves and their families out of the country as quickly as possible. You saw it everywhere—Cuba, China, North Korea. All the leaders in government and the military fled, leaving everyone else to fend for themselves. Democracies had gotten their acts together and were faring better, but large portions of the globe had gone black, no communication in or out.

" 'Amazing,' Jason said to me as I stood inside the war room watching the map. 'One second we're the dominant species on the planet, the next we're shrinking dots on a map.'

" 'I need to know I'm not wasting my time, Jason, what little I have left of it. I need to know that you believe there's an answer in the Congo.'

"He nodded. 'There's definitely an answer. I'm just not sure it's the one you want to hear.'"

BOOK TWO:
Africa

16

NORAD, the North American Aerospace Defense Command, wasn't uniquely American, as most people thought. Pete Brass remembered when he'd first come from the Air Force and joined NORAD, he'd been amazed to see half the staff in his office were Canadians. It was a joint agreement between the two countries that they needed each other to defend their air space.

The command center in Peterson Air Force Base just outside Colorado Springs was the nicest military installation Pete had ever hoped to work at, all chrome and shine. NORAD, truth be told, didn't really do much, so there weren't many opportunities to have crowds of people mucking up the building. Everything was in prime condition and pristine, just how he liked it. Given how the rest of society looked, coming to work was a welcome relief for Pete.

One of the senior airmen, a man named Bryce, walked past him as he stood in the back of the room.

"Bryce, what are you doing here? I thought it was your son's birthday."

"It is, sir. I couldn't get anyone to cover my shift."

"No," Pete said, "go home and be with your family. I'll take up the slack."

"Are sure, sir?"

"Yeah, go home. Have some cake for me."

He smiled widely. "Thank you, sir."

Pete took a sip of coffee as he headed over to Bryce's station to cover his shift. He sat down, brought up the monitor, made sure no emergencies were occurring, and then began reading on his iPad, something he knew most of the rest of the world was unable to do anymore.

He read for another hour before he heard, "Sir."

"Yeah?" he said, without looking up.

"You better have a look at this."

Pete sighed and put the iPad down. He was in the command center, at a station in the back. Before him were about fifteen other desks, each staffed by men in green uniforms with a NORAD insignia on their shoulders. On each desk, five computers sat monitoring everything from satellite surveillance to air currents. On the wall at the front of the room were five of the biggest monitors the US government could provide. On the wall next to them were two more monitors, where cable news never turned off: CNN and Fox. After the outbreak, both had gone off the air and only recently returned, the crew broadcasting from an undisclosed secure location.

Pete rose and strolled over to the airman's desk. The airman stared at a black screen that had a map of the US superimposed in neon green.

"What am I looking at?" Pete said.

"Right here, sir."

Pete looked where the airman's finger pointed. On the screen were several blips, one not far from NORAD, a few on the East Coast, some on the West.

"That a glitch?"

"No, sir. I've run diagnostics."

"Well, run them again," he said, straightening up to head back to his station.

"Sir, I ran them three times. I also checked the satellite."

"And?"

The airman swallowed and then pressed a button on the keyboard. One of the monitors switched to a magnified satellite view of the United States. The blips were clearly visible now and completely in US airspace. They seemed to hover motionless over multiple cities.

Pete thought of those Looney Tunes cartoons where a black cloud followed people around just above their heads.

He leaned forward, staring at the satellite feed. "What is that?" he said quietly.

The airman shook his head. "Whatever they are, there's a lot of them. And they weren't there a second ago."

It'd been two and a half hours since the objects, which was all they were calling them for now, had been spotted. Pete paced from one end of the command center to the other. He'd taken off his jacket and rolled up his sleeves. Suddenly, it seemed hot in there. No windows were allowed, so every few minutes he would stop at his desk and use the little paper fan his mother had gotten him as a birthday present. The gift was from another time. Even with all his credentials and clearances, Pete didn't know if she had survived the outbreak. Communication had been all but cut off to most of the states on the coasts.

The doors suddenly opened, and in walked the assistant secretary of defense for special operations, Daniel Clover, a brooding, middle-aged man in a military uniform with a brow the equal of any Neanderthal. At least, that's how he'd always appeared to Pete.

"Master Sergeant," Clover said by way of greeting, "please tell me what my meeting with the chief of staff was interrupted for."

Pete cleared his throat and hoped he wasn't turning red. "Um, sir, we have unidentified objects in our air space. They appeared about two and a half hours ago."

"You realize," Clover said, his voice rising, "that I have more important things to do than fly halfway across the country to come look at a damn blip on your radar."

"You don't need to look at the satellite feed, sir." He paused. "You can look outside now."

The assistant secretary's brow furrowed, and he spun on his heel and headed out the door. He'd probably been driven in without even bothering to look up at the sky. Pete followed him out. It took a few minutes, as they had to pass several security checkpoints.

Once outside, the sun shone down and the sky was blue. Off in the east, a black mass floated in the sky, almost like a plane that wasn't moving.

Clover placed his hand above his eyes to shield them from the sun. He then lowered his hand and put on his glasses, then took the glasses off and stared at it with the naked eye again.

"What the hell is that?" he said.

"Unidentified, sir."

"A meteor?"

"No, sir. It reduced its velocity and is now… hovering." Pete swallowed. "I think it might be a vessel of some kind, sir. We're seeing them spread over major cities across the country."

Clover looked at him, and the two men held each other's gaze. "Get the secretary of defense on the line as quickly as you can, Master Sergeant."

Pete looked up at the motionless black mass, a trickle of fear going up his back. "Right away, sir."

17

The sky glowed a dim orange as the sun sank behind the clouds. Mitchell watched Dr. Samantha Bower with detached curiosity. "You know," he said, "I think you and I would've hit it off quite well in private. Before all this… mess."

She didn't respond. Rather, she looked out at the horizon and the setting sun.

"Well," he said, "you never made your flight out to Africa, did you? Instead, you ended up in Miami helping the dying for no reason at all. Sisyphus pushing your stone up the hill."

"We didn't make the flight because there wasn't one for a long time, a couple of months. So I thought I could do some good here."

Mitchell nodded, a slight grin on his face. "I see that about you, that drive to do good. Hasn't really helped you so far, has it?" He sighed and pulled out the pistol tucked into his waistband. He placed it on the table. Samantha's eyes drifted down. The smooth steel, a silencer built into the end, reflected the dimming sunlight. She'd seen an identical gun before.

"Ian failed," she said. "And I get the sense that he was much better than you."

"Actually, he was in the organization a lot longer, more training. But I'm right about up to snuff now. You know, he was a friend of mine. I was very saddened to learn you killed him."

"I didn't kill him."

"Really? That's not what I'd heard. Doesn't matter. There's only one way this ends anyhow."

She looked up, into his eyes. "Why does Hank Kraski want me dead?"

"That's not his real name, you know. Hank is... he's quite an amazing man. He's fierce, willing to do anything to achieve what he needs to achieve, a Napoleon. It's a shame he doesn't have the army he needed to do what Napoleon couldn't." Mitchell chuckled. "Although I suppose the virus is the army, isn't it?"

"Why me?"

"He thinks you might actually develop a vaccine, and *that* we can't have, not yet, not until humanity can't fight back anymore." Mitchell leaned forward, crossing his hands on the table. "Hank is the type of man who would stomp the world under his feet if he could rule over the dirt afterward. He doesn't see civilization the same way you or I do. He has a long-term view of it, of the species as a whole. He thinks we're weak, and he is going to make us strong."

"Strong?" Samantha motioned to the devastated buildings around them, the fires that dotted the landscape randomly like erupting geysers. "Does this look strong to you?"

"It looks like a crucible, and when man does finally emerge from it, he will be strong, yes, willing to do what it takes to survive without distractions."

She shook her head. "Hank is insane just like Napoleon. One driving ambition blinds him to everything else. Napoleon brought destruction to the world, too. That's all he's giving you; destruction."

Mitchell shrugged. "I suppose only time will tell." He paused. "You know, there is a way you can prolong your life, if you would like to. Right here on the table, let me fuck you. That would buy you an additional half hour or so."

He chuckled. The look of disgust on her face was priceless.

"I suppose that's a no. I could rape you, but I'm not in the mood for a fight right now. I think I'd rather put a bullet in your head and then find a hot meal. And thanks for allowing the interview. I knew it'd be an easy way to get close to you. Everyone wants to tell their story." He lifted the pistol and then felt a muzzle against the back of his head. He instinctively spun just as the round caught him near the ear. Years, almost decades, of training saved his life with one jerk of his head.

Jason Shafi stood behind him.

Mitchell leapt to his feet. He thrust out with his hands, trying to knock the pistol away, gouge Jason in the eyes, or land a fist to his jaw, anything. The round had grazed his head, causing a ringing in his ears, and his vision spun. Jason easily moved away from his blows until he finally caught his fist, twisted the arm around, and snapped Mitchell's wrist.

Mitchell screamed as Jason got him down to his knees.

"Didn't think I'd see you again," Jason said. "I thought you were dead."

"Not yet."

Mitchell slammed his foot into Jason's ankle, knocking him nearly off his feet, and then came up with a quick blow to Jason's neck. Jason backed away enough for Mitchell to side kick him in the chest, his heel crashing into Jason's sternum and sending him flying back. Mitchell didn't pause. He leapt into the air and came down with a knee. Jason rolled away just as the knee hit the soft covering of the roof. Jason spun and landed two kicks to Mitchell's face before he lurched to his feet.

Jason, wrestling style, sprinted at him and tackled him around his waist. Both men hit the roof, Jason landing sharp elbows to Mitchell's jaw. Mitchell was feeling loopy by this time but managed to slip out the knife hidden in his sleeve. Jason saw it and caught his arm just as Mitchell tried to thrust it into his neck. The two men pushed and pulled, grunting like animals, the knife slowly slipping closer and closer to Jason's throat. Mitchell had him. He knew it. The knife would enter the throat and he would twist, ensuring a wide wound that would bleed out.

Just as the tip of the blade touched Jason's throat, Mitchell saw movement above him. Samantha lifted her glass and slammed it down into his face. Mitchell, the move catching him off guard, lost his grip. It only lasted a fraction of a second, but for someone like Jason, it was all the time he needed.

Jason grabbed the wrist that held the knife and turned it toward Mitchell. Using both hands, Jason put all his weight on the hand and wrist, the knife slowly entering Mitchell's throat. He screamed, and then the scream went silent as his larynx was sliced in half.

The last thing Mitchell saw as the warm blood pooled around him, running down his shirt, over his chest, and spurting out over the roof as Jason removed the knife, was Samantha Bower, a doctor, standing over him and not moving to help him.

18

Samantha watched as Jason dragged the corpse over to the side of the roof and tossed it. The body hit the building before looping down and hitting the ground. Several infected rushed for it from the mounds of debris they hid behind, tearing at it like coyotes over carrion.

"He's not the last," Jason said. "Hank will keep sending people over and over, until either you're dead or he's outta guys." He turned and looked at her. "I can go to the village by myself. I'll bring back samples of their blood for you to analyze. We can find somewhere new for you to hide. Somewhere Hank's influence doesn't reach."

She shook her head. "I'm tired of running. I wanna know why this happened, Jason. I wanna know why the world turned into this."

"If you're sure."

"I am."

He nodded. "Flight leaves tomorrow." He hesitated. "We can't take her with us."

"I know."

"This hospital's about as safe a place as any to leave her. They get resupplied every month, plenty of troops guarding the entrances, she'll be safe here."

"No, she won't be safe anywhere." She turned and headed back through the door leading down into the hospital.

The clinic-cum-hospital, which had once been for physical therapy and several other paramedical professions, consisted of sixty staff, not counting the marines that guarded the entrances, and now served as the local military hospital for an area covering almost a hundred square miles. As part of the deal the medical staff had made with the military, civilians would be served here as well, as long as resources were available and soldiers were the first priority for the beds.

Samantha had spent the past two months trying to bring ritual and routine back into her life. She had never known how much she needed those things, how much she relied on them. With a life of routine, your brain could almost go on automatic pilot, and you would have mental resources to focus on other things. When every second of existence had to be carefully thought out and planned, she found that by the end of the day, she couldn't think. All she could do was lie in her cot and take sleep aids so she could actually stop having nightmares for a few hours.

Jessica had been doing much better. The hospital staff all lived there in the building, and several had children, even two girls who were near Jessica's age. The three of them were inseparable, and their giggling and mischievous laughter that sometimes filled the halls comforted Sam in a way she didn't think something like that would.

A rudimentary laboratory had been set up in the hospital's basement. Nothing anywhere near a BS4 lab. Those days, at least for people outside the military, were gone, but she had enough equipment to study the virus. Several times a day, the hospital would be attacked and corpses of the infected would be burned after being shot by the marines. She would occasionally collect tissue and blood samples, trying to isolate the virus and track its mutations. With the equipment she had, however, it was nearly impossible. It felt a bit like grabbing things in the dark, hoping to land on something useful.

Jason stepped into the laboratory and sat down on a couch pushed against the wall. He rubbed his temples. "We're ready. Just gotta wait till the morning."

"Good."

"There's something I should tell you, Sam, about Tristan."

Samantha turned to him. "What?"

"She's… unique. I don't know. I don't know what I'm trying to say. I'm just so tired."

Samantha sat next to him on the couch and held his hand. Neither of them spoke or moved, not until the sun came up and Samantha realized they had both slept on the couch. She rose and checked her watch. The plane would be ready for takeoff in less than four hours, and before that, she would be entering the depths of Miami to get to the airbase.

19

The empty roads reminded Sam of the barren wasteland of Death Valley. She'd been there for a marathon once, seemingly in another life when training and competing in those actually seemed important.

In the tepid morning light, car after car stood on the sides of the interstate. The buildings beyond them were deteriorating so quickly that she couldn't believe her eyes. Windows were broken wherever they could be broken, and she wondered why people, during all this, would take the time to break them and find amusement in doing so.

"We need to switch cars," Jason said. "This one's almost out of gas."

He took an exit that led to an intersection. The traffic lights, covered in what appeared to be dirt, swung in a strong breeze. The lights in Miami no longer worked. Turning left, Jason parked on the side of the road. "We'll move on foot until we find something else. Stay close."

Sam exited the vehicle. If they were caught by a crowd of ips, no one could help them. Police didn't exist here. They were scattered to a few hospitals and financial centers or other places deemed worth protecting. The military patrols would be their only help, but they were few and far between as well.

"Let's move," he said.

They hurried up the sidewalk, Sam at Jason's side. He seemed single-minded, his eyes focused ahead of them, taking in their surroundings, considering every option, a soldier bred for war.

Jason nodded in the direction of a large building, and they took the corner and strode over.

The building, large and gray and at least twenty stories tall, had a massive parking structure next to it. They headed for the parking structure. Sam guessed the cars on the sides of the roads had had their tanks siphoned dry a long time ago and hoped they could find something in the structure that still had some gas left. Jason stopped at the entrance, closing his eyes.

"There are people in here," he finally said. "I don't know if they're hostile or not. If something goes down, you just run. Don't wait for me. Run."

She swallowed as they entered the building, the butterflies in her stomach nauseating her.

The structure had a ramp leading to the other levels and rows upon rows of cars. When Miami, like most major cities, had been evacuated, the roads had been shut down afterward. Cars were obsolete anyway because gas was nearly unaffordable. Everyone left had to walk—everyone who didn't have connections. The well connected could get out of any city.

"You should probably know something else, Sam. It's Hank's plan... the last phase isn't done yet. There's one more component to it."

"What?"

He hesitated. "The clouds again. It was, like, his obsession. He believes he can wipe out everyone if he can find a way to infect the clouds more efficiently. I think he may have found a way, but I'm not sure."

Jason began checking all the cars. When he found one he liked, he'd search it for keys. If it didn't have keys, he would break open the steering column and hot-wire it to check the gas gauge. They would then move on to the next car.

They checked the entire first and second floors of the parking structure. The gasoline had been siphoned from the cars long ago, leaving just a trace in each one.

As they approached the top level of the structure, Sam could hear voices, a lot of them. Jason motioned for her to stay back as he quietly took the stairs leading up.

She crossed her arms and paced around. The memory of what had occurred in Los Angeles was fresh in her mind. A man like a machine, who wouldn't stop no matter what pain he was put through, to carry out a single mission: kill her.

Her boyfriend had been killed in that fight, and the thought of Duncan filled her like a gray weight in her stomach, as though she had swallowed concrete.

On the outskirts of the parking level, she saw movement. She whipped her head around, but the movement was gone. Scanning the structure, a chill went up her back, a primal warning that she wasn't alone. A noise came from behind her and she looked back, catching sight of just the heel of someone scurrying behind a truck.

Samantha backed away, toward the stairs leading to the top level. The noises grew louder. Someone, or several people, was closing in around her.

Her heart pounding, she turned to run and froze. A man in tattered clothing stood before her, his hair gray on a rectangular head. He grinned and produced a knife hidden in his clothing. Behind her, two other men appeared, sinister smirks written across their faces, their fingers wrapped around a screwdriver and a length of steel pipe. Not ips, not enough blood covering them, but not friendly, either.

"You lost, Little Bo Peep?" the man in front of her said.

Samantha said nothing. She took in her surroundings. Only two routes away: down or up.

"Keep away from me," she said.

"Or what? Hm? What you gonna do?"

She broke into a run, as fast as her legs could carry her. She dashed past the man, headed for the ramp leading down to the lower levels. The other two men behind her were sprinting as well, their footfalls echoing against the walls. The tall man casually stepped away, letting the other two do the work.

Sam pumped her legs, making it halfway down to the other level before the men overtook her. One tackled her at the legs, slamming her down into the pavement. A burst of pain exploded inside her, but she didn't stop to consider it. She pushed up to her hands and knees and was on her feet again before the one with the pipe came at her. He swung wildly. She ducked and then kicked his groin. He grunted like a pig from the sudden pain, and she was gone. Turning around and heading in the opposite direction, she was almost to the next level by the time the men were dashing after her.

On the third level, she could hear their shouting. Their words were filthy, horrible things. Descriptions of what they were going to do when they caught her. One of them said they would wear her skin.

She sprinted past a few cars and jumped over the hood of one, landing hard on the ground. Covering her mouth with her hands, not trusting that a scream wouldn't escape her lips, she attempted to control her breathing, to remain still and quiet.

The running behind her stopped. The men were breathing hard, the one with the pipe letting it dangle in his hand and run along the pavement.

"Come out, come out," he said. "You can't run forever." He turned to the other man and said, "Go by that ramp so she can't get out. I'll look for her."

Hidden behind a tire, she poked her head underneath the car. One set of feet moved toward the ramp leading down to the second level. Another began going in between the cars, stopping near the windows a moment before moving on.

Eventually, they would find her.

As quietly as possible, she lay flat on her stomach. As she crawled underneath the car, her belt scraped against the pavement. She held her breath, her eyes on the feet not four cars away. They didn't show any reaction, just kept going from car to car.

Her entire body could fit underneath the car, a large SUV. She curled up so as to have all her limbs in the center of the vehicle and less likely to be seen by someone walking by. If he passed there without seeing her, she would crawl back to the ramp leading up and find Jason, or maybe to the set of stairs on the far side of this level and head down to the street, and attempt to find a military patrol.

The feet were two cars away now. They hurried around the next car, and she could see the man peering in through the windshield. His fingernails were black with grime and oil. She didn't know why that would be the thing she would notice above all else, but it was.

She held her breath as the man got to her car.

He paced around it and then looked inside before moving on to the next car.

Before she could release her breath, she felt his grip on her ankle and screamed. He began pulling her out from underneath the car, giggling. His grip was tight, and his fingernails dug into her skin.

When she was out and on her back, he climbed on top of her, laughing, strands of drool dribbling down onto her.

"We gonna know each other now," he said with a large grin.

The man was holding her arms, and he let go of one and grabbed her pants, attempting to rip them off. With her free hand, she reached up and thrust her nails into his eye, so far in that the eyeball nearly dislodged.

The man screamed and sat up, his hands to his face as blood began to flow. Sam pushed him off and ran. The other man hurried after her. She headed for the door leading to the stairs. Her lungs burned, and her heart pumped acid through her legs, but she didn't slow down.

She hit the door, grabbed the doorknob, and turned. It was locked. The man held the screwdriver like a sword and came at her.

Then, suddenly, he stopped.

His eyes went wide and he stared at her as a small trickle of blood dribbled down his lip and over his chin. He collapsed onto the cement, a knife sticking out of the back of his neck, the same knife Mitchell had tried to stab Jason with.

Jason stood at the ramp and jogged over. The man was writhing, attempting to pull the knife out. Jason pulled it out for him, slammed it back down into his throat, twisted, opening the wound, and pulled it out again. The man, quiet now, slowly bled out.

"I found a car," he said. "Let's go."

The car was an old sedan, something used by the people that squatted in the parking structure. As Sam followed behind him and got into the passenger seat, she glanced over at the people huddled together against the walls. She didn't see any women or children, just men staring blankly at them as Jason turned the car around and headed down the ramp.

"How'd you get the car?" she asked, afraid of the answer.

"I killed the guy who owned it."

Sam sat quietly a few moments, staring at him. He had said it so matter-of-factly, as if it were the most normal thing in the world, that she wasn't sure how to process it.

"Jason..."

"I know. It was necessary, trust me."

She looked out her window at the sky. Gray clouds had overtaken the sun, and it gave the city a sick pallor. "What if I can't do it? What if I get antibodies and I can't develop a vaccine from them?"

"One thing at a time. Let's just make our flight for now."

20

Planes, particularly commercial planes, were not something that held people's trust any longer, especially Samantha's. She'd seen commercial planes fall out of the sky, crashing into the ground in a fiery ocean of twisted metal and whatever they happened to land on. One flight had slammed into a residential neighborhood, taking out at least sixty homes. The pilot had been infected with Agent X but didn't want anyone to know. He attacked the copilot and they lost control of the plane. Military transport planes had even more of the infected. The military wasn't as kind to the infected in their ranks as the civilian population was, and there were rumors of executions for those that tested positive. It gave soldiers an incentive to hide the illness as long as possible, infecting dozens or even hundreds of others before being discovered.

As Sam crossed the Atlantic, the sparkling waters underneath her, she thought about the last time she'd been in the jungle, a jungle in South America as dense as anything Africa had to offer, a jungle that had almost killed her.

When they landed at an airbase in Brazzaville, the capital of the Democratic Republic of the Congo, she was amazed by how large the city actually was. When she thought of the Congo, she pictured sprawling villages interspersed with jungle, not a city that looked as though it might have been pulled out of Europe.

"There're no fires," she said, staring out the window.

"No," Jason replied. "The city's on military lockdown, for sure, but the infection didn't hit here like it did in the States. Not yet, anyway. The military's been able to keep the ips in the jungles."

Once on the ground, Jason took over. He knew where to go and who to speak with. A guide drove them to the drop-off point near the Congo River, and from there they loaded packs and began the hike through the jungle flora.

The Congolese jungle oozed darkness, a general sense of unease gripping Samantha's guts and tightening them. The vegetation, though dark green and red, spattered with yellows and browns, was foreboding, like the woods from *Grimms' Fairy Tales*, where monsters and demons dwelled. The afternoon warmth melded with the humidity of the jungle to create a wall of heat that hit Sam like an entity, as if it were a thing that she could touch and see. The taste of warm grass, soaked by the fetid water and heated by the brutal sun, sat on her tongue and filled her nostrils. She knew lots of different species of fauna were in there, but she couldn't hear them. The wilderness dampened the noise, as though they were being watched by the animal life. In other areas, the animals grew so loud it was deafening, like being at a rock concert where you can't hear the words being sung.

"How do you know where you're going?" she asked after a couple of hours.

"Just being here before, for training. They used to fly us out to different places, places with snow and mud, water, war zones, anywhere we had to fight to survive. Then they'd drop us off with nothing and we'd have to make our way back."

After another two hours in the heat and humidity, Samantha felt like passing out. She stopped in the middle of trudging up a particularly steep hill, taking a moment to gaze at the landscape before her: vines and valleys, mountains, hills, and dense canopy. "What're the people in this village like, Jason?"

He breathed deeply a moment as he came over the crest of the hill. "Normal folks, but I always felt like they had secrets. They never really trusted anybody from the outside. These are people who don't send their kids to school or read books. They've detached from civilization."

"I'm not sure I blame them."

Sam hiked another half an hour, then stopped and drank from her canteen, every muscle screaming for her to lie down and rest. Her head pounded with a coming migraine, and she considered stopping underneath the shade of a tree. But she thought of Jessica, a young girl stuck in a hospital, surrounded by violence and death. If there was a way to stop that, Sam would do everything in her power. That would give her the strength to keep going.

Pushing through the brush, they crossed a massive clearing and came to a gathering of thick cypress trees with branches that nearly reached the ground. She moved them aside with her hands, feeling the soft branches against her skin. Stopping under the trees for a few minutes, they ate a light meal of jerky then kept moving.

Dry land took up most of the landscape, and then suddenly a lake or pond would appear, the water a murky brown, concealing whatever was underneath. Once, she thought she saw a crocodile, but as she fixed her eyes on it, she saw it was just a log.

"Do you know how far?" she asked.

"Probably best you don't know."

The hike turned brutal as the land elevated within minutes. The trees and shrubbery thinned out, and all that was left was long grass that came up to their knees. In the distance, lush green mountains tore into the sky, their peaks covered with white clouds like icing on a cake.

The ground seemed to sink under her feet, making movement problematic, and soon sweating became more difficult, as she had already lost most of her body's moisture. As far as she knew, none of this water was drinkable. The parasites would make them so sick they would just vomit up any moisture they consumed.

At evening, Jason dropped his pack in a small clearing surrounded by African oak trees. "This is good," he said, "protected by the trees and nowhere near a water source."

Sam didn't argue. She dropped the pack that clung to her like a wet shirt. The ground was dry grass, and she collapsed and lay on her back, staring at the clouds slowly drifting by overhead. The howling of monkeys in the distance unnerved her, reminding her she was someplace unknown.

"The ips stay deeper in the jungles," Jason said, pulling out a small tent from his pack. "You'll hear 'em screaming at night sometimes. When they do come out, they rush for the cities. As long as we don't build a fire or make a lot of noise, we'll be safe."

"I'm not worried about them," Sam said. "I'm more worried about the insects."

Jason nodded, though his back was turned to her. "Buddy'a mine got bit by an unknown insect. His heart started giving up. In two months he went from two hundred pounds to ninety-five pounds. Got a heart transplant, but that didn't do much. He died from it, and they couldn't even tell him what kind of insect did it."

Sam turned her head toward him. The tent was up, and he walked over and took hers out of the pack without asking and began putting it up.

"You know," he said, "if you do create a vaccine or a cure, you'll be one of the greatest scientists in history. They'll have you in the same books with Newton and Pasteur."

"I doubt that. People tend to forget things quickly. Abolishing smallpox the first time was one of the greatest accomplishments of science. Can you name one person who took part in that?"

Jason flopped onto the ground next to her. "No. This is different, though. This thing will eventually wipe us all out." He looked at her then, and their eyes locked. A brief moment, just a moment, passed between them. Jason leaned in and kissed her, a quick kiss lacking passion but a small token of something that could've been.

"Night falls in a second out here," he said. "You should get some grub in your stomach and get to bed."

He rose and went to his tent, leaving Sam staring at the surrounding jungles. A small voice, extremely distant, echoed through the vegetation, a scream.

21

The overhead lights had been turned off, transforming the space into one lit blue by all the computer screens. Pete reclined in his chair, rocking manically back and forth. He rose and paced around the edge of the room a bit as though walking around a circular track. No one said anything to him, but he was certain his looming presence bothered a few of the techs monitoring the screens.

Assistant Secretary Clover came back into the room. Pete beelined for him and caught up as he stared at the monitors on the far wall.

"Well?" Clover said.

"They're still hovering, sir. No movement."

"The squadron ready?"

"Yes, sir. They're taking off right now from McClellan."

Airman Clyde Andrews climbed into his fighter jet as though slipping into a convertible. He had one back home, and every time he got into his F-22 Raptor, he thought of his car sitting in the garage gathering dust.

"Big Poppa," he heard on the intercom in his helmet, "we got you a clearance for take off. Over."

"Roger that," he replied.

The Raptor was one of the most advanced jets in the United States military. It had both stealth technology and supersonic capabilities. The jet was meant for a war that Andrews knew wouldn't be fought. Not a single air force in the world had anything like the Raptor with the exception of Israel, who got it from the United States. No one was a threat anymore in the way this jet was meant to fight, and soon it would be obsolete. The new war didn't need them. With ips, jets were useless. You killed an ip with bullets and blades, not jets and tanks.

Andrews, as he prepared for takeoff and began pulling the 43,000-pound plane out of its slip and onto the runway, realized he was envious of the pilots that served during the Cold War. They had a distinct enemy, someone to put a face to, to be the epicenter of all their fears and hatred. Now they fought scattered bands of insane people, preying on women and children hiding in closets. It was a different world, and not one he felt would get much better.

"Big Poppa ready for takeoff. You keep them pizza bagel bites warm for me."

"Will do. You're clear. Good luck."

The pressure in the Raptor was unlike anything else Andrews had ever experienced. Nothing in training had prepared him for it. The closest thing he could think of was being smashed by a tractor.

The jet lurched forward with so much force that his organs compacted, and the blood rushed out of his limbs. As the plane left the ground, the pressure slowly easing off of him, he wanted to shout, to holler at the top of his lungs. He wanted to do that every time and never did.

The object wasn't more than a couple of klicks away. He curved around and increased the altitude gradually. He caught a glimpse of the city below him, a city once bustling with people. Now it looked abandoned, cars left on the road, trains stopped mid-shipment, factories that no longer poured smoke into the air. He turned away, focusing his attention instead on the object in front of him.

It was black, but it didn't really appear to be a vessel. He'd studied aeronautical engineering for two years on the government's dime, and he knew the ship, or whatever it was, hadn't been designed to minimize air resistance. It was an oval shape, something more like a container than a vessel.

"Homebase, I'm near. The unidentified vessel appears to be unprotected. Doing a fly-by now, hang tight... it looks made of plastic or something similar."

Pete Brass listened to the pilot. *Looks made of plastic or something similar.*

He shook his head, staring at a still image of the object on one of the monitors. Clover was standing with his hands behind his back, flanked by two of his assistants, or what Pete guessed were his assistants. His face was stern and didn't change as the pilot reported back.

"Homebase, it looks completely unguarded. Awaiting further instructions."

Clover smirked. "Well, that was easy."

"What was, sir?" Pete said.

"Determining if it was a threat. If we can just take it out, I'm not too worried."

Pete looked from Clover to the monitor. "Why would we take it out? We don't know what it is."

"Oh, I know what it is. I've seen it before. I'm going to order it shot down. We'll see how they like that."

Pete thought a moment. "Sir, it's completely unprotected. Why would it be unprotected? Unless they, whoever 'they' are, wanted us to destroy it. I'd like your permission to study it a bit further before taking any action."

Clover looked at him, running his eyes up and down as though noticing him for the first time. "And what if it attacks us while you're studying it, Master Sergeant?"

"Sir, if it intended to attack us, it could've done so already."

Clover grunted and turned his eyes back to the screen. "You got two hours. Make them count."

22

The NORAD command center seemed to close in around Pete, confining him as if he were locked in a box. The claustrophobic pressing in of a room built underground without windows was too much. He decided to go for a walk.

"Where you going?" his assistant, Debra, asked.

"For a walk."

"I'll come with."

They headed up the elevator and then out of the building. The sun hung in the sky, but clouds blocked the light. Pete put his hands in his pockets and strolled along the perimeter of the base, just beside the fence. Something he'd done a thousand times.

"You know, Nietzsche said all great thoughts were the product of walking," Pete said.

"You trying to impress me by quoting dead philosophers?"

He grinned. "Are you impressed?"

"A little."

She looked at the object in the sky. "What are those things?"

He shook his head. "I don't know. But they've been reported over all the major cities—Tokyo, Shanghai, London, Madrid—at least the parts of those cities that can still communicate with us. If you wanted to kill off our species, you'd only need to take out the major cities. Without leadership, everyone else will divide and be easier to conquer."

"This is crazy, I know, but what if they're aliens? You think they'd come here to conquer us?"

"No, an advanced civilization... if that's what they are... no. We just assume that because that's what we've historically done. Whenever we've encountered a new, more primitive culture, we've enslaved them, whether in real chains or by making them think they need blue jeans and Coca-Cola to be real people."

"What do you think Clover meant when he said he knew what they were? That he's seen them before?"

Pete saw a colony of ants swarming over an old crust of bread. He stepped over them, never taking his eyes off the ground. An icy chill ran up his back at their movements. "I don't know. But it makes me think we're not dealing with anything extraterrestrial, as much as I would prefer that to the alternative. Whatever's happening is above my pay grade. But one thing I do know: we shouldn't blow them up without knowing what they are."

"In about five minutes, Clover's going to do just that. You got any ideas?"

He shook his head. "Nothing. I've tried communicating, we've run searches through every database in the world containing aircraft... it's something new, whatever it is." He checked his watch. "We better head in. They should be launching soon."

Back in the Raptor and up in the baby blue sky quickly turning gray, Clyde Andrews looped around the black object, leaving a stream of white contrail across the sky like a scar. He dipped the plane low and then raised it high again, testing whether the object would have any reaction to his movements. Nothing happened. The black mass was as motionless as a statue.

He was given clearance to fire, and that's exactly what he did. The first missile released, throwing the balance of the Raptor off for only a split second. The projectile sped to its target in less than two seconds, impacting with enough force to shatter it.

The object fragmented and fell to the earth.

"Homebase, target is neutralized, repeat, target is neutralized."

"Roger that, Big Poppa. Come on back to base. Good work."

"Roger that. Big Poppa comin' home."

Pete paced the floor nervously. Clover was sitting with his back straight as a board in Pete's chair. They'd given the order to take the thing out.

Homebase, target is neutralized, repeat, target is neutralized.

Cheers went up, though they were muted since a commanding officer was in the room. Clover smirked and stood up, straightening his uniform. Pete strode next to him, awaiting his orders. This was Clover's show, and Pete had come to realize that what he said didn't matter. But that didn't help the knot in his gut that told him they'd made the wrong decision.

"See, Sergeant-Major, nothing to worry about," Clover said.

"Yes, sir. I'd like to see what's left up close, though, sir."

Clover eyed him. "I'm not sending a team out. It would cause too much attention. But feel free to have a look if you're so inclined."

"Yes, sir."

Pete turned and crossed to the elevator.

23

The drive had taken longer than he thought it would. Pete Brass sat in the passenger seat of the jeep while Debra drove. He stared out at the landscape. People had been ordered indoors after T-Zero to eliminate contact with each other. Add the ips on top of that, and no one came out for any reason. It created a ghost-town effect where everything looked abandoned, like the cities themselves were living organisms and slowly dying.

"I used to think America would be around forever," Pete said, not taking his eyes off the city passing in front of him.

"Nothing lasts forever," Debra said.

"But it seems like it does, doesn't it? There were people born during the Peloponnesian War who grew up, lived, and died during it. They thought that's what life was, one continual state of war. I wonder all the time if we're living in something like that, some epoch that future generations will see as a fluke."

"I think maybe you wonder about things too much. You gotta just relax and live in the moment, Pete."

"Children and criminals live in the moment. Adults plan for the future. Besides, is this the moment you really want to live in?"

She didn't reply.

Up ahead, farmland took up the next dozen miles or so. Pete was familiar with the scenery. His grandfather had been a farmer. He remembered long summer days when his parents would drop him off at the farm and his grandfather would put him to work. The work was backbreaking, and all he could think about while doing it was when it would be over. Now, after ten years behind a desk, all he could think about was the feel of sunshine on his face and working with his hands, having something to show for a good day's work in the evening. If someone asked him what exactly he did, he wasn't certain he could define it.

"Look at that," Debra said.

Pete looked. In the middle of a green field of crops, a smoking heap of parts took up space, an unwelcome scar. The jeep pulled into a road that led back there, and Pete kept his eyes on the heap. He scanned the surrounding area. The military patrols did a good job eliminating ips, but they couldn't get them all.

Ips.

He hated having to call them that. They were people, people suffering from a horrific disease, but he had to create that cognitive dissonance. He had to feel they weren't people at all but things. Otherwise, how could they kill millions of them?

"So, there's seriously not going to be, like, a military response or anything? No doctors or scientists to examine this stuff?" Debra said.

"If we see something interesting, we'll call it in."

The jeep rumbled to a stop on the dirt road and parked maybe thirty feet from the heap. Pete stepped out and around the vehicle and stared at the smoke. The coloration wasn't white or gray—it was black. Like burning rubber.

"Stay here," he said.

He began making his way through the crops. His shoes sank in the ground, soft from rain a few days back.

When he was within ten feet of the object, or what was left of the object, he stood still and watched. Uncertain what he was looking at, he knew one thing: it looked familiar. He walked closer, cautiously and methodically analyzing anything out of the ordinary. The heap looked like a pile of refuse someone threw out and lit on fire. There was nothing particularly extraordinary about it. Behind him, he heard footsteps and turned to see Debra.

"I told you to wait."

"Our possible first interaction with ET and you think I'm going to wait?"

He turned back to the heap. "No, guess not."

Pete circled around, taking a couple of steps toward the object with each pass. He stopped when he was no more than five feet away and put his hands on his hips. "This isn't aliens." He reached into the pile as Debra gasped, as if he was jumping through the fire or something. He glanced over and then continued reaching for what he wanted.

The hunk of material burned his fingers, and he had to hold it by the edge. He pulled it out a few feet and dropped it. A long piece of black plastic, shaped something like a car bumper. He bent down and examined it.

"This is plastic," he said. He tapped it with his fingers. It didn't sound or feel like any plastic he'd ever encountered. "Some sort of unique polymer to give it better cohesion, but just plastic." He leaned in close. In the corner, he saw a stamp.

Pete's heart dropped and his eyes drifted off the object and back to the heap. He stood up, his gaze fixed on the smoke billowing up into the sky.

"I know what this is," he said.

"What?"

"This is a drone."

"Seriously?"

He looked at her. "I also know why Clover said he recognized it."

"Why?"

"Because it's one of ours."

24

Pete Brass paced outside the massive office. It was the largest one in all of NORAD, and Clover had taken it over. Pete had hoped Clover would leave after destroying the drone, but he'd decided to stay a while. Now he was making Pete wait to see him.

Finally, the door opened and someone in a military uniform stepped out. Pete stormed in. Clover sat with his back straight, staring out a window at the hallway.

"What the hell, Danny?"

"Problem?"

"You knew that was a drone."

"So what if I did?"

"And I'm guessing you know it's one of ours?"

"I do."

Pete folded his arms, staring the older man in the eyes. "What else aren't you telling me?"

"I'll tell you what you need to know."

"Don't give me that need-to-know bullshit. What is going on?"

Clover straightened the top of his uniform, brushing away a bit of string on the chest. "Those drones were sanctioned for use by the NSA and DIA. They disappeared after their acquisition. They've turned up now."

"That's it? 'They've turned up'? Turned up from where?"

"I don't know."

"But you have a guess."

"I do."

Pete waited a beat. "What, are we playing charades?" Pete sat down across from him. "What the hell is happening?"

"We had someone at the DIA who thought he was king. He's toying with us right now. Showing us what he's capable of."

"Who?"

"His name is Kraski. He's about the most weaselly son of a bitch you could ever meet. His division was shut down, funding cut, and he hit the roof. He consolidated his department so that it could run without strings from the DIA and Congress. Now he's making his move for power."

"With empty drones?"

Clover waved his hand dismissively. "It's a power play. He's showing us he can put something in the air over every major city if he wants to."

"Well, who is he?"

"He's never been military. Direct recruit for his language skills. He's a polyglot, speaks ten languages. After a stint in the CIA, he went to the DIA and rose through the ranks until he carved out a little empire for himself. That's where I know him from. He handled the intelligence in the first Iraq war." He paused. "He and his team specialize in things we might find distasteful."

"So what does he want?"

Clover shook his head, picking up a stress ball from the desk and squeezing it in his palm. "How should I know? I think he's unstable, always have. No moral compass." He placed the ball back on the desk. "I'm ordering all his drones shot out of the sky."

"Why?"

"To show him how I feel about his power play."

"They're just plastic. Who cares if they're up there?"

"I don't know what he's got planned, but I'm not playing along. Now if you'll excuse me, I have a few calls to make."

Pete rose from the desk and headed out the door. At the last moment, Clover stopped him, saying, "Pete, I want full response units at the sites of the crashes. Just in case. You didn't touch anything when you went out there, did you?"

"A hunk of plastic. They're empty."

"Hm," he said, nodding. "Well, just in case, then."

25

After a breakfast of corn cakes and water, Sam followed Jason through the jungles again. The terrain varied among rainforest, grassland, and what appeared to be swamps, marshes full of brown water. Several times they'd had to swim, and all she could picture was what Shui had told her, people in the water disappearing suddenly with the infected below them. And then she wondered if Shui ever got back to Shanghai as he had planned.

Near the top of a steep hill, she saw a wake of vultures swooping above them.

"That's not a good sign," she said, huffing.

"There's a body down there. The vultures know where everything is. Some people out here think they're telepathic."

"You think that?"

"No. But one thing I do know about 'em is they taste like shit."

Over one of the hills, they approached a lake, and Sam saw children playing in the water. They were nude, white skin, blond and brunette hair, not natives, and had fishing poles made of wood and string.

The instant they saw the two adults, they ran into the brush and disappeared. A little beyond that was a village.

The village seemed like a town that had died. Everything was made of wood or tin, looking like it could fall apart at any moment. Old, rusted trucks lined the passageways that passed for streets, and several people were out on porches, sipping drinks and talking.

A group on the porch of a home near them quieted, and the men rose, ushering the women back into the shack. One of the men pulled out a shotgun and approached them. Most were black, but many were white. Maybe even American, Sam guessed. They'd been out here so long that they appeared as much a part of the jungle as the trees and the sky.

"Who you be?" one of the men said in clear English.

Jason stopped walking, locking eyes with the man. "I'm here to see Tristan."

"She ain't here."

"Just tell her Jason Shafi is here. She's expecting me."

The man backed away and spoke to another man on the porch. That man ran off and disappeared into the village. When he returned, he spoke in hushed tones with the first man.

"Well?" Jason said.

The first man lowered the shotgun and set it back on the porch. "She'll see ya."

26

Pete Brass stepped outside the building and sat on a curb, an empty parking lot before him. It was lunchtime. The only place to eat nearby was the commissary, though some people had taken to bringing food in. Though an ip hadn't been spotted nearby in weeks, no one risked travel when they didn't have to.

He wasn't hungry. In fact, he felt a general malaise, something akin to working out really hard and having the body force the mind to slow down. An itch had developed in the back of his throat, and it annoyed him. Several times he had to wipe sweat away from his brow, though the day wasn't hot.

"You okay?" Debra said, sitting down next to him and handing him an unopened can of soda.

"Fine. Thanks. Just a scratchy throat."

She sipped her drink. "Clover's taken over your office. He liked it better."

"Fantastic," he said dryly.

"You don't like him, do you?"

"I've just known a lot of men like him. They think they can't be wrong. It's dangerous to have men like that in power."

"Is that sour grapes I'm hearing?"

He shook his head, popping open the can. "No, I'm fine where I am in my career. I got another nine years left on my twenty, and I'm going to get a cushy desk job and ride it out until retirement, as long as some ip doesn't tear my throat out before then. But it just gets to me sometimes that guys like him are the ones calling the shots."

She shrugged. "They've always called the shots. You and I can't do anything about it." She paused. "That was kinda weird this morning. I mean, I know they were just drones, but thinking that they were from some other planet was crazy. It made me... I don't know. Giddy, I guess, that we weren't alone."

"Well, it's probably fortunate that we are. Imagine our barbarity but with advanced weaponry we stole from another civilization."

"Is that what you thought they were? Weapons?"

"What else would they be? They hovered above population centers, just waiting for..."

Pete's heart dropped. The itch in his throat, the sweat... He jumped to his feet and said, "I need you to drive me somewhere."

"Where?"

"The hospital."

All hospitals still operating had testing centers screening patients that had shown symptoms for the presence of *Variola major*, better known as smallpox. Traditional smallpox, Pete knew, took anywhere from seven to twelve days to develop to the point where the host began showing symptoms. But this strain, and others like it, had mutated, and it seemed the incubation period for each strain was shorter than the last. It was entirely possible a strain had evolved that had an incubation period of hours rather than days. He'd seen something close to it in the ips.

As Pete sat in the passenger seat of the jeep, Debra going much slower than he would've liked, he felt the acute discomfort of body aches. He had a slight fever, he could tell from the heat emanating from his face and the sweat that wouldn't stop rolling down his back and scalp.

"What are we going to the hospital for, Peter?"

He looked away from her so he wouldn't breathe on her. "I think…"

The words wouldn't even form on his lips. The possibility was too horrific.

The hospital was busy, as all hospitals were, even though triage declined most people. Unless an injury or illness was life threatening, the hospital wouldn't take you.

Pete had Debra park near one of the five or six trailers in the parking lot, where the tests were performed for smallpox infection, a pinprick. The site of the injection would inflame if the patient was infected, creating a bubble-like pustule. He'd seen it several times in his colleagues who'd tested positive and were bedridden afterward. But this new development, the insanity that now followed infection, was the most terrifying aspect. He decided if it came to that, if he felt himself losing his mind, he would end it by his own hand.

"Pete, what's going on?"

"I think I'm infected," he said, his eyes unable to move from the trailer.

A long silence between them.

"Does anyone know?"

"No. But you need to come with me."

"Why?"

He looked at her. "Because I think you're infected, too."

Neither spoke for a long time. Pete eventually got out of the jeep and waited for her. She followed him in silence to the first trailer. A physician was inside with a single assistant. They wore what looked like spacesuits, even while relaxing on chairs. A chain ran across the entrance to the trailer, and one of them rose and unhooked it.

"I need a test, please," Pete said, "for smallpox."

27

Waiting for the results of the test, for any test, was always the worst part. Pete decided sitting around at work being eyed by Clover wasn't where he wanted to spend the next hour, so he drove around the city with Debra.

The thing that had caught him off guard, that had caught everybody off guard, was how few people needed to die for society to begin the process of disintegration. The virus had only wiped out perhaps 15 to 20 percent of the world's population, though numbers varied widely depending on which nation you asked, and yet it seemed like the other 80 percent could not function without them.

The buildings were dark without power, and the streetlights didn't work. Cars, too expensive for the general public, were abandoned like leftovers in every nook and cranny where they could fit and stripped of any useful or valuable parts. The skyscrapers had been stripped just as thoroughly of anything useable and now were just hulking skeletons needlessly taking up space. The whole thing gave Pete a chill, and he remembered why he didn't like coming into the city.

"You okay? Debra asked.

"No," he said, reclining in the passenger seat. "No, Deb, I think I'm definitely not fucking okay."

"Easy, don't bite my head off."

He swallowed. "I'm sorry."

"I'm scared, too."

Pete shook his head. "I'm not scared of dying. I'm really not. It's what has to come before it that scares me. I'll be in that much pain and I still won't want to die. I'll still fight just as hard. And then I'll lose my mind and attack anything that moves. I don't want that. I want to go in peace. My dad died in a bed surrounded by everyone he loved. He got to hold hands… say a prayer, listen to his favorite album." Pete grinned. "*Led Zeppelin IV*. He could've listened to anything he wanted, and he chose that. He said it took him back to his childhood."

"You miss him?"

"Every day. He was my life for a long time. The person I'd call when I had a problem and didn't know which direction to turn." Pete exhaled. "I could sure use his advice right now."

"We don't know that we're sick."

"I don't feel good. And the doctor said he's seen the incubation period go down with every passing week. The virus is mutating quickly. It's not natural, Deb. It's engineered. Most people think it's a punishment from God, like a hurricane or something. It's not. It was made in a lab by men too insane to see what they were really doing."

Debra stopped the jeep and reached over. She lay her hand on his lap and looked him in the eyes. "We don't know if we have it, Peter."

He nodded. "I'm so sorry I took you with me to that site. I should've gone alone. I could've at least worn some protective gear and—"

"You didn't know what you had on your hands. Don't beat yourself up."

He looked out over the city and could see a baseball stadium down the road. Now it was used as a makeshift prison and, something not everyone knew, an execution chamber. Ips were brought in by the dozens, shot, and burned. So many of them were crammed in there that he could hear their screams even from half a mile away. "I used to watch games there, a minor league team, the Bees or Raptors or something. I don't even remember now. Isn't that funny? I went there a few years ago and I don't remember anything about it."

"Traumatic events can do that to us."

He looked at her. "I don't want to die alone."

"You won't. I'll be here."

"They said we shouldn't be interacting."

"They don't know anything." She rested her head on his shoulder.

Just then, an entire relationship flashed in Pete's mind. Debra had always been the one, the one that he called when he was lonely, the one that went to movies with him when he couldn't find anyone else. He had always figured she agreed to see him outside of work because he was her boss, but he could see now there was something else between them. His biggest regret was that he saw that now, when it was too late for him to do anything about it.

"I'm sorry I never... I should have made this happen sooner."

She lifted her head and kissed him. Everything inside him said to stop, that if one of them was infected and the other wasn't, they would now infect the other. He couldn't stop. The kiss felt better than anything he'd ever done in his life, and he didn't want it to stop.

She pulled close and they held each other, staring at the abandoned buildings in front of them. "The tests should be ready. We need to head back."

She started the jeep and turned around.

28

By midafternoon, Samantha had sweated out the last of her moisture. Now dehydrated, her lips cracking, a pain had developed just underneath her ribcage. Her kidneys. But the immediate pain was the skin peeling off her lips. She licked them, even though she knew it would only make them worse.

The villagers wouldn't let them inside their homes, so they had to sit out in the dirt road that passed through the town and wait for Tristan. Jason kept his eyes closed as though he were meditating.

Sam had been watching the people in the town. They seemed happy, oblivious to the chaos going on around them. None of them appeared sick, and she was surprised they let anyone from the outside world in at all. A single infected person could easily kill everyone in the village in a matter of days.

Eventually, she saw a woman step out of a building. The woman was strikingly beautiful, more so because Sam didn't expect to see someone who looked like that here, of all places. Her hair was bright red, almost the color of red crayon. A large man with a rifle followed her out, and they strolled over. The woman grinned and said, "It's been a long time, Jason."

Jason rose. "You look the same."

"No stress. Stress is the great killer of modern humans." She looked at Sam. "And you must be Dr. Bower?"

Samantha forced herself up. "I am."

"We welcome you to our village. I hope we can be of some assistance."

The woman seemed ethereal. Maybe it was the way she spoke, maybe her beauty, or the elegance of her movements. But behind her eyes was something else, something mischievous or maybe even malicious.

"You have a lot of animals here," Sam said, noticing the pens filled with wildlife.

"Yes, we're entirely self-sufficient. I don't want my people to rely on the outside world in any way. We don't even have electricity. It's difficult at first to grow accustomed to, but once you do, it's difficult to imagine living any other way."

Tristan began strolling around, and Sam got the impression she was expected to follow. She followed Tristan as she sauntered by a large pen holding some sheep.

"So you want to devise a vaccine based on our antibodies," Tristan said, more a statement than a question.

"If it's possible. I don't know that it is."

"Must be a noble career, finding vaccines and saving lives."

"I also take them."

She stopped, the interest in her face showing brightly. "How?"

"The smallpox vaccine is a live virus and causes at least one pustule. If the pustule oozes, it's contagious. It's also causing people with weak immune systems distress or death. I would anticipate about 1 percent of everyone that takes it will die. Most vaccines for hot viruses are similar, and I've helped develop a few."

"Take a few lives to save a great many more… I don't think there is another way to save people, is there? Everything has a consequence. Every action goes beyond where we think it does."

"Jason told me the same thing."

"Jason and I have a lot in common in our thinking. We're both children of reality. Anything mystic doesn't appeal to us." She paused, watching several sheep as they ran over to see if any food was about to be thrown. "We don't want any contact with the outside world. I hope you understand that. None of my people will be leaving the village. You're free to study a few of us, take blood samples, but nothing more."

"I understand. Is it true you haven't had a single case of the virus here?"

"Not a one."

"Is it simply a matter of exposure?"

"Oh, no, we've had exposure. Several people have come through here, attempting to get away from the cities. One was infected and we couldn't tell. He coughed on the woman tending to him and several of her children. None of them were infected. Of course, we've had the insane. For them, there's nothing that can be done. They simply have to be killed. But we are immune to their virus."

"And how do you explain that?"

"I don't. Some things in nature are just unknown. Maybe we're lucky, or perhaps purity in our genetics has built a resistance."

Sam noticed that most of the people in the village had dirty boots. But Tristan's boots were clean, even sparkling in the sunlight as though freshly shined.

"I've seen people that have naturally fought off the smallpox, but I wouldn't call what they have now life. I've never met someone who might actually be immune," Sam said. "And this new mutation, the one causing insanity, I don't even know what it is. I just don't know if your blood will help me at all."

She smiled. "Then we should hurry and get you a test subject. I'm curious myself."

As Tristan left, the man with the rifle following her, she said a few words to Jason. He approached Sam and said, "Just so you know, there are no laboratories here. You get what you need from these people and I'll take you to another lab."

"Not the CDC?"

"Atlanta's still off limits. But we might be able to set something up with the army." He hesitated. "Hank isn't here."

"It's fine," Sam said, absently looking out over the town.

He hesitated again, averting his eyes. "Tristan told me he's not done. He doesn't want anyone unaffected."

Variola major could be turned into a mist. She had known that as a graduate student. But to get it into the clouds, it seemed so unnatural, so monstrous, that the thought hadn't even entered her mind that other men would be willing to do it. Now not only had it been done, she had just been told it would happen again.

"They tried to terminate it," Sam said, staring off at some children.

"What?"

"Smallpox, in the nineties. We abolished it from nature in the seventies, but the US and Russia had stockpiles. The World Health Organization tried to exterminate it as a species entirely. They wanted to destroy the stockpiles. But the militaries of the US, UK, and Russia were against it. A lot of scientists were, too. They thought exterminating an entire natural species, even smallpox, was immoral. If they had done it, this wouldn't have even begun."

"Don't kid yourself. Every nation with a laboratory has smallpox. It's a weapon too powerful to give up."

"It's not a weapon. It destroys its user in the process. No man-made weapon does that. It's a force of nature, like lightning. We can't control it. That type of control doesn't exist. We're the only species that doesn't live with nature but tries to conquer it."

He gently placed his hand on her shoulder, drawing her attention back to him. "You can save a lot of lives with this."

She nodded. "I don't know if I can, but I'll try."

29

Pete couldn't look at the pustule, not for a long time. He didn't really know what he was looking at, but he figured the larger and more colorful it was, the more likely he had smallpox. He sat in the trailer as the physician cleaned his arm. When he was done, he sat down across from Pete. Without having to say it, Pete knew.

"How long do I have?" Pete muttered.

"I don't know for certain yet. The pustule seems to indicate an infection, but I'll need to get your blood results back to make certain. That takes days."

"If I do have it, how long?"

"I don't know. I've never seen an antigen like this one. It adapts and evolves, mutates... probably no more than a couple of days before you get the headaches and intense fever. You'll be bedridden by day five or six and the pustules will appear, or you'll go insane. Those are the two roads. We can give you the smallpox vaccine now since it's so close to the time of infection, but the vaccine hasn't been working. This strain is resistant. We just do it because we don't know what else to do."

Pete nodded and rose, unable even to blink. He stumbled out of the trailer and stood in the dwindling sunlight. The day was coming to a close, and with it, he realized, so was he. This was the worst day of his life, and all he could think of was that he wished he could have a few more hours of sunlight.

And then a sudden, powerful thought pushed itself into his consciousness. The drones were filled with *Variola* mist. Being shot down, the drones would expose the mist.

Pete jumped into the jeep. Debra ran out of one of the trailers.

"Are you…"

"No," she said, relieved. "Negative."

"Then you can't be near me. Goodbye, Debra."

"Goodbye? Wait. What do you mean goodbye? Pete! Pete!"

He peeled out of the parking lot and got back on the road, shooting through the streets and heading back to NORAD.

The simple pleasure of driving wasn't something Pete had felt in a long time. It was odd to be behind the wheel of a car and not have anybody else on the roads. The streets were dirty and the buildings more so with no one around to clean them up anymore. He'd never appreciated how much that meant to him, to have cleanliness, until that moment. He figured everything was like that: you had to lose it first, and then you'd value it. You could never appreciate something while you had it. *What a sad little joke*, he thought.

The jeep roared up the interstate, and by the time he got off, he realized there wasn't much fuel left. Seeing the needle so close to empty filled him with unease. Several times, he'd been in military transports that had run out of fuel. Those angst-filled hours while they waited on the side of the road for another military vehicle to bring fuel, the screaming of the insane echoing around them, were some of the most terrifying of his life. And now they didn't compare with the thought that he would be one of them.

He parked next to the entrance and jumped out. Just as he was about to run into the building, he caught a glimpse of himself in the jeep's side mirror. The sweat had soaked his collar and his eyes were rimmed red, as though he hadn't slept in a great while. And he remembered what was coursing through him right now. He couldn't go into the building. He could potentially infect everyone there.

In the back of the jeep, as in all military jeeps now, was an infection protection kit, a red container that held everything someone would need if they were going to deal with a potentially infected person. Pete opened it and searched the contents. He found what looked like a rubber fishing suit and a transparent gas mask. He put them on over his clothing and then snapped latex gloves over his hands. Even though he knew it was impossible to transmit smallpox through hair, he took out the surgical cap and put it on before hurrying inside.

Everyone stopped what they were doing when he walked in. People turned at their desks, phones still in their hands with voices coming through on the other end. A few stood up, as though he were a wild animal that was about to attack. Pete guessed they didn't know whether he was infected or whether someone else was and he was protecting himself. Either way, their fight-or-flight responses had been triggered. The reptilian brain had taken over, and they were just waiting for the moment to either run or subdue him. He had no doubt that his long-time friends would hurt him if they thought their lives were at risk.

Pete quickly jogged past the main floor and to his office. He found Clover on the phone, one of his assistants standing behind him like a slave waiting for commands. They both looked up at the same time and Clover said, "I'll call you back" into the phone.

No one said anything for a moment. Pete felt his throat in a way he never had, dry and sticky at once. He swallowed, feeling his breath heat his face in the confines of the gas mask.

"I'm infected," he said.

Clover sat silently for a moment. "From the drone?"

"Yes. You can't shoot them down. They contain the poxvirus, Danny. Whoever put them up there *wants* you to take them down."

Clover considered this before leaning forward and rubbing his brow. "Son of a bitch."

"What?"

"I should've killed that bastard when I had the chance." He looked at Pete, as though noticing him for the first time. "You're relieved of command, Master-Sergeant. I'm sorry."

"It's fine. What about the drones?"

"I'll figure something else out."

Pete nodded, looking around his office. He thought briefly he should pack up his things, then remembered that he wouldn't be needing them. He turned and shut the door behind him, glancing at the giant monitors on the wall before walking out and sitting in the jeep. After stripping off the gas mask, he removed the gloves and suit.

There was a small canyon nearby. Pete started the jeep and headed there.

The farther up into the mountains he went, the cooler the air became. The green in the foliage was dappled gold from the setting sun. He figured he had maybe twenty or so minutes of sunlight left.

He came to a clearing. The last time he had been there, the clearing was filled with cars. People parked there and hiked up the small hill off to the right, sightseeing. A panoramic view of the valley below waited for them at the top of the hill, along with white boulders that seemed otherworldly. Pete had sat on one of the boulders with a girl he'd been dating, Papaya. He remembered her name because it was so unusual, and he finally got the nerve to ask her if she was actually named after the fruit, which, it turned out, she was.

As he got out of the jeep and trekked up to the top of the hill, he wondered what had happened to Papaya.

At the top of the hill, he saw the white boulders and approached them. They weren't dull white or cream or anything diluted; they were a pure, bright white, like snow, an aberration of nature. He sat on one and watched the valley below him. How different it looked now. More trees, no cars, no glimmering stoplights or street lamps. A perfect oasis of nature with remnants of civilization left.

Pete curled his legs up to his chest, and before he could stop them, tears flowed down his cheeks, and he wept.

30

The apartment seemed more isolated than usual. Pete normally didn't even notice the dilapidation or silence, but now that was all he could see when he looked around his home: the rust on the faucet, the tear in the couch, the crack in the window over the sink. All of it told him one thing: he'd worked his entire life and had nothing to show for it. He drew a good salary, or had drawn one, anyway, but he had no luxury possessions to speak of, no wife or family, not even the memories of such things to comfort him. His entire life was crammed into a studio apartment.

The building was surrounded by razor wire and had a guard at the entrance at all times. He'd noticed a trend where apartment buildings that weren't guarded were filled with squatters in a matter of days. Then an ip would break in. The infection would spread, and the squatters would have to be killed by the military patrols. His building paid for security after a similar incident in another complex up the block.

He rose from the couch and stared out the window onto the street. Other than the military patrols, he never saw any cars. People had occasionally walked by on the sidewalks, but even that had stopped months ago.

He paced his apartment, but it was so small that only took a couple of minutes. Staying indoors wasn't going to work. He would need to find something to hold his interest, to keep his mind off the organism inside of him, for as long as was possible. Otherwise, he would drive himself insane thinking about it.

He left the apartment. Two flights of stairs led down to the ground level and the jeep he'd taken from NORAD—a vehicle they'd probably come for, eventually. He didn't have a car of his own, since NORAD provided them to their officers. He decided to pass it up and walk.

The air cooled his skin. The moon was barely visible. The sliver of it that did show doused the city in a pale white light. Without light pollution, it was breathtaking. Even the mailbox he walked past shimmered. The windows of buildings reflected a speck of moonlight in a shiny epicenter like a glowing diamond. Mirrors up on a business storefront reflected the light back up to the sky.

Pete did four rounds of his block. No one was out. No one drove by other than the patrols. Of the two he saw, both stopped and checked his identification. A curfew was in effect, and all nonmilitary personnel were arrested on the spot. He didn't want to be that close to them, even with their biohazard suits, but he couldn't bring himself to tell them to keep away because of infection. If he did, he would be joining the dying at the stadium, a bullet to his head before being burned in a pit with thousands of others.

He stopped at an intersection and tried to plan his best course for the remaining time he had left in life. It didn't matter, not really. Whatever he did, his mind would be somewhere else, on the virus multiplying within him.

As he passed along the sidewalk, his thoughts took him back to that drone. A few things didn't sit well with him, mostly how they actually stayed in the sky. They'd been up there a long time, and nothing had flown up to refuel them, which meant that someone, or something, had discovered a way to conserve massive amounts of fuel and refused to share it with the public. Or maybe they would share the technology with the public for a price.

As Pete passed a bank, he saw the clock on the street sign, a digital clock with red lettering. Almost every building had the power cut, but the clock was still on. He turned his attention back to the sidewalk and froze. He looked up at the clock again. Something about it looked familiar. The small light bulbs, the displays to show the time… He'd seen several pieces at the drone crash site that…

He hurried back to the jeep, started it, and sped away.

31

Samantha had been given the freedom to wander around the village. It reminded her of the villages she'd seen in Eastern Africa whenever she was there because of a fresh outbreak of Lassa virus or some other hot agent. The shacks were predominately homes, with only two communal buildings that she could see: a "hospital," which was nothing more than the doctor's shack, and a city hall, which, again, was just a hut converted for a different purpose.

One thing that impressed her was the joy in which people went about their work. It consisted almost exclusively of tending to livestock, farming, or carpentry. The latter group seemed to be attempting to build a wooden house rather than a hut, but the people seemed content.

The animal life varied tremendously, and she saw something she never thought she would see in the middle of the jungle: camels. The village had three camels, or rather, she was told, one of the village's citizens owned the camels. Sam saw the owner come out and speak to the camels, running a brush through their hair. The camels had little black spots, almost like leopard spots, running the length of the body and the mouth.

"I didn't think I'd find camels in the middle of the jungle," she said.

The man glanced to her and went back to his brush. "The moisture ain't good for 'em. Messes with their skin. But none of us is comfortable, is we?"

"What made you choose camels?"

"I'm buildin' an ark."

"An ark?"

"That's right. Gotta include all the animals I can."

Sam watched as he finished brushing one of the camels and then took out a white, gooey substance from a black container and applied it over the animal.

"Why are you building an ark?"

"World's comin' to an end. Figure it can't hurt."

Sam watched the man a long while before she left and found Jason sitting on a porch, sucking on a homemade cigar. He kicked off his boots and leaned back in the chair. "We're staying here tonight. No one else lives in this hut. They'll leave us alone."

"They're saying the world's ending," Sam said, walking over and sitting down next to him. "If they actually believe that, I don't think they'd care much about whether or not we were harmed."

"These are good people."

Sam looked back at the camels. The man was quietly speaking to them now. "How do you know Tristan?"

"She…"

"Oh. Sorry, didn't mean to pry."

"No, it's not that. It just feels weird saying it. It was so long ago it feels like it happened to a different person." He reached into his pocket and pulled out another cigar, offering it to her. She took it, and he cut off the tip before she could put it in her mouth. "Now you can actually taste it."

"Thanks." The first puff tasted almost toxic, like paint thinner. Samantha coughed, causing Jason to grin. "Not for everybody."

The substance burned, and Sam knew it wasn't just tobacco. It had been cut with another ingredient. She took one more puff and then put it down on the porch. One of the children of the village ran across the street and hid from them, his head sticking out of his hiding spot as he stared at them.

"Why are they scared of us?" she said.

"They don't want any confrontations. They try to avoid those as much as possible. The ones that do want to get into a confrontation, you can see it on their faces when they look at you. Most of them just want to be left alone."

"It feels odd here, as though we've stepped back in time or something."

"We have."

Samantha looked back at the hut. The structure appeared sturdy and large, built of good material.

"You sure no one lives here?" she asked.

"Yeah, it's ours. I'm going to get some weapons from Tristan, a couple pistols and rifles. I want you to start carrying a pistol with you at all times. Just tuck it into your waistband."

"I don't know if I'm comfortable with that."

"Comfort has nothing to do with it." Jason rose and said, "Mind helping?"

They strolled past the hut and back into the road. A few people watched them from the huts, but as soon as they were noticed, they hid themselves back inside again.

"Any guesses about why the virus hasn't touched this town?" Jason asked.

"I would guess they just haven't been properly exposed. I'll run some tests as soon as she allows me to see people. Separate the blood cells from the plasma cells and test for *Variola* RNA. It'll tell us if they carry the virus and it just isn't active or if they've never been infected."

Jason stopped and looked at her. "Jessica told me back in Wyoming that you lost your mother. I'm sorry."

She nodded and started walking again, Jason following a step or two behind. "In the final months, my mom didn't recognize me. I didn't get to say goodbye."

They walked in silence a moment. Finally, Sam stopped and turned to him. "Please be honest with me, Jason. Why me? Why did you guys choose me?"

"Hank thought you had the best chance at a vaccine… and most of the other top virologists in the world are dead. Hank had dozens of them killed right before he came after you. He shot one guy in his kitchen while he was eating breakfast with his family. Did it himself because the guy had insulted him somehow, refused to work for him or something. Hank doesn't care about people. He doesn't see them the same way we do. They're materials to him, curiosities."

"He's a psychopath?"

"Terms like that don't really apply."

Across the street, the man who had come out with Tristan stepped outside. A rifle hung from his shoulder, and he tucked his thumb under the strap and spit on the ground. He strolled over to them and said, "Tristan's ready for you. She got some people that volunteered."

Jason looked at her. "Firearms can wait. I'll be here when you're done."

She nodded and followed the man back to Tristan's home.

32

Pete's biggest fear was that someone had already gotten to the crash site. The military, after he'd told Clover, had no doubt sent a biohazard team, but the team wouldn't be there to clean up the mess. They would cordon it off and then probably burn it. If they had already done so, he wouldn't be able to test his hypothesis, though something in his gut told him he was right anyway.

As Pete approached the field where the drone had crashed, he stopped the jeep and scanned the area. Not a single vehicle was there, no cleanup crews, no military vehicles, nothing. He drove to where he remembered the debris was, at least some of it, and it took a moment for him to find it in the dark. When he did, he got out of the jeep and guessed that it was all there. Clover hadn't sent anyone. He was either grossly incompetent or something else was going on.

Pete, despite the fact that he'd already tested positive for the virus, got some latex gloves out of the jeep along with his gas mask and snapped them on before rummaging through the debris.

He held up pieces of the drone in the headlight beams of his jeep and found the one he was looking for. Four slots made up of little burnt bulbs—a clock. No, not a clock, a timer.

In addition to the timer, he saw a piece of a solar panel. That explained how the drones could stay up without being refueled, but it didn't explain their purpose. Also, solar power on something this size couldn't keep it in the air very long. Probably not even through the night, unless of course they weren't meant to get through the night.

Pete took out his cell phone, dialed into the secure line at NORAD, and asked to speak to Clover.

"He's retired for the night," a female voice said. "May I take a message?"

"Where is he?"

"I'm not sure, sir. Would you like me to find him?"

"Yes, please, as soon as possible, and call me back."

Pete stood over the debris a minute, kicking away a piece with his foot. Whatever had been inside it, a mist or cloud or spray of the virus, was gone. Absorbed into the air. The virus couldn't live long exposed to the elements, no more than eight hours. It needed a host. Luckily, no homes or buildings were anywhere near, but if it drifted on a breeze, about ten miles away was a concentration of family houses. Rather than sitting around waiting for a call, he got into the jeep and headed to the road leading out to the homes.

When Pete arrived at the cluster of suburban family houses, he was shocked by how normal it all looked. Fences and yards, toys strewn on driveways, a kite stuck in some power lines, almost like nothing was wrong at all. He stopped the jeep near the curb and just sat for a while. The neighborhood was dark other than the light of the moon.

A burning sensation rose up in his throat, intensely hot, then mild. It felt a little like the beginnings of strep throat. It shattered the moment of tranquility he'd been having and reminded him why he was there.

He got out of the jeep and marched up the porch of the first home, then stopped. If these people weren't infected, he could potentially infect them. Unsure what else to do, he knocked several times as hard as he could, and then stood off the porch, away from whoever answered.

He couldn't hear anything, so he knocked again. After a couple of minutes of knocking and waiting, he went to the next home.

Within the first few seconds after knocking, someone answered: a woman in a bathrobe, holding it closed with one hand. She didn't open the screen door.

"Yes?" she said meekly.

"My name is Master-Sergeant Peter Brass. I'm with the United State Air Force. I'm sorry to bother you so late. I just had a couple of quick questions."

She didn't move or speak, but he could see that she clutched her robe tighter.

"Ma'am, have you or anyone that resides with you experienced any flu-like symptoms recently? Fever, headaches, sore throat, uncontrollable sweating… anything like that?"

She shook her head. "No."

"Did you notice anything out of place early today, a smell in the air maybe, something like that?"

"I don't think so. What's this about?"

"Just looking into something. I appreciate your time."

Pete had turned to walk away when she said, "Is this about the virus? Is there something happening here with it again? We just got rid of those damn ips. I couldn't handle the virus coming this way again."

"We were concerned… I was concerned, that the pox may have spread in this location, yes. Just stay indoors and you'll be fine. Thank you for your time."

Once she shut the door, Pete sat down on the steps. This was a waste of time. Maybe the mist hadn't even arrived yet? Maybe they were infected and just not showing symptoms? Without running tests, there was no way to know, no way to protect them.

He pulled out his cell phone. Clover hadn't called. He tried NORAD again and got the same operator.

"I'm sorry, Mr. Brass, the assistant secretary has informed me that you are no longer with USAF or NORAD and your privileges have been revoked."

"Revoked? They haven't been revoked, I'm on leave."

"I'm sorry, sir. That's what he told me."

"Where is he?"

"I'm afraid that's all I can say. Have a pleasant night, sir."

The line went dead. He slipped the phone back into his pocket. Why would Clover revoke his status so quickly? Pete needed to get in touch with him. Clover might be in the barracks, but there was a decent hotel nearby as well. He would have to check the hotel without potentially infecting anyone else with the pox.

There was only one place he could think to go.

The night closed in like a veil. Debra sat on her porch. She used to sit out here and watch the children playing in the streets or the cars that would speed by, some of the local teenage boys smiling and waving at her. Now the streets were empty. The sound of crickets, so loud it sometimes kept her up at night, was the only thing she could hear.

Before she could get up to go inside, she heard a car engine up the street. Headlights appeared, and a military jeep sped down the block. It stopped in front of her house, and Peter Brass jumped out and jogged up her front lawn.

"Pete, what are you doing?"

"My clearance has been revoked. I need you to listen to me, Debra. No! Don't come any closer. Stay on the porch... please."

She stopped, remembering that inside of him, a germ was slowly spreading. One that would shut off his immune system and then devastate his body in a way she hadn't thought possible even a couple of years ago. "Okay," she said.

"It's Danny. Whatever's going on, I think he's a part of it. No response team was sent to the crash site, even though he knew I'd been infected. The debris is still there. And he revoked my clearance and won't take my calls."

"That's not entirely unusual, Pete."

"He left potentially infectious material out in public." He paused. "And it gets worse. Those drones have timers."

"Timers for what?"

Pete didn't say anything.

"For what, Pete?"

"They're going to release whatever infected me, a type of mist probably, when that timer runs down. I'd bet everything on it. They're bombs. And I think Danny knows that."

"He wanted to shoot them out of the sky. You're the one who stopped him."

"I think he knew I would. He doesn't want to shoot them down. He only shot the one to calm everyone, to let everyone at the DOD know that these things were easily destroyed and not a threat. I think he's playing us, Deb."

She shook her head. "Why would he do that?"

"I don't know, but I don't have a lot of time. In a few days... I need to see him now. I don't have anyone else to help me."

Pete, normally confident to the point of being pushy, appeared defeated. He was soft-spoken and unable to maintain eye contact for long.

Debra said, "Let me get my jacket."

33

Sam walked into Tristan's hut and stood by the door. The space was clean, almost immaculate. Bearskin rugs covered the floors, furniture appeared hand made but comfortable, and the walls were decorated in paintings of natural scenes from the jungle: a bird on a tree branch, rushing water over a small hill, ants coating a piece of fruit. The hut was nicer than most apartments Sam had had through school.

Tristan sat on a wicker chair, her legs crossed, a grin over her lips. She rose and took Sam's hand, leading her to the back of the hut.

"You seem like Alice in Wonderland for the first time," Tristan said.

"I just didn't think places like this existed anymore."

"Places like what?"

"That are cut off from everything else."

Tristan glanced at her as they made their way outside through a door in the back of the hut. "Is that really such a bad thing? It certainly helped us when this virus showed itself."

They stepped out into the bright sunlight. Two men sat on wooden chairs, young, perhaps nineteen or twenty. Tristan said, "These are your volunteers, strong men willing to help if they can."

"I appreciate it," Sam said to them. The men didn't reply.

"We secured some rudimentary medical equipment for you, just a doctor's traveling bag. But it has syringes and vials and a few other things you might find helpful."

"Thank you."

Tristan nodded. "Some people here don't believe this outbreak was a bad thing. They think humanity needed to be cleansed and reborn. You should at least consider that as you hunt for a vaccine."

Sam looked out over the landscape. It was cultivated and decorated, almost like a park set up for the village. Several people were milling around, sipping from tin cups filled with a drink they were getting out of a barrel. "I saw a gymnasium full of children vomiting so much blood they died of exsanguination before the virus actually killed them. I've seen ips tear people apart while they're still alive. There's no redeeming quality to it. This virus and man cannot live on the earth at the same time. It has to be eradicated."

Tristan smiled. "I have no doubt it would feel the same way about us." She turned to go back inside. "Let me know if you need anything."

When she was gone, Sam turned to the two men sitting in front of her. Making a vaccine was, in essence, not that difficult. The creation of the first vaccine by Edward Jenner in 1796 was a breakthrough that, in Sam's mind, rivaled the moon landing, the wheel, or even fire. Without Jenner's discovery, humanity would have been wiped out by the deadly strain of Spanish influenza in the early twentieth century, or polio, or smallpox. Then again, man had made it two hundred thousand years without vaccines. Maybe humans were more resilient than scientists gave them credit for.

The first method of creating a vaccine was the egg-based method. Virologists took strains of weaker virus and created a seed virus by implanting the weakened strains in hen eggs. The virus multiplied in the egg, and each egg produced a couple of doses of vaccine.

The second method was the cell culture, in which the virus was added to a growth solution, usually mammal kidney tumor cells, and then the virus was separated from the growth solution. Its RNA and structural proteins were removed, leaving weakened surface proteins that were then given as injections or nasal spray. This method was quicker than the egg-based method, as it only took four or five months or so to develop rather than the six to nine months the egg-based method took.

The final method was the recombinant-DNA method, the most complex of the three. Essentially, a species of fall worm was infected, and a portion of the worms' genetic code was replaced with a section of code that would force them to produce proteins matching the virus for which a vaccine was sought, usually a flu virus, as it had never been tried on smallpox. The worm was then introduced to other worms, where it reprogrammed them to produce the same protein by infecting them. Then the proteins were harvested and used as vaccines. This method could produce a vaccine within six weeks. It was the only method Sam hadn't tried yet.

She would try it, but she wasn't hopeful. Agent X had shown itself to be resistant to every method of developing a vaccine, mutating, in some instances, within days. The only method Sam could think of that might produce a vaccine was to get the antibodies of somebody that had developed an immunity or had a genetic predisposition to immunity and synthesize it on a large scale. Immunoglobulin therapy, or using the blood of one person to heal someone else, had been used for various autoimmune diseases in the past, and theoretically, it should work on smallpox as well.

Sam searched through the small doctor's bag and pulled out two syringes, latex gloves, a tourniquet, cotton balls, and iodine. She looked from one young man to the other.

"So who's first?" she asked.

34

Pete sat in the back of the jeep, covering his face with a surgical mask. Debra didn't seem frightened, though she was sitting not two feet away from him, driving the jeep. She kept turning around to check on him. She made it seem as if she were looking for other traffic or at passing piles of junk, but he knew she was taking care of him.

"You don't have to do that," Pete said.

"What?"

"Look out for me. There's no cure, Deb."

She shook her head. "Why didn't I get it? Why would—"

"Because that's just life. It's random. Looking for purpose in it is a waste of time. Don't do it. And after tonight, I don't want you seeing me again."

She glanced back at him. "Too bad."

"I'm serious, Deb. I don't want you to see me... I don't want you to see me weak."

She laughed. "You men. I swear, Pete, whether you're fourteen or thirty, you act the same."

"Just don't try to see me after this. Please."

Pete didn't know Clover that well, but he knew what type of man he was. Pete had known that type since he was a child. Being sickly as a kid, he had been picked on constantly. As a method of survival, he had developed a sixth sense about bullies, the type who would derive satisfaction from the pain of others. He learned who they were and what to say to avoid getting beaten by them. He remembered one incident vividly in which he had convinced a bully who had picked on him regularly to attack another bully. The two beat each other to such a bloody pulp that both had to be taken to the emergency room. That was where he learned that these types of men would rather die than be perceived as weak.

Clover would not be at the barracks, he decided. It would be perceived as thinking he was on equal footing with his men. He would want to make sure everyone knew he was far superior to them.

Though most hotels had closed up or gone out of business, some still remained that catered to the scientific researchers and wealthier military officers who came through the region. A Hyatt Regency wasn't far from NORAD.

As the jeep stopped, Pete hopped out and circled around the passenger side, staying as far away from Debra as he could.

"Wait here," he said. "If I'm not back in fifteen minutes, leave. Leave and don't go back to work."

He turned to walk away and she said, "Peter?"

"Yeah?"

"Be... careful."

"I will."

The hotel's interior was a mix of plush modernity and expensive antiquity. Luxury items were somewhat commonplace now.

Just days after the explosions and the harsh military response of absolute martial law in all fifty states, the price of certain items had dropped to next to nothing, and others shot through the roof. Batteries were fifty dollars for a pack of four, but iPods were the same price as a combo meal at any of the fast-food restaurants. Some states didn't even have electricity. Most companies manufacturing luxury items simply couldn't sell them anymore, and people were practically giving the goods away. But soon the supply would dwindle and the demand would rise, and even the cheap goods would be too expensive for most of the world's populations. The only thing Pete saw in the future was cycles of deprivation and starvation.

He approached the desk clerk. Pete had worn his uniform for this specific moment. "I need Assistant Secretary Daniel Clover's room, please. I'm to brief him on an ongoing matter."

The girl behind the desk said, "I'm sorry, sir, but I don't have a list of permissible visitors for him."

"Oh, he knows I'm coming."

The girl stared at Pete's surgical mask. He considered taking it off, but infecting some poor girl just trying to earn a few bucks wasn't on his to-do list today. He'd rather find another way in. But ultimately, she didn't say anything about it. The power of a uniform, particularly in a situation where the police didn't exist and the military had taken over, gave him a lot of bargaining power.

She picked up the phone, and Pete watched the keypad. She dialed "0" and then "6 1 6." After speaking softly into it for a few moments, she hung up and said, "Sir, he's refusing to see anyone."

"I understand, thank you."

Pete pretended to walk out of the building and then turned around at the last moment. The girl was back in conversation with a male employee, as she had been before Pete had disturbed her. The elevators were across the hall, so Pete hurried there. He went up to the sixth floor and stepped off. Room 616 was just down the hall, across from floor-to-ceiling windows looking down on the streets. Pete pressed his ear to the door. There was an ice machine down the hall a bit. He got an armful of ice, brought it back, and dumped it in front of Clover's door. Then he pressed the doorbell and stepped to the side so someone looking through the peephole couldn't see him.

The door opened. Pete saw Clover's face staring down at the ice. Pete took a deep breath, attempting to calm his jangled nerves, and spun in front of Clover.

Pete grabbed him by the lapels and pushed him into the suite. Clover twisted and flung Pete into a closet, breaking the doors. Clover came at him with a kick, connecting with his chest. The breath left Pete instantly. Clover kicked at him again, and Pete caught his foot and twisted, sending the man to the floor.

Pete got to his feet. He jumped on Clover's back and attempted to pin him down. Clover swung back with an elbow that caught him in the face. Pete stumbled back, dazed, as Clover turned. The older man grabbed a vase sitting on a desk and lobbed it at Pete. He ducked, letting the vase shatter on the wall behind him.

Clover shrieked like some Amazonian warrior and rushed at Pete. He tackled him at the waist and slammed Pete into the wall. Pete wrapped his arms around Clover's midsection and tried to take him down, but the older man was much stronger than he was. Pete couldn't budge him.

Pete reached for the phone on the nightstand next to him. He grabbed it and bashed it into Clover's head, over and over, until the phone was in pieces. Clover shot blood across the room then backed away before coming in again with a wild haymaker that probably would've broken Pete's jaw.

Pete moved just as the fist was going to connect. Instead, Clover's hand went through the drywall. Pete swung up with a lamp, smashing it into Clover's face, loosening his hand from the wall and sending the older man onto his back.

As Pete went to grab something else, Clover got hold of his ankle and twisted him off his feet. Pete's jaw hit the nightstand, and he tasted blood and felt bits of tooth in his mouth. He tried to rise when he felt Clover's arm around his throat, squeezing the life out of him.

The loss of air was instantaneous, and Pete was amazed how limp his body went. He could scarcely move his hands to pull at Clover's arm. But he could still move his head. He tucked his chin low enough that his mouth was over Clover's forearm and bit down with everything he had.

Clover screamed as a ragged chunk of flesh tore from his arm. He pulled away as Pete collapsed onto the ground, panting so hard he thought he might pass out. Clover buckled into a chair against the wall, holding out his arm as though it were a war injury and he were waiting for a medic. The blood from his head and arm soaked the carpet. He took off his shirt and wrapped it tightly against his forearm. The older man leaned his head against the wall, and the two of them just breathed for a long time.

"What do you want, Pete?" he said, still out of breath.

Pete clutched the covers of the bed and pulled himself up. He fell onto his back and stared at the ceiling. "You knew... what those drones were. You knew they had the virus."

Clover breathed deeply a few times. "I did."

Pete watched the man. He had no remorse when he admitted it, no sense that he had done anything wrong.

"You're going to kill a lot of people," Pete said. "Why?"

"*I'm* not doing it. I just played my part."

"What part?"

"To keep everybody calm until..."

Clover grimaced as he tightened the shirt on his arm. Pete swallowed blood and wasn't sure if it was from his injured mouth or Clover's arm.

Pete said, "If not you, then who did this?"

"You wouldn't know him."

"Terrorist organization?"

"No. This goes beyond terrorism, Peter. This goes much beyond that. This is about a power struggle that was started a century ago. About reshaping the world."

Pete had just enough strength to pull himself up. "You're a soldier. You're an American soldier, Danny. How the fuck could you do this?"

"There are no countries anymore. We're interconnected, everyone a nation unto themselves. When shit hits the fan like this, you gotta look out for yourself. That's all I was doing, looking out for me and mine."

"How?"

"In this war, we're all going to lose. I have someplace now for me and my family. When things hit their worst, we'll be there, away from all this... shit."

"Money? You sold out your own country for *money?*"

Clover shook his head. "You think too much in the old ideology. You have to adapt, Peter. That's all that matters. That's strength, adaptation. Nothing else is important." He paused. "If you wanted, I could get a spot for you. I could reinstate your credentials and we could work together."

Pete grinned, blood running down from his mouth onto the floor. "You forgot something, Danny."

"What's that?"

"I'm infected."

Clover's eyes went wide. In the adrenaline of the fight, he had forgotten he was fighting someone infected with smallpox. Pete stood up and fell back onto the bed from the pain. He leaned forward, his elbows on his knees.

"Well," Pete said, "you should probably get tested."

The look of fury in Clover's eyes was something that normally would have terrified Pete. But now he took it in passively. Clover didn't have the power to hurt him anymore.

Finally mustering the strength to stand, Pete got to the wall and leaned against it. He turned to Clover, whose eyes were locked onto him. "Out of curiosity, Danny, who is this man you sold everything out for?"

"Hank Kraski. I didn't lie to you about that. I thought you might run across his name eventually."

He nodded. "I may pay him a visit, too."

"I don't think you'll need to, Peter. He may just call on you."

35

With the top of the jeep off, Debra enjoyed watching the sky. As a little girl, she'd lain with her sister in the backyard and counted the stars. Then the next night, they would do it again, wondering whether the same number of stars would appear. And if they didn't appear, they would wonder where they went. No Google existed then, so they couldn't look up why some nights only a few stars would appear and others the sky seemed coated in shining diamonds. They imagined that the stars would hide some nights, and others, when they felt brave, they'd come out.

Pete stepped out of the hotel. He was limping and holding his side, his face bloodied.

"Peter!"

She jumped out of the jeep. He recoiled and shouted, "Don't get close!"

Debra stopped. They stood far apart. He straightened and said, "You need to get the cities evacuated. They're planning something big."

"How am I supposed to do that?"

"Go to Jacob's house. Tell him about the drones. Tell him he has to get the cities evacuated. He'll listen."

Debra took a step forward. "I'm not leaving you."

"You have to."

"No," she said, emotion tightening her throat, "no, not like this. It can't end like this."

Pete grinned. "You wanna know something? I was going to ask you out the first day I met you. I got right up there, behind your table when you were eating lunch in the mess hall, and then I chickened out. I said to myself, 'there's plenty of time...' There's never plenty time."

"Pete, don't do this. You can fight."

"I'm a danger to everyone I'm around," Pete said, his mouth overflowing with liquid. He spit a glob of blood onto the pavement. "Go to Jacob's house and tell him everything. He'll believe you."

She nodded and turned away, wiping the tears from her eyes as she climbed into the jeep. She started it, and Pete took a few steps back. He didn't say anything as she pulled away, She tried to watch him in her rearview mirror, but all she could see was darkness.

Pete watched until the taillights of the jeep faded into black. A piece of garbage fluttered in the street. Other than that, there was no motion, no sound, not even the wind blowing through the abandoned buildings.

Pain had an off switch: apathy. All Pete had to do was not care anymore. If he turned off that part of himself, he wouldn't have to feel it anymore, but he wanted to feel it, to know that he was still alive. *Not dead yet*, he kept saying to himself. *Not dead yet...*

He leaned against the wall of the hotel and slid down. Closing his eyes, he felt sleep washing over him, but he knew it wasn't sleep. He was losing consciousness from the blows he had taken to his head. He had to stay awake because he wasn't sure he would wake up if he closed his eyes. But then again… there were worse ways to go than in your sleep.

Pete wasn't certain how long he sat there, but something roused him. Screaming.

He jolted awake. The screams echoed over the empty streets, like waves rolling over them. And they were getting closer. Pete forced himself to his feet. Around the corner up the road, a single person appeared. It was too dark to make him out clearly, but Pete could see the blood soaking his shirt. The man screamed and sprinted at Pete.

Pete turned, the pain so acute it made his knees wobble. He leaned heavily against the hotel's exterior, trying desperately to claw his way to the entrance. The man kept screaming, each scream painfully closer than the last. Pete slammed through the revolving doors. There was a lock on top of the doors, and he pushed the pin inside the lock, preventing the doors from turning.

The man crashed into the doors, nearly breaking the glass. Covered in blood, shrieking, his face pale, his eyes black, he looked like a devil.

Pete stumbled into the building, one hand pressed against the wall for support. People were gathered around a television. One woman had her hand covering her mouth while tears streamed down her face. One of the men's jaws dropped so far he looked like it was stuck that way.

Pete made his way over, shouting, "I need a gun," and no one even moved. He stood behind them, away from them so he wouldn't get blood anywhere, and his eyes locked onto the television. A video was running, taken on what looked like a cell phone. A plane clipped one of the drones. The drone dropped from the sky and exploded onto a busy Manhattan street, releasing a light-green mist. No one was reporting any illness or injury, but everyone knew what it was. At least two hundred people had been in the radius of the mist. With an R-naught of twenty, that meant those two hundred would infect about four thousand people, and those four thousand would infect eighty thousand, and so on. There were at least thirty other drones over population centers. Isolation could only go so far. Eventually, everyone would be infected.

Pete felt pain and exhaustion pour over him. He didn't have the strength to fight anymore. He limped away and sat on one of the hotel lobby couches and then lay down and closed his eyes. Before he even knew what he was doing, sleep overtook him, shutting out the rest of the world.

36

The dinner laid out before them was unlike anything Samantha had ever had. All the food was fresh, the meat untouched by antibiotics, growth hormones, or corn, which practically no animals were meant to eat in the quantities they were force-fed in modern industrial societies. It gave the meat a flavor she'd never tasted.

Jason spoke with Tristan, who was seated at the head of the table. The rest of the village, the adults anyway, sat around them or on smaller tables set up in a separate dining room inside the largest hut. Sam had initially thought the feast was for their benefit, but she could see this was a nightly ritual, one that was important to them. Though the townspeople behaved stoically during the day, now, with a little bit of beer, they let their hair down and relaxed.

A hierarchy definitely existed. Based on the way some of the men responded to some of the women, Sam guessed that this was a matriarchal society, with Tristan at the head.

"You've hardly touched your drink," Tristan said to her.

"I'm not much of a drinker."

"I think you'll find this particular drink pleasant. It's a mixture of beer and a special juice from a local berry. It's quite flavorful. You must try a little."

Sam, to be polite, picked up the cup and took a drink. "It's good, thank you."

Tristan smiled and bowed her head.

As the night wore on, Jason turned to her and said, "You okay?"

"Yeah, why?"

"You seem sad."

"It's hard not to be."

He shrugged. "You gotta make the most of the little moments, you know?"

She nodded, though she felt nothing of the sort. The devastation and chaos were too recent. She still remembered the way things used to be. When she awoke in the morning, it was the world of two years ago that she expected to step into, and every day she would have to look out her window to see that her nightmare was actually real.

Within a few minutes, Sam noticed an odd sensation, her vision blurring at the edges. At first she thought it was a trick of the light, there being only candle and an oil lamp, light she wasn't used to. Soon she saw it wasn't the light. The blurriness coincided with general vertigo, a buoyancy to her body that made her feel as though she could float away.

"I don't feel well," she said.

Jason looked her way, and his eyes rolled back into his head. He fought it, but eventually his head just collapsed onto the table.

Everyone stopped talking. They had their eyes fixed on her. Her limbs felt as though they had to move through sand, and heaviness descended over her, making even the slightest movement difficult. She pushed herself away from the table and nearly fell over as she got to her feet.

"What'd you... do to me?"

"It's best not to fight it, dear," Tristan said. "You could harm yourself. Just lie down and let it take over. It's not entirely unpleasant."

Sam tried to get away, but the room spun. She hit the wall, bouncing her head off it, and collapsed onto her back.

The last thing she saw was Tristan's smiling face over her.

37

A commotion woke Pete. He sat up and saw a man arguing with one of the clerks. The suited man had puffy blond hair and was wearing an overcoat, even though it was summer. The man was growing frustrated, as evidenced by the constant tapping of his fingers against the counter. Finally, he shouted, "Tell me where Daniel Clover is or I will kill both of you!"

Pete ducked low as soon as he heard it. The clerk stammered, "Six sixteen. He's in six sixteen."

The man stomped over to the elevators and took the next one up. Pete pushed himself up. Every bit of him hurt and his head was spinning. He had to take a moment to adjust.

When he'd regained his equilibrium, he looked to the revolving door. No one stood outside of it anymore. Pete staggered over to the clerk. "Do you have a gun?" The clerk, terrified, nodded. "You need to give it to me. That man is not here for a party."

"I don't..."

Pete went around the counter. A small safe sat before the woman. "Open it," he said. Slowly, she took a key from her pocket and opened the safe. A .38 lay there, and Pete grabbed it. He took the elevator up to the sixth floor again.

When the doors opened, he stepped off. He couldn't hear anything. He slowly made his way over to Clover's door, which was wide open. Pete stuck his head in. He could see feet sticking out against a wall, but the rest of the body was concealed until Pete got closer.

Rummaging through the pockets of Daniel Clover was the blond he had seen downstairs. Clover was dead. One gunshot wound to the side of the head. The blond was frantic, tearing through his pockets until he stopped at the waist. Behind the belt was what looked like a small pocket, something that would've had to be customized on Clover's pants. The blond man pulled out a set of two keys. He eyed them a while then closed a fist around them. Pete raised the gun.

"I assume those must be valuable to kill an assistant secretary of defense."

The blond looked up but didn't turn around. "Very valuable," he said.

"What are they to?"

"A warehouse."

"Warehouse of what?"

"Of something very important."

Pete took a step back and leaned against the wall, his legs feeling wobbly. "And what is that?"

"Death."

The blond spun and rushed him. Pete got off one round, blowing away a bit of the man's shoulder. The man struck him with a fist and then an elbow in quick succession. He kicked out at Pete's throat, and Pete moved. The foot kicked through the wall, raining a cloud of drywall over the man's leg. Pete stumbled backward and fell. The gun the man had used to kill Clover was on the floor next to the body. The man rolled over it, picking it up along the way, and was in a crouching stance before Pete could blink.

Pete fired twice, as did the blond. One of Pete's shots hit the man in the throat. Bits of flesh and blood exploded over the walls behind him, and he choked. His hands went up to his throat in the universal sign that he was unable to breathe.

Pete had been shot, too. One round had missed his head, but the other had connected with his arm. The pain was excruciating, like being stabbed with a blade that was on fire. When he tried to move his arm, agony blasted through his body. He dropped the gun, trying to stop the flow of blood.

The blond man choked to death, a pool of dark blood soaking the carpets around him. Pete was breathing heavily, and the sweat wouldn't stop. His body felt hot, like he'd been in a furnace, and the injury made his arm nearly useless. The keys were on the floor in front of him. He stared at them a long time before picking them up. On one of the keys it said, "Harboro Storage."

He forced himself to his feet. There had to be a first aid kit downstairs somewhere. Stumbling forward, he made his way to the elevator and then down to the first floor, leaving a trail of blood behind him. The front desk clerk, her eyes wide, said nothing as he struggled up to her and said, "I need the first aid kit, please."

Pete sat on the couch in the lobby. He bandaged the wound as well as he could, at least enough to slow the blood until he could get to a hospital. Then again, going to the hospital seemed a little like plugging a hole in a sinking ship.

Besides, he had to go somewhere else first. He had a feeling Harboro Storage had something to do with the drones, and killing Clover was just a measure of cleaning up.

"I need a car," he said to the clerk. Though he didn't point his weapon, the sight of him holding a gun, covered in blood, must've been terrifying, and he didn't do anything to change that impression.

"We have a van," she stammered.

The van was used for transporting equipment and various items to and from the hotel. It was filled with linen when Pete climbed inside. He started it, flipped on the headlights, and pulled away. No one tried to stop him. But when the patrols came by again, he was certain the clerk would be outside waving them down. He had to hurry.

Though he couldn't connect to the military server, the general server for the US government was still up. He had access to the Internet through his phone, and he looked up the address for Harboro Storage, a facility about fifteen minutes outside of town.

Pete drove the van like he was ninety years old. Pain radiated from his arm, distracting him. He couldn't concentrate on the road or anything else. He stopped once and checked the bandages and layers of gauze that he'd soaked in Betadine. The bleeding hadn't stopped, only slowed.

The warehouse sat in a field of long grass surrounded by a ten-foot-high fence topped with razor wire. Only one gate led in, and a guard booth sat in the middle with retractable steel arms on either side. Pete pulled up to the guard gate. The guard was a soldier, a pistol strapped to his hip. He stepped out of the booth and came to the window, glancing inside the van.

"Identification, please."

Pete pulled out his NORAD identification from his wallet and handed it to him. The soldier went back into the booth for a minute and then came back out. He handed the ID back and said, "Head on through, sir."

The arm pulled up and Pete drove through.

Gravel surrounded the warehouse and crunched underneath the tires. No other vehicles were around. The warehouse looked rusted and old, something he could've driven by dozens of times and never noticed. He stopped the van in front of the door, which bore several chains and two padlocks. He got out of the van and looked back to the guard booth. The guard was staring at him through the windows of the booth. Pete turned to the locks and took out the two keys.

The two keys opened the two locks. He paused a moment before doing anything else. A cool breeze was blowing, and in the sky, the moon was starting a slow retreat as the sun began its ascent.

He felt weary and hot. A general malaise had fallen over him, and the itch in his throat had turned to pain that rose to his ears. The pox was building momentum. In a couple of days, he wouldn't be able to do anything but lie in bed. After that, he would be one of *them*. As he stared at the doors, he wondered why he even cared what was in there. It made no difference, ultimately, to him.

But he knew he couldn't just walk away. He had to know why this was happening.

Pete opened the doors and stepped inside.

The warehouse was large, far larger than the exterior let on. As he moved, the droplets of blood that dripped from his arm, down his hand, and off his fingertips onto the pavement were not lost on him. He was a walking virus, and everyone around him was at risk. Maybe a better approach would've been just going somewhere isolated and dying alone… but the thought was so horrific that he couldn't fathom it—to die alone and in pain, no one even knowing he was gone.

Pete trudged through the warehouse. Lining the walls were shelves of equipment. He didn't recognize them, but they were clearly for manufacturing something, vehicles or machines, something that required large engine parts. Eventually he reached shelves that were cleared. There wasn't enough light to see them in detail, so Pete had to get close. As he did, he noticed something else on the far side of the factory: large containers.

He went to them. They were vats of thick plastic. White. He'd seen these vats before…

"Sir," someone said behind him.

Pete turned to see a soldier in the Weaver stance, the pistol aimed at his head.

"Do you know what this is?" Pete said.

"You're going to have to come with me, sir."

Pete looked at the vats. "It's poxvirus, tons and tons of it, enough to wipe out every human being on the planet. And it's sitting in a warehouse with two locks." He looked back at the soldier. "Has the entire world gone crazy?"

"Sir, I'm going to need you to come with me."

Pete shook his head. "This was the plan, wasn't it? To wipe everyone out and start over? Why would someone do this?"

"Sir, I'm not going to ask you again. I have been given authority to take you into custody by any means necessary."

"You should run, soldier. I'm infected, and just by breathing the same air as me, you might become infected, too. Run. Run now!"

The soldier appeared shaken, his eyes wide. He didn't lower the gun right away, but Pete could see the terror in his eyes—terror no doubt brought on by watching the final moments of someone dying from the strain of smallpox that had come to be known as black pox, Agent X: sheets of skin falling off the body, blood, nearly all the blood in the body, draining from every orifice, the vomiting, the organs that liquefied and came out of the anus, and then the victim turning into a demented predator. It was Hell itself.

The soldier backed away a few steps and then ran out of the warehouse. He might be back, he might bring others, but that would take some time.

Pete searched the shelves. Many of the containers had chemicals in them, but they were unmarked. He had no idea if they were flammable or not. He'd have to guess.

He went outside and got into the van. He drove it through the double doors, knocking the doors off their hinges, scraping the body of the van against the walls in a shower of sparks and groaning metal.

The van stopped just inside the doors. Pete felt his stomach on fire. Before he could stop it, he vomited a spattering of dark blood. The incubation period had accelerated even more than the doctor who'd tested him knew. The blood clung to the steering wheel and the windshield. It dripped down over his thighs. He looked in the rearview and saw only a dark outline of his face.

He drove the van over to the vats. When he got out, he had to lean on the van and place his head against it. Only the sweat dripping into his eyes and the sting that accompanied it woke him from his stupor. He didn't have long before he'd be useless.

Pete gathered as many of the chemicals as he could, dumping the contents out over the vats, over the van, and over the warehouse floors and walls. He took off his uniform jacket and tore the sleeves off, creating a long piece of cloth. The warehouse stank strongly of chemicals, like an overwhelming amount of paint thinner. He opened the gas cap to the van and began running the cloth inside the gas tank, as far in as he could get. He pulled it back out, saw that the end was soaked in gasoline, and then shoved it back inside the other way.

Now, all he needed was a lighter.

He searched the van but didn't find one. The guard may have had one in the booth, and Pete headed out that way. The breeze that whirled around him cooled his skin. The pain in his stomach had faded, but the one in his arm had increased. With every movement, it felt like he was tearing the wound open again.

The guard booth was abandoned. Inside, a paperback novel sat on the counter, along with a package of cigarettes and a drink in a plastic bottle. Thirst rang inside of him more powerfully than he had ever felt. He drained the bottle, juice of some kind.

He searched the drawers underneath the controls. In one of the drawers was a book of matches with a few left. Pete held them in his hand, running his fingers along the edge. He turned back to the warehouse.

In the distance, not too far on the only road leading to the warehouse, he heard vehicles, the rumble of engines, military vehicles. As he limped back inside, he saw their headlights on the road.

The warehouse was lighting up as the sky lightened outside. He wished he could see the sun rise one more time.

Pete knelt down near the cloth sticking out of the gas tank and struck the match. He held it in his fingertips a long time, long enough that it burned him. He pressed it to the cloth. The material ignited instantly, creating a large flame that began to consume the cloth. As it burned, it ran up the length of the material, into the gas tank.

Pete shuffled over to the hood of the van. He climbed up, his arm screaming from the effort, and pulled himself to the roof. He lay down on his back and stared out the windows of the building. He could hear the sizzle of the cloth, which was overtaken by the engines that roared to a stop in front of the building.

The sizzle softened, and he knew the flame had reached the fuel. He closed his eyes and thought of Debra. Then there was a bright light and a moment of pain.

38

The pain pierced her consciousness before anything else. Sam felt her eyes flutter open. She took in her surroundings as if in a dream, curious but not concerned. It took voices to snap her out of it. She felt groggy and weak, unable to even lift her arms. When she tried, there was resistance, and she saw the ropes that went from her wrists to the metal loops in the wall. Feed lay stacked near her in neat piles. The smell of horse dung was overwhelming. She was in a barn.

Next to her, Jason lay on his side, his hands tied behind his back and his ankles bound to the wall. Across from them, leaning against a stack of hay, was a young man of maybe twenty. He was bound with rope as well.

Across the barn, Tristan spoke with another man. They were discussing something in hushed tones. She glanced over and saw that Sam was awake.

Samantha's tongue felt like it weighed twenty pounds, and her mouth was sandpaper. Her throat dried after every swallow, and a burning in her stomach told her she'd been poisoned.

"What did you do?" she said, hardly able to speak, her head lolling to the side.

Tristan strolled over to her and looked down. "I'm afraid you won't be devising that vaccine after all, my dear. You'll be staying with us."

"Why?"

"Let her go," Jason spat.

He lifted his head, his eyes fixed on Tristan, who simply grinned and moved over to him. She placed her fingers gently on his chin and brought his face up.

"Your time has passed, Jason. The military-industrial complex doesn't exist anymore. We're nothing more than tribes again. And I will do whatever I have to do to ensure my tribe's survival."

He struggled against the ropes, grunting as Tristan took a step back and motioned for one of the men to come over. The man slammed the butt of his into Jason's head.

"No!" Sam yelled. "Stop."

Tristan turned to her. "He's too dangerous to let live, my dear. I am sorry if you cared for him." She looked to the man with the shotgun and nodded. The man lifted the weapon.

"Wait," Sam bellowed, "wait, what do you want? What do you want with us?"

"With him, simply to die. With you, another fate."

"What?"

"As you may have noticed, there are not that many women in our little village. We need breeders, and that shall be one of your tasks." She knelt down, looking Sam in the eyes. "I'm afraid it will be quite uncomfortable at first, taking on man after man until you're with child, only to do it again once you deliver, but it is simply the way things must be. You have to think of the good of the village. With your age and strength, I wager you'll birth a dozen children. That will make you a powerful figure here."

Sam tugged on her ropes, but they were so tight they cut into her wrists. "Let him go, then," she said. "Let him go and I'll do what you say."

She chuckled. "Are you falling for him? Oh, you poor dear. You have no clue who he is, do you?"

"I don't care. Just let him go and I'll comply."

"Really? You will comply willingly?"

Jason shouted. "Don't do it. Fight with all you've got."

Sam swallowed. "Yes, I'll comply if you let him live."

Tristan smiled. "Roger, take Jason out into the jungle and release him. Put a single shot in his leg so that he can't come back here, but let him go."

"Yes ma'am," the man with the shotgun said. He lifted Jason with the help of another man, undid the section of rope fastening him to the wall, and carried him out.

"You see," Tristan said, "I can be reasonable. I will treat you how you treat me. You show me respect as the leader of our tribe, and I will show you respect as the mother of many."

Tristan reached down and undid the ropes on her wrists.

"How many children do you have?" Sam asked.

"None, my dear. That was not meant to be my role." She helped Sam to her feet. "We'll get you settled in your new home. I hope you understand, at least for the foreseeable future, I must have one of my men guard you at all times. Just until you've earned my trust."

Sam glanced down at the boy. "Who is that?"

"Oh, he misbehaved in a way that I'm afraid is unforgivable. Isn't that right, Earnest?"

"What did he do?"

Tristan, as though she were an expert assassin in the Middle Ages rather than a tired woman in a dark jungle, slipped a knife out of her skirt, slit the boy's throat, and let him bleed out over the wooden floor.

"He tried to escape, if that's even the right word. No one leaves here, Samantha. You are now a part of that. Should you attempt it, I'm afraid the same fate would await you."

Sam watched as the boy died, his eyes empty, the floor coated in his blood, which mingled with the dirt and created a semidry mud. "I won't run."

"Good," Tristan said, taking her hand, "then let me show you to your new home."

39

The night air cooled Jason's skin. Jungles were humid, intensely muggy, but for some reason this section felt just right. He thought perhaps the drugs had affected his temperature regulation.

"Hurry up, boy," one of the men pulling him along said. "We gotta set you free."

"We both know," Jason said, his voice still shaky from the narcotics, "you're not setting me free."

The man chuckled. "Smart boy. Chuck, right here's good as any."

They stood Jason in what he guessed was a stream. The water was cold against his ankles and feet, though his legs and arms felt numb. One of the men stood in front of him and rubbed his own belly.

"Well, you wanna do it?"

"Nah, you go ahead," the other said.

Jason moved like a cobra, slipping his arms over his legs and pushing against the ropes to pop them off. He grabbed a stone from the stream, slick and cold, and hurled it at Roger. It bashed into his skull, sending bits of teeth and bone spraying into the cold water. The other one shouted, "Holy shit!" and went to raise his rifle, but it was too late.

Jason grabbed the man's mouth with both hands, his fingers inside. He opened Chuck's mouth wide, wide enough that he heard the pops as the jaw muscles tore from the strain. Jason leaned in and bit into his tongue. He ripped it away, leaving a bloody stump as the man screamed a gurgling, frothy shriek before Jason flipped him off his feet and held his head underwater.

Chuck struggled, but Jason put his weight onto his head. Soon, he stopped moving. Jason held him there a while longer, just to make sure, and then sat back into the stream. He felt exhausted, as though he'd been through a boxing match. The drugs drained him, and all he felt like doing was lying down on the soft muddy bank and falling asleep. But Samantha was still back there. He rose to his feet and started stumbling back.

40

Tristan had calmness, a detachment to the things around her that Sam thought might've been what saints or the insane felt. One thing she knew for certain: the woman's touch sent waves of revulsion through Samantha like an icy chill.

As they walked through the town, Tristan took Samantha's elbow. The town was quiet, even the children hiding away.

"It really won't be so bad," Tristan said, "once you get used to it. Think of it as having multiple husbands. And these are good men. They've come here from all nations of the world to find a better life."

Sam's stomach churned at the thought of these filthy men violating her night after night. She decided right then that if it came down to it, she would die first.

"Are all the women here treated the same?" Sam said.

"The ones that can breed are revered, as they should be. The ones that can't are put into other positions. I guess you'd call them administration."

"Did you grow up here?" Sam said. As long as Tristan was talking, Sam could think. Devise a way to get out of here and find Jason.

"Heavens, no. I was a professor, actually. Folklore and mythology. When the virus first hit the Hawaiian Islands, I read the writing on the wall. I knew we couldn't contain something like that. So I found elsewhere to be, somewhere away from everyone else. My husband and I found this property and, well, here we are."

"Where's your husband?"

She was quiet a second. "You've met him."

They came to the same hut Jason and she were supposed to have slept in. Tristan helped her up the stairs and through the door. Sam's vision and balance were still affected. Tristan led her to a wicker couch with thick cushions on top, and Sam collapsed into it. The comfort of the cushions lulled her toward sleep almost instantly, and she had to fight the urge.

"Just sleep now."

"Please," Sam said, "let me go. Just let me go."

"Sorry, dear. I told you, we're just tribes now. And you're going to be part of my tribe. And I swear to you, I will do everything in my power to protect you, and you'll one day swear the same thing to me."

Sam felt emotion rise up in her belly, and she felt as if she could cry right then. Everything in her life had been devoted to others—her career, the sacrifice of her love life, having children, everything—so that she could help those who were sick and afflicted. And what had she gotten in return? A life of death and slavery.

"Please," was all she could say.

Tristan pushed away a strand of Sam's hair. "You rest now, dear. I'll be back in the morning, and we'll start your new life. There'll be a man posted at the door if you need anything. If you try to run, and I know you won't, but if you do, he has orders to bring you back any way he can, dead or alive. Do you understand?"

Sam felt the warmth of tears on her cheeks, saltiness on her tongue. Her vision swirled, and she couldn't focus on anything for long. The world felt like it was melting away from her. She closed her eyes and fell back onto the couch, Tristan lightly brushing her hair like a loving mother.

Sam saw her own mother, not toward the end when most days she couldn't remember Samantha's name, but when Sam was a child and her mother was a strong, independent woman who always told her she didn't need a man or money to be happy. "Happiness is a habit," her mom would say, "and the more it's practiced, the easier it comes."

Sam admired her mother and couldn't bear to see her withering away. She would make excuses so that the nurses would have to stay late and she could be out, and then she would sit by her mother's bed all night and weep when she got home, a mixture of guilt and pain—guilt because she didn't want to see her mother like that and pain because she knew there was no one else to take care of her.

The image of her mother faded, and Sam saw a bright light. Her eyes didn't move from it for a long while until she recognized what it was: an oil lamp hanging on the wall. She sat up and found herself still on the couch. The hut had two lamps, which were enough to light it well. A migraine pounded inside her skull. Her hands went up to her head, and she rubbed her temples.

The first time she got to her feet, she found her balance off, but she didn't topple over. Whatever narcotic they had given her must've been enormously powerful to knock her out in one drink, unless while she was unconscious, they'd injected her with something more powerful.

She walked as quietly as possible to the front of the hut. Peering outside, she saw a man with a rifle sitting in a chair, sipping something out of a cup. Sam backed away.

She scanned the entire hut from top to bottom. Nothing there that could be used as a weapon, not even a decoration or piece of kitchenware.

She was trapped, and a tight, pressing feeling, as though she were being crushed, came upon her. She slumped down to the floor and didn't move.

41

The narcotics faded quickly once she was up and moving around. Within half an hour or so, she guessed, because her watch was no longer on her wrist when she awoke, she felt well enough to walk without wobbling. The hut and village were quiet. She didn't hear anyone or anything other than the occasional plane going by overhead. The man out in the chair appeared grizzled in the lamplight and was chewing on something, a piece of straw or reed. The rifle rested next to him, leaned up against the chair, and he had refilled his cup from a whiskey bottle. Apparently some modern luxuries wouldn't be left behind.

Samantha approached the entrance. She stood there, a light breeze blowing over her, the semisweet odor of rotting vegetation wafting in the air.

"Excuse me," she said quietly.

The man nearly dropped his glass. He fumbled with his rifle and rose to his feet, pointing it at her, his eyes wide.

Sam held her hands up. "Tristan said I could ask you if I needed anything."

The man didn't say anything at first. Then he glanced down to his glass, which was laying on the ground, its contents spilling out in the dirt. "You made me spill my drink."

"Sorry, I didn't mean to startle you. I just have to use the bathroom."

The man grumbled something, took his cup, and set it on the chair before picking the rifle up and slinging it over his shoulder.

"Come with me."

She followed him around the hut and into the darkened jungle. Eventually, nothing but moonlight bathed them. An outhouse sat about forty feet from the hut, and the man trudged toward it.

"Have you lived here your whole life?" she said.

"I ain't your friend," he said. "So shut your mouth." He looked back at her. "Though you and me gonna get to know each other a little better soon 'nuff."

The revulsion that coursed through her was palpable, like a poison. But she didn't react. Not now.

They arrived at the outhouse, and the man stood by. When she opened the door, the smell nearly made her gag. She swallowed and breathed through her mouth before stepping inside. She turned toward the door. The outhouse wasn't built well, and there were gaps between the slats. She could see the man trying to peer through them at her. Not that there would've been much light for him to see anything by anyway.

She closed her eyes a moment and then opened them.

The man stood near the entrance. She backed up as far as she could, took a deep breath, and rammed her shoulder into the door. It flung open and belted him in the face. He grunted and dropped the rifle, his head snapping back.

Sam dashed from the outhouse and toward the thicket of trees. The man cursed behind her, and she heard the rifle chamber before a shot rang out that echoed off the trees. She didn't slow down, but she pivoted and ran in another direction before pivoting back and sprinting into the cypress trees. Another shot rang out, and bits of bark flew off the tree she ran by.

The man was older and drunk and couldn't keep up. He fired two more rounds, but neither of them came close.

Sam ran until her legs hurt, until her lungs screamed for air and she couldn't breathe. She stopped near a stream and nearly fell over. Leaning down, she retched, but nothing came up. Her stomach heaved and churned, and finally a little bile leaked from her mouth, but nothing else. She wiped her mouth with her wrist and kept running.

The water was cold against her legs. The stream wasn't deep until about halfway through, and then it came up to her waist. The swirl and power of the stream moved her back and forth, and she felt that if she didn't fight every inch, it could've swept her away.

"Got you, bitch!"

She turned to see the man taking aim. He lifted the rifle and fixed on her. Sam ducked underneath the surface. She heard the round enter the water above her. The current was flowing south, and she swam with it as far as she could. She burst out of the water and sucked in air, the man about ten feet away. He jumped into the stream, holding the rifle above his head. Another deep breath and Sam went under.

The stream narrowed and grew shallower. Soon, it wouldn't cover her.

Sam thrust out of the water one more time and he was right there. He raised the rifle.

Sam lurched at him, knocking the rifle away. He backhanded her, sending her flying into the stream, and scrambled to find his rifle in the water. Under her feet, she felt the heavy stones, jagged and slick. She reached down and lifted one. As the man was turned away, pulling the rifle out, she shouted and slammed the stone down into the back of his head.

He dropped instantly, crumpling as though he was nothing but a sack of gelatin. Facedown in the water, he began to drift away with the current.

She pulled herself out and ran into the darkness.

The blackness welcomed her. People in the village must have heard the shots, and she had no doubt they were after her. They would have dogs on her trail, and the only way to avoid them was to keep moving. She wouldn't be able to hide for long.

The jungle lit up in places with moonlight but in most others was black as tar. Howls, grunts, and chirps filled the night like some monstrous symphony. Sam had run so much that all she could do was lean against a tree and listen, panting. Normally, the noise might unnerve her, but so much adrenaline coursed through her that she could ignore it. Finally, she pushed herself off the tree and continued walking.

Jungles at night held no beauty for her. The trees, reflecting the moonlight and glimmering like sparks of white light, were about the only beautiful thing to look at. Everything else was wet, dark, and slimy.

As she pushed through a particularly harsh brush, the branches like sandpaper scraping across her arms and face, she heard something, something too rhythmic to be another sound of the swamp. Stopping and ducking low, she listened... footsteps. Someone was walking toward her.

Her breathing quickened, and she tried to calm herself, panic was setting in. Memories came to her: a man with terrifying eyes rushing at her in a hospital, a long fall and the impact that seemed to knock the life out of her, men screaming and dashing for her, bits of bloody flesh hanging from their teeth.

Samantha started hyperventilating. The footsteps stopped and then rushed forward. They'd heard her. She got to her feet, trying to run, panic making her chest feel like a car sat on top of it. The bushes behind her separated and she screamed as she sprinted for the darkness of the cypress trees again.

"Sam!"

The voice was familiar. She glanced over her shoulder and saw Jason just as her foot hit a root, and she tripped. She hit the ground hard on her hip, her hands preventing her head from hitting the ground. The panic had turned to tears, and they poured out of her as she sobbed.

"It's okay," he said, putting his arms around her. "It's okay."

42

Gerald pulled himself from the stream. He sat up, his hand to the back of his head. The woman had gotten him good, so good that he'd have to make up a story about her escape so he wasn't punished for his gullibility.

He sat on the bank of the stream a long time. The sound of rushing water calmed him, soothed his nerves. Less than a year ago, he'd been working the oil fields near Vernal, Utah, twelve-hour days, six days a week in the hot desert sun, so burnt and drained of water even his eyeballs felt hot. The sound of water, no matter how long he was here, would always be a relief.

The trees welcomed him when he finally rose and stumbled back to the village. Jungle heat wasn't like desert heat. It had moisture in it, and there was always water around you. Had to be careful of the water, though. Someone from the village had been killed by a water snake a month ago. Pissing right into the river and the snake nabbed his ankle. Shot so much venom through him that his heart stopped before he even had a chance to call for help.

As Gerald stopped at a tree, his head pounding from a migraine, the noise behind him rent the air. As clear as a jet engine in his ears, a scream emanated from the darkness.

"Shit," he mumbled, as he pushed off the tree and dashed for the village. "Shit, shit, shit." He was the lookout tonight for the village, the first warning signal in case of an ip.

The screams closed in around him from every side, a pack of wolves closing in on the injured deer. Gerald pumped his legs. The darkness of the jungle hid the predators well, but it also hid him from them. It'd take some time for them to just happen upon him. As long as he stayed quiet, there was a good chance he could make it back.

The screams circled him. One even went in front about ten feet, and he saw a shadow run right by. Gerald dropped to the jungle floor, flat on his belly, and heard the rustling brush around him as they ran past, searching and screaming. He put his face in the dirt a second, quietly saying a prayer, then got to his knees, his feet, then burst into a full sprint.

Breath seemed to be squeezed from his body. He sucked air through his mouth in huge gulps, hoping for just enough so he didn't pass out before reaching the village and the safety of their guns.

Coming out of the jungle, he saw the lamps hanging on the huts. They were welcoming beacons, and he thought he could die right there, he was so happy. He slowed down, not because he wanted to, but because his heart felt like it might explode. He got all the way to the first hut before the screams came out of the jungle.

There were dozens of them, maybe hundreds, a full swarm. They rained down upon the village, their screams drawing people out of the huts. Gunshots began to ring. Gerald saw one woman, the nurse of the village, make a run for her hut where her two children slept. An ip, a Congolese man in fatigues, leapt into the air and landed on her with his full weight. He ripped into her face, tearing away her nose and an eyeball. Another man got tackled hard into the ground by three of them, the ips reaching into his stomach and removing organs while the man screamed.

Gerald turned just as an ip bit down into his neck. He yelped in pain, trying to push the man away, but he was too strong. He had a frantic strength, like some Viking berserker. Gerald reached for the only thing he could, an oil lamp. He broke it over the ip's head. The flames instantly engulfed both of them and the nearby hut.

43

The fire was visible from the jungle. There were no fire departments out here, no one rushing to quell the flames. Only the village and the surrounding brush.

Sam stood next to Jason on the outskirts of the village, watching the devastation. She could see bodies from there, in the middle of the dirt street where the fire couldn't reach. They could've died from smoke inhalation, but she didn't think so. They'd gotten out. They could've run out of the town and would've been fine. Something else had killed them. And given the amount of blood that had poured from the bodies, she thought she knew what that something else was.

They walked closer. More bodies were visible now, dozens of them, torn apart, but no screaming. The ips had moved on.

The intense heat made Sam squint. She backed away, and Jason followed her.

"I lost the blood samples," she said. "They took them from me. I need to get some more from one of those bodies. Two vials' worth."

Before Jason could respond, they heard a groan. Sam looked in that direction and saw Tristan on the ground. She was on her stomach, mumbling to herself. Jason ran over. He knelt down over her. Sam thought he would have a violent reaction, considering she'd tried to kill him, but he was gentle as he turned her onto her back. They saw two open wounds where her eyes should have been.

Tristan screamed and clawed at him. Jason tried to calm her down, but she had lost it. Sam turned away from her and ran into the village.

The first hut had been largely consumed, but the last was still up and relatively untouched. Sam dashed for it, covering her face with her arm. She got there quickly and ran inside. Fire ate up one of the walls and reached the ceiling. She grabbed two tin cups.

When she got back, Tristan was hoarse from screaming. Jason had backed away and was standing over her, watching, his brow furrowed in helplessness.

"What're you doing?" he said.

"We need blood."

"Hers?"

"No, we're going to take her with us. I'm going to get it from the bodies."

Jason looked down to Tristan, who was wildly clawing at the air. "We're not taking her with us. She's infected now."

"I'm not leaving her," Sam said.

"We have to."

Sam looked at him. "Jason, I'm not leaving her to die."

Jason exhaled and looked down at Tristan. He knelt, grabbed her head on both sides, and twisted her neck so that her face was almost planted into the ground. Sam could hear the crunch of sinew and bone.

"She's infected, Sam. There's nothing else we can do."

Sam ran over and attempted to check her pulse. Jason had snapped her neck so harshly it had stopped her heart. Sam stood up. "That was unnecessary."

"No, it wasn't. And the sooner you see that, the longer you'll survive." He took one of the cups from her. "I'll get a cup from someone in the street. You get one from her. And then we need to get outta here."

After securing the cup of blood, Jason found an old pickup truck in one of the barns. It ran and had nearly a full tank of gas. The keys were hanging up on the wall next to it. He started the car. Before getting in, Sam wrapped the tops of the cups with large leaves and then tied cloth over the leaves so they wouldn't spill.

"You should know something," Jason said as they sped down the road back to the city. "I didn't want you to know. You had enough to worry about. But I think you need to know now. In Hank's last phase, the final part of his plan, was drones. He's put a drone over every major city in the world, filled with liquefied *Variola*. They're gonna detonate at the same time, releasing the mists over the cities. Whatever people we have left right now, the drones will finish off. That's why it's so important for you to find a vaccine, why I was willing to come out here. If what he set up works, he'll kill every person on the planet." He glanced at her. "Every person who isn't loyal to him, anyway."

44

The drive seemed less rushed than everywhere else they had been. Sam watched the passing landscape. She looked at the moon and the stars. She stared at the jagged mountains against the sky in the distance, like black scales thrusting up from the ground. The two cups were secured at her feet, and she used her ankles to hold them in place. The entire notion of carrying cups of blood from the dead back to a lab revolted her, but she had no choice. This was the last thing she could think to do. After this, if she failed, she was powerless.

"I need to get to the CDC labs," she said.

Jason shook his head. "No way. Atlanta's nowhere near as secure as here."

"I need a BS4 lab and equipment that only two laboratories in the US have. One's in Maryland, the other is the CDC in Atlanta."

He glanced at her. "What if I told you there was another lab?"

"Where?"

"Here. Brazzaville."

"That's impossible. Unless we're talking about a rogue state like Iran or North Korea, the WHO has to sanction a BS4 lab. It requires years of observation and licensing, review by the UN and intelligence services… there's no way a lab could just pop up under the radar."

"Well, it's here. I'll take you to it. The drones will detonate soon. We don't have time to go to Atlanta." He glanced at her again. "Your head's bleeding."

She reached up and touched the side of her head and came away with a smear of blood.

"How'd you get away?" she asked.

"Those men weren't desperate. I was. In a fight, the most desperate usually wins. Shame, though. Tristan and I spent time together. Hard to see someone you did that with die like that."

"Who was she?"

"Just an old, old friend."

Sam wished she knew the time of day it was. It was still nearly black outside, so she guessed it wasn't that long after midnight. She wished the sun would come up, but she also wished for sleep. Neither would be happening right now.

She lay her head back and watched the trees on the sides of the road. "I used to be scared of forests and jungles. We had a forest near our house, and my brother would tell me monsters lived there. They were just waiting for me to pass by so they could grab me and eat me. They especially liked little girls, he said. They liked to hurt children."

"Most of the world hurts children."

"I didn't know that at the time. I thought the only dangerous place was that forest. I didn't realize the forest wasn't trying to kill me. It was just doing what it did. Only humans *tried* to kill each other. Nature was indifferent."

"This virus doesn't seem indifferent."

Sam stared off into space. "It's easy to anthropomorphize, but ultimately it's just like a tree or a star. It just exists the best way it knows how. And it didn't try to extinguish our species, but we tried to extinguish it."

Jason reached over and gently placed his hand over hers. Neither of them moved, just sat quietly as the rhythm of the road lulled them to calmness.

Once in Brazzaville, Samantha initially felt at ease. She was back in a city, surrounded by buildings and businesses and a sense of normality. But it only took a few minutes before the gnawing anxiety roared back. The businesses were closed and the buildings empty. Population centers didn't really exist anymore.

Brazzaville, even empty, maybe especially empty, had the feel of a big city but with a small-town soul. The businesses looked as though they dated back decades, if not centuries, small shops selling herbs and spells, a few bars with the lights still on but no one inside. They didn't pass the red-light district, where allegedly tourists could purchase anything and anyone they desired, but Sam could see it as they crossed a bridge over a river.

Once on the other side, Jason said, "It's not far now."

Now that the adrenaline had waned, every muscle ached. Her head pounded with a coming migraine, and her fingers felt bloated and tight, as if she'd taken in too much salt. Her mouth was dry, and her tongue stuck to her teeth and the roof of her mouth as she moved it around.

The building didn't look like anything, just a three-story office building. The door had a large padlock, but no more security than that. Jason rolled to a stop in front of it. He stared at the building.

"This is it."

"There's a BS4 lab in there?"

He nodded. "Fully equipped. Maybe more than the CDC."

"How?"

"'Cause one hand in government doesn't know what the other one is doing. Come on."

Sam stepped out of the car, the pain in her legs severe now that she'd rested. She stretched them and felt tightness in her back, something that pulled the rest of the muscles. She had possibly slipped a disc.

They went up to the door. Jason lifted the lock. There was no keyhole. Instead, on the back was a series of buttons. He pressed them in a certain order, and the lock clicked open. Jason pushed open the door and they went inside.

Sam stood in the front room as Jason locked the door. The place was decorated like a home, complete with photographs on the walls. Jason crossed to the kitchen, Sam following. He switched a light on. Another door, this one thicker than the front door, sat next to the pantry. It looked out of place, like it'd been put in there after the house had been built. Only when Jason entered another code on this lock and pulled the door open did Sam realize the door was made of steel and only coated with a layer of thin wood.

Stone stairs led down into the dark. Jason flipped another switch, and the stairs lit up. Carefully, Sam followed him down.

At the bottom of the stairs, she took in the large space. First there was a chain-link fence with another lock on it, which Jason opened. Past that were rows of computers, laboratory equipment, chemical-processing equipment, refrigerated storage units, and a separate room with spacesuits and biohazard gear, a complete BS4 laboratory.

Just past the fence were another series of spacesuits and air hoses to create negative air pressure inside the lab. Jason opened the fence, and Sam stepped inside.

The laboratory equipment was unused, fresh and polished, the spacesuits still smelling of new rubber. Everything she would need was here.

"This place has never been used," she said.

"No."

She turned to him. "How can a fully functional BS4 lab be here?"

"Beyond my pay grade," Jason said dismissively. "Bedrooms are upstairs. Get some rest. We can start tomorrow. I don't know about you, but I'm taking a shower."

"No," she said, walking to the spacesuits. "I'm going to start now."

45

An antibody titer test was the most accurate way to determine the level of antibodies in blood from a host that had been infected with a virus. An enzyme-linked immunosorbent assay, or ELISA, used the antibodies and a simple color-change technique to determine the presence of a particular antigen.

As Samantha performed the tests, she could only hear the soft hum of the sterile air pumping into her blue spacesuit. The equipment in the laboratory was identical to what was present at the CDC, just newer and more updated. If she'd had one assistant, she would not have been at a disadvantage here.

She placed antigens from an Agent X sample on the surface of a growth dish. Then she applied an antibody derived from the blood they'd gathered from Tristan, allowing the antibodies to attach to the antigens. Finally, she bound a protein enzyme and a substrate of the enzyme, causing it to activate.

Then she waited, unable to leave or even take her eyes away. The minutes ticked off as she stared down, and the color began to change.

To her shock, she found that Tristan's blood contained Agent X.

She had been infected, but the virus had been fought to dormancy by her antibodies as though she had been vaccinated.

She ran the blood of the other person and found the same thing. Both samples were infected with Agent X.

A high-powered digital microscope sat on the counter near where she worked. She took the dish and placed it inside the microscope. A monitor above the microscope lit up with the antigen and antibodies. She had seen Agent X under the microscope dozens of times. It was nearly identical to the original strain of smallpox, an oval with an hourglass shape in the middle made up of genetic material. This wasn't identical to smallpox, not really. The genetic material was too wide and the oval shape more circular. It was certainly a strain of *Variola*, but not *Variola major*. This was something new, and a part of it looked familiar, as if it had been crossed with another virus she couldn't identify.

She sat down in a chair and stared at the image on the microscope. She had seen that strain before, in her research somewhere.

Camels.

She rose and looked at the image more closely. Camel pox was the closest strain of pox to *Variola major* in nature. The strain that infected camels was even more closely linked to the human strain of pox than the one in monkeys. It had never even crossed her mind that a possible vaccine could be derived from it.

Jason had fallen asleep on a cot outside the laboratory. Sam quickly stripped off her spacesuit and went through the decontamination showers. She rushed over and woke him up.

"What?" he said, immediately sitting up. "What is it?"

"I have it," she said, breathless. "I have a vaccine."

Samantha paced the corridor outside the lab and explained the process to him. Infection with camel pox acted as a vaccine that triggered the body's own antibodies. Tristan had injected herself with camel pox, and it hadn't killed her. It wasn't similar enough genetically to create the cytokinetic storm of *Variola major* that would shut down a person's immune system. But it was powerful enough to create antibodies that fought Agent X.

"That's why they had camels in the middle of the jungle," she said. "I didn't recognize the pustules on the camels because I wasn't looking for them." She folded her arms, staring at the floor as she paced. "We'll have to do human trials with camel pox. I won't ask anyone else to do it; I'll do it myself. But we need some of the camel pox first. There's a species of camel pox in the fridge at the CDC. I just need to get back there."

Jason chuckled and shook his head. "I can't believe that's all it was. I was so mesmerized by how Tristan did it. She wouldn't tell me. Even though we'd been married once, she wouldn't tell me."

Sam stopped pacing and looked at him. "You were the husband?"

He nodded. "Before she left the program, yeah, we were married." He chuckled again and pulled out his phone. "He's not going to believe how simple this was."

Sam's stomach dropped. "Who are you calling?"

"Sit down, Dr. Bower. I think we're going to have a long night."

46

Samantha sat in a chair across the room from Jason, who was now the one pacing. He stopped and planted himself in front of the chain-link fence leading into the lab. He folded his arms and didn't speak. His entire manner had changed, his presence, the way Sam felt around him.

"Jason, what's going on?"

"Probably better you speak to him."

"Who?"

He glanced at her. "Hank."

Within a short time, she heard a car roll to a stop in front of the building. The door upstairs opened, and she heard people, though she couldn't tell how many. The door by the pantry opened as well, and now she clearly heard two sets of footsteps coming down to the lab.

A young man came down, followed by an older man in a suit. The older man smiled when he saw her, his hands in his pockets as he stood in front of her. He took one hand out and lifted her chin.

"So nice to meet you, Dr. Bower. I didn't think I would be coming out here so quickly. We expected a couple of weeks of research at least."

She brushed his hand away. "You're Hank Kraski?"

"Ilari Kuzma. But I like Hank. So American, don't you think?" He sat down across from her in a chair.

"Who are you?"

"I was born in St. Petersburg and emigrated to the United States when I was twenty-three." He rubbed the side of his nose a moment. "It's amazing, the questioning the intelligence services in the US had at the time. The Cold War was in full swing, and they were worried about KGB operatives infiltrating their ranks. That was the holy grail of intelligence, to infiltrate an enemy country's intelligence service. When I was hired, after they already knew I was KGB, I remember the CIA's polygrapher asking more questions about American culture than anything else. That's what got everybody else caught. If they weren't *American* enough, they'd be cut from the program. But I loved American culture. I was actually born in Miami. My favorite show was this one called *Greatest American Hero*. Did you ever see it?"

"No."

"Fantastic show, that, and the *Incredible Hulk* and *The A-Team*. No one has ever topped the US for entertainment."

She glanced at Jason, who was standing behind Hank like a bodyguard. The other young man, out of nowhere, shoved him and bellowed, "My arm is infected."

Now Samantha recognized him. He was one of the men who'd attacked her in the garage, one of the men that Jason supposedly had stopped.

"Part of the game, brother," Jason said. "I had to make it look real."

"What game?" Sam said.

Hank grinned. "The game we put on for you, Dr. Bower. We figured you had the best chance of developing a vaccine, and we were not wrong. But force can only get you so far. That's what every tyrant in history has misunderstood. They think with force, you can get a person to do anything you want them to. But that's not true. You cannot force their mind to work. They'll go through the motions, but the true breakthroughs won't be there. For the mind to work properly, there has to be internal incentive. And your mind worked perfectly." He looked at Jason. "He told me about camel pox. Isn't that amazing? A vaccine, a natural vaccine, has been right in front of us the entire time, and no one except Tristan could figure it out. I'm sorry about her, Jason. I know she was special to you."

"Not anymore," Jason said.

Sam shook her head, going from one man to the other. "Why would you do this?"

Hank took in a deep breath. "Everyone was under the impression that the Soviet Union fell. Do you really think that a wall tumbling down ended one of the largest empires the world has ever seen? Do you know the one thing people can't sacrifice? They can sacrifice almost anything—people they love, possessions, their own lives—but they can't sacrifice power. Abraham Lincoln said anyone can overcome adversity, but if you truly want to test a man's character, give him a little bit of power. He was right. The KGB was the most advanced and powerful intelligence service in the world. We did not care that a wall came tumbling down."

"I don't understand."

"I began as a KGB operative, the only one ever to infiltrate as high as I did in American intelligence. We knew our moment would come one day. It's a shatterpoint. That's what nations are like. Diamonds have a specific spot, a shatterpoint, where if you apply even a little bit of pressure, it will crack the entire diamond. I knew America's shatterpoint would come, and I was right." He leaned back in the chair and crossed his legs. "The WHO tried to abolish smallpox. It was the first time in the history of the world that one species tried to eradicate another. Think how odd that is, how unnatural."

Sam looked at Jason again. The other young man was standing to the side of him, tending to the wounds on his arm. His arm appeared swollen and leaking puss. The wounds were infected, badly from the looks of it.

"I don't understand what you want," she said.

His face briefly contorted in anger. "I wanted the United States to choke on its own arrogance. I wanted my empire back." A smile parted his lips, the anger dissipating as quickly as it had come. "But there are always unintended consequences, aren't there?" He paused. "The violent aspects were something we bred. Did you catch on?"

Sam hesitated and said, "Bovine spongiform encephalopathy. I recognized it under the microscope."

He grinned. "Just simple mad cow disease. The beef industry actually named it. It sounds almost cute, doesn't it? In humans, it causes violent insanity. It wasn't difficult to cross with *Variola*."

Sam swallowed. "Mad cow with a shorter incubation period."

"Yes, though the bred virus didn't trigger in a lot of people, like you and Jessica. I don't know why. Just one of those mysteries of nature, I suppose."

When he said the name *Jessica*, Sam's stomach tightened. If he knew about her, he also knew where she was.

"The virus became too virulent," Hank said. "We tried to destroy its entire species and, for lack of a better word, it fought harder. The mutations you've seen were not engineered, they were spontaneous. Somehow this damned thing knew it was fighting for its existence." He leaned forward, interlacing his fingers. "And now it's come home to roost. Come back to my home country and her allies. It's... unstoppable. We needed a vaccine, and this, I thought, was the best way to get one. You're quite a brilliant pathologist, Dr. Bower. If only you had worked for us... the things we could've achieved."

Hank checked his watch.

"We should celebrate," he said.

"Celebrate what?"

He smiled. "The drones will detonate soon."

Samantha's heart dropped. She must've had a physical reaction to the words, because Hank laughed.

"The drones weren't filled with smallpox, not all of them. One was shot down that was, and that one, I thought, might be tested for the virus. But the rest aren't," he said. "They're filled with anthrax, not transferable from one human to the next. I had no intention of a widespread release of Agent X on the world again without having a vaccine for my people. The anthrax will kill a few hundred people, but that's it." He held up his finger. "But now, we're ready to release Agent X in a way no one could've imagined, forty tons of it. We're going to reshape the world, Dr. Bower. If you join us, I'm happy to allow you to live in it."

"The anthrax is a spore. If the drones detonate, you won't kill hundreds, you'll kill thousands, maybe tens of thousands."

"And why should I care?"

"Stop the detonation… and I'll work for you."

"You'll work for us?"

"I'm dead anyway, right?" Sam said. "I'll work for you."

Sam tried to keep her face as steady and calm as possible.

He nodded. "If you betray me, I'll kill you and everyone you've ever known. Play me right, and I'll even allow your sister and her family to live. Maybe even that brother of yours who's a beach bum."

Sam swallowed. "You'll stop the detonations?"

He took out a cell phone from his pocket and sent a text message. His phone beeped a moment later. "They're stopped."

Slowly, she rose. "Let me gather a few things."

47

Sam walked back into the BS4 lab. Hank looked at Jason and said, "Go with her."

Hank's phone rang, and he answered, walking away so no one could hear. Samantha continued into the lab. She swallowed, forcing herself not to look at Jason. She got down a spacesuit and began putting it on.

"What're you doing?" he said.

"I need to gather the samples. I might be able to synthesize a pure vaccine rather than infecting us with camel pox. I can purify it, turn it into a spray mist, get it to work quicker."

He eyed her. "And you're just doing this out of a sudden change of heart, huh? I don't buy it. You're going to try to betray Hank. I know. And I'll be there to snap your neck when you do."

"Like your wife's?"

"She made her choice," he said. "She abandoned us and scurried off to hide in the jungle like a rat."

"She discovered a vaccine."

"I'm sure it wasn't her. She had microbiologists, too, some of the best in Eastern Europe. They probably did the work and then she had them killed. She didn't want any connections to her former life."

Sam pulled the suit over herself. In the BS4 labs at the CDC, all a person could wear underneath the blue suit was scrubs, socks and gloves. Underwear wasn't permitted. She pulled the suit over her jeans. She had no intention of following procedure right now.

Snapping her helmet into place, she began a slow check over the suit, pretending to search for any tears. Suddenly, she heard Hank shouting into the phone. Jason's head snapped in that direction. Something was wrong; Hank was ranting and cursing, saying something about a fire. Jason headed that way.

Sam quickly entered the lab. Bolted to the counters were a series of Meker burners, an advanced type of Bunsen burner that was soundless and reached temperatures of two thousand degrees. The burners typically ran on methane or liquefied petroleum gas. Some of the more antiquated ones used natural gas. She checked the cupboards underneath the counters and found large white cylinders marked as LPG, liquefied petroleum gas, a volatile mixture of propane, butane, and other flammable gases. She looked back at the three men. Hank was still on the phone shouting, while the other two stood around, waiting for orders like lemmings.

Sam grabbed the needle valve that adjusted the level of gas and opened it fully on all three burners. The gas had a smell that not entirely noticeable until higher levels were reached. When the gas was pouring out, filling the lab and the house, she walked over to the microscope and began slowly gathering supplies from the experiments she'd conducted.

The three men were discussing something, and then the young man ran out. Jason and Hank remained. Sam searched the lab for anything to ignite a flame and found a thin lighter in one of the cupboards near the burners. The Kevlar gloves made moving less than easy. She took them off and just wore latex gloves.

It took a good five minutes to gather everything, and then she exited the lab, bypassing the showers and leaving her spacesuit on. She got out to the room where Jason and Hank stood and took out the lighter. Neither of the men spoke for a moment, and then Hank chuckled.

"Well, would you look at that," he said. "I thought I smelled gas. Interesting. I was going to kill you at some point soon. I knew there was no way you'd ever work for me. But I have to say, I didn't think you'd betray me this quickly."

"This ends now," she said, her voice echoing in her ears inside the suit.

Hank shrugged. "So do it. We're both here. No one's stopping you. Kill us both."

Sam lifted the lighter.

"But you die, too," Hank said.

She looked at Jason. "Your daughter. Was that true?"

He shook his head. "No. I thought you'd be more sympathetic because you lost your mother."

She looked down at the lighter. It was actually lovely, appearing to be made of smooth steel, without blemishes.

"You won't kill us," Hank said. "You can't kill. You're a doctor. You've devoted your entire life to healing people. So cut this nonsense out and get what you need so we can go."

The movement was almost imperceptible, but Samantha saw it. His left hand had fallen and reached behind him.

She struck the lighter just as the knife came out, and Jason rushed forward, his hands wrapping around her wrist.

Hank came at her with the blade, but the lighter had already ignited. A loud hissing followed, and then Sam saw a flash.

The flash was beautiful, white and then red. Pain echoed in her body, but it was distant, happening to someone else. She felt heat and the sting of the suit melting to her body as the house burst into flames, the fires raging across the ceiling and floors, beams of wood collapsing around them.

She was still conscious, and she was on her back. The explosion had flung her into the wall and she'd broken ribs. The agony was nearly unbearable, so much pain that she wanted to lie there and not get up, to let the flames consume her, but something inside kept pushing, an image of her mother.

She saw her mother in her last days, confused and in anguish yet not willing to give up. Her mother had fought until her last breath. Life had been precious to her, even a life of pain. Sam turned toward the stairs and crawled. The suit, with its air pressure inflating like a bubble, had saved her life.

As she made each painful movement, fully aware that the burns covering her body would be deadly if not treated soon, she kept thinking of her mother, the sweet smile on her face even in the face of imminent death, and of Jessica growing up, getting married, and having children of her own, and Sam would pull herself up one more step. Her hands were burned so severely she couldn't use them and had to use elbows and forearms to climb.

When she reached the top of the stairs, she saw the building eaten alive by the fire. She glanced back and saw two charred bodies. Hank's face had been burned nearly completely off. Jason lay in a mangled heap, his legs and arms shattered and going in different directions.

Sam turned back to the door and crawled through.

48

Samantha lay in the hospital bed, staring at the ceiling. She had placed a call to the director of the CDC and informed him of the anthrax in the drones. Many of the drones were falling out of the sky. Ciprofloxacin, if taken soon after exposure, could prevent the onset of anthrax. The CDC was developing huge quantities of the drug and shipping what they already had out to those cities that were affected. The public was told to stay away from any drones or debris from drones that plummeted to the ground.

She had also informed him of the vaccine, and Ngo Chon was busy at work synthesizing a mist spray. The people already infected wouldn't survive, not in huge numbers, but billions would be vaccinated and live. Humanity, ultimately, would go on.

The burns were primarily first degree, but on portions of her back and thighs, where the plastic from the suit had melted to her skin, she had suffered second- and third-degree burns. She was in an isolation unit now, the burn unit of Saint Joseph's in Johannesburg, a transparent plastic sheet covering her bed. Every three hours, a nurse would come check on her, and immediately afterward they would sedate her, but she would live.

She had heard from the CDC that the Russian government had completely disavowed the work of Hank Kraski and proclaimed him a terrorist working without approval. Whether it was true or not, at this point, didn't seem to matter. What mattered is that his connections, his money, and his men were gone. Once the disease ran its course and everyone was vaccinated, the world could begin to heal and rebuild.

Right now, she was in that dreamy state where she'd been given the sedative but wasn't unconscious. In fact, over the past seventy-two hours or so she'd been there, she felt she already required more narcotics for the same effect.

The pain, initially, had been itching and discomfort. Now, even with morphine and Vicodin, it still felt like her skin was being pulled apart. Between the analgesics, the anti-inflammatory steroids, the antibiotics, and the cleanings and dressing changes, she felt as though she would never leave, as if her life was now as a trauma patient in the hospital and no other options were open to her.

A moment of panic overtook her, and it required a sedative to calm her. Now she lay there, waiting for the inevitable sleep that would have to come. Then something happened. A nurse walked in and said, "We have a phone call for you, Dr. Bower."

The nurse held the phone close to the plastic that shielded Sam. "Hello?" Sam said, her eyes nearly shutting from the narcotics.

"Sam? It's you! Are you okay?"

"Jessica..." she said with a weak smile.

"Don't ever leave, okay? I don't want... I don't want you to leave again. Just hurry up and come back."

"Jessica, I'll be home soon. And I promise, I'm never going to leave you again."

AUTHOR'S REQUEST

If you enjoyed this book, please leave a review on Amazon.com. Good reviews not only encourage authors to write more, they improve our writing. Shakespeare rewrote sections of his plays based on audience reaction and modern authors should take a note from the Bard.

So please leave a review and know that I appreciate each and every one of you!

CPSIA information can be obtained at www.ICGtesting.com
Printed in the USA
BVOW08s1856090215

387003BV00016B/478/P